**Bolton
Council**

Please return/renew this item
by the last date shown.
Books may also be renewed by
phone or the Internet.

Tel: 01204 332384
www.bolton.gov.uk/libraries

TWISTED THERAPY

S. J. Magson

Matador
9 De Montfort Mews
Leicester LE1 7FW, UK
Tel: (+44) 116 255 9311 / 9312
Email: books@troubador.co.uk
Web: www.troubador.co.uk/matador

ISBN: 978-1905886-876

Cover illustration: Ian Legge

Typeset in 11pt Book Antiqua by Troubador Publishing Ltd, Leicester, UK
Printed in the UK by The Cromwell Press Ltd, Trowbridge, Wilts, UK

Matador is an imprint of Troubador Publishing Ltd

This work is dedicated to Marko and Devon.

*With thanks to Julie, Gail, Lesley Millward
and friends in 'The Swamp'.*

Contents

Prologue

Dr Milner's Introduction

The dark recesses of the psyche are surely enigmatic. Certainly, the primary aim, of members of my profession, is to objectively study the opaque regions of the brain. By so doing, they deem that it is humanly possible to classify what they find under a limitless barrage of specialist terms – terms that leave even the experienced practitioner baffled and bemused. In the end, I have to confess to believing that all such signs signify nothing, nothing that is, apart from the doctor's own twisted psychology.

Therefore, before I even begin to catalogue the narratives of some of the warped individuals I have interviewed over the last few years, I feel it is only just that I outline certain particulars about myself.

My name is Dr Helen Milner and I have worked at Hollbury Psychiatric Unit for five years, in the position of Psychiatric Registrar. My duties in this post have entailed producing an initial Psychiatric Report on all those referred to the unit. This has involved formulating and scribing a preliminary diagnosis for each and every patient.

As you would probably expect, during the course of the last five years, I have seen many deluded, deceitful and depraved individuals walk through the welcoming doors of Hollbury. Some of these 'residents' have been successfully treated and have managed to escape into the outside world. Many have not.

Regardless of the actual recovery of these patients, one feature has become perceptible above all others: every one of them had their own story to tell; a story which just so happened to delve into the sphere of, what we are inclined to call, the paranormal. This fact alone struck me as notable and worthy of study.

What follows is thus a history, if you will. It is a history of the personal experiences of certain individuals who have been classified as mentally ill. For the most part, the texts given have been written in their own words; words scrawled during therapy, when the said patients were asked to write about their experiences from their own viewpoints. There are just two exceptions, which, for reasons that will become clear later, have been transcribed by someone close to the patient.

Note to the reader

Given the sensitive and confidential nature of this study, it has been necessary to change certain particulars. Thus, names and dates have been altered.

Moreover, I have to confess, as with anyone who has had to type the writings of another, I have not been able to refrain from correcting the grammar of each tale, here and there. I also have to admit to slightly toning down the language of certain 'authors,' such as Mr David Lowe and Mr Dylan Holt. In addition, despite my best efforts, I am sure that, on occasions, my own style of writing has coloured the texts of my subjects. Still, I have remained as faithful as possible to the manuscripts I received.

Finally, to establish that each of you has all the necessary facts, in order to form your own opinion on the topic, the stories have been preceded by my own personal diary entries. These thoughts were penned during the twilight hours, when I reflected upon the patients in my care.

So, now for those narratives…

Mr David Lowe

Dr Milner's diary entry: 3rd October, 2005

Today, for the very first time since I took the position of Psychiatric Registrar at Hollbury, I encountered a truly twisted individual, one Mr David Lowe. It appears, from his records, that this man was a former inmate of H.M. Prison, Bradshaw; surely, a fine establishment, if ever there was one – just full to the brim, with murderers, rapists, fascists and fools!

It's hard to describe exactly how I felt, when the convicted murderer and paedophile entered my room. Certainly, I had expected to see a monster, a heinous looking beast. In the event Mr David Lowe's appearance lived up to and exceeded my expectations. He was an aged, tatty, torn and hunched individual. As he spoke, his cheeks puffed and bloated, pushing the obnoxiously protruding whiskers that covered his face out even further. For the most part, he wretched and squirmed as he attempted to answer the initial questions put to him.

I know that I wanted to hate this man. I wanted to remain the aloof professional making notes. I sorely did not want to find myself actually listening to anything he had to say. Though, I have to acknowledge, as the interview proceeded, I found his psychology fascinating. Typically, there was the overbearing whining about a troubled past: in Lowe's case a strict father and the premature death of a mother from cervical cancer. However, when it came to outlining the details pertaining to his crimes, the depth of conviction that Lowe presented was most beguiling.

Without any doubt, his arguments in themselves were completely incredible. For example, he maintained that black-outs occurred during his vicious assaults. Further, he proclaimed that an evil entity was, indeed, the real culprit of the attacks. Yet, I would swear that, the more I heard, the more he apologized over and over for the actions of another, the more credible Mr David Lowe became. It was his eyes. How he stared with those deep, penetrating, ice-blue eyes.

Maybe I was simply tired today, more susceptible to psychological molestation. Essentially, I suppose it's what they all do – negate responsibility. It's the only way they can live with what they have done. Given this, perhaps the only truly astonishing feature of the interview with Mr David Lowe was when I discovered that someone had actually allowed this animal to work as a teacher in a public school. I mean, really! The only lesson he will be learning in future is a hard one.

In the end, I scribbled, 'Anti-Social Personality Disorder,' on his admittance form, reported that staff should observe the patient for further evidence of auditory and visual hallucinations, and consigned him to Ward 14: Secure Forensic Unit.

Note on the text: The narrative that follows is an accurate reproduction of the manuscript I was given by Mr David Lowe after his admission to the unit.

Dr Milner, Psychiatric Registrar.

Chapter 1

Mondays

I had always struggled to meet the tight deadlines that my *vocation* required of me. For 20 years and more, I had survived the demands of teaching History and Mathematics; a curious combination of subjects, which had forced me to switch between the two distinct and often contrary fields of the logical and theoretical. Still, the pressures of coping with lesson planning, ever-changing assessment schemes and pupils' undisciplined behaviour, hardly accounted for the descent into madness that took hold of my very being from the 9th September, 2004.

The morning of the 9th September began in much the same way as any other day – the aroma of freshly ground coffee roused me from my dreams. However, it was not just any Monday morning. It was, after all, my first day back at school with the pupils in attendance; a day that had arrived much too quickly, for my liking, after a *holiday* spent on preparations for the new Entry Level Certificate papers for the reluctant Year 10s. I was, therefore, slightly flustered at the prospect of a full teaching day, cluttered with all the consequential hassles of school life. So, I showered, shaved and donned my new black suit with a certain amount of trepidation.

It's simply the beginning of term blues, I told myself, as I headed for the kitchen to enjoy a few moments of peace with *The Times* and a coffee. I scanned the *Educational Supplement* with one hand, whilst I called a local taxi firm with the other. Much to my irritation, the local train station was under repair, necessitating the use of one a few miles away in Leeds.

So it was that, before I had even finished my drink, a frustrated and impatient driver was blowing his horn outside the door and, within moments, I found myself speeding through the streets of Bradford and towards the M62. Now, whether the velocity of the means of conveyance increased my nervous state that morning I cannot say, however, as I approached Leeds Willston station I felt increasingly uneasy. All the same, I alighted from the taxi with a sigh of relief – at being delivered to my destination in one piece.

Carrying my overloaded briefcase and a slowly burning cigarette, I made my way to the information desk. There was no queue, which was fortunate, as a flustered looking assistant was currently foraging her way through a mountain of paperwork, searching for something, which, judging by the exasperated expression on her face, proved to be quite elusive.

'Excuse me,' I interjected, 'I need to get to Castleton by 8:30am. I've not travelled from this station before and I would like to know which platform the York to Manchester train leaves from.'

Mrs Coldwhich, as I perceived from her identity card, continued with her work, completely oblivious to my interruption.

'Excuse me,' I exclaimed, 'I was just wondering, to what use do you think I could put my *invisibility*? If you could think of one it would be rather nice, after all, I wouldn't need to be rushing around on a Monday morning trying to find a train then, *would I?*'

Now there was a response. 'I will be with you in a moment, Sir,' she clipped, through gritted teeth and a painted, polite smile. She also pointed to something on the wall behind me, which, on inspection, turned out to be a notice reminding passengers that Leeds Willston was now a no-smoking station.

I hesitated at first then proceeded to crush the offending butt underfoot. Admittedly, I was somewhat annoyed that Mrs

Coldwhich had belittled my clever speech and had gained the upper hand in the confrontation.

The next few minutes were spent watching the enlarged digital clock that hung over the notice board. All the while, I tapped my left foot on the floor in frustration. It was not that I was normally a foul tempered person. Rather, it was the prospect of having to teach the Year 10 and 11s, the more 'mature' students in the school, all day. Moreover, even though this alone was enough to cause anyone with a slightly nervous constitution night-sweats, I also had to make more than 60 photocopies of each of the following: the trench system utilized during World War I − a 'cloze' procedure on the dangers of the trenches; secondary sources covering different interpretations on Fidel Castro's success, and a spider-diagram on the causes and consequences of the Cuban Missile Crisis. Since the only photocopier was inconveniently positioned at the opposite end of the school to my classroom, it was essential that I arrived at the school in good time. I knew, all too well, once the school day had commenced, there would be little chance of gaining a spare minute to complete such tasks.

Eventually, Mrs Coldwhich looked up from her papers, pulled her glasses further down her nose, for a superior effect, and began:

'There's been a change of platform for the York to Manchester, owing to an accident on the line. It's now running approximately 33 minutes late, which is just as well for you. If you proceed to Platform 13c, it's due there in five minutes.' She then gave a list of directions to 13c, which was at the far end of the station, beyond the Café Latte outlet and over the old mainline bridge.

I thanked Mrs Coldwich, apologised for my earlier rudeness, and set off in all haste to catch the train.

As she had described, 13c was quite set apart from the rest of the station. It took at least six minutes of pushing and panting before I reached the platform. Once there, I deliberated whether there was time enough to return to the Café Latte. I was excruciatingly groggy and parched. Yet, I decided against this course of action, through fear that the York to Manchester would pass me by. I was thus left to scan my surroundings, there being precious little else left to do.

The decoration of platform 13c was entirely black and decrepit. The only colour that could be perceived was the musty copper of the rail tracks themselves, which seemed to be past their prime by almost a century. Somehow they conjured in my mind most alarming thoughts as to their safety. *Well, they must just use this part of the station in emergencies. Yes, she did say there had been an accident. I'm not surprised on this line. What a mess! Surely, with the amount I alone have spent on travel they could have sorted this out?*

As I thereby debated the rights and wrongs of rail expenditure, suddenly, my thoughts were interrupted when an icy shot of morning wind swept through 13c. I quickly wrapped by arms tightly around my chest, to defend myself against the cold. Momentarily, the cruel wind calmed, almost as quickly as it had raged. The platform fell deadly silent again.

It was through this numbing silence that I became acutely aware of a constant thudding, a pounding, that was increasing in audibility. I also sensed, with creeping conviction, that I was no longer alone on the platform. I turned brusquely, to catch the interloper by surprise. I was, however, left feeling more than a little foolish. There was no one in the darkness of platform 13c. The pounding was only that of my heart, responding to an over-active imagination. *For goodness sake, what's got into me this morning?*

About time! The York to Manchester came sluggishly along the track. At the same time, a strange, although seemingly familiar, thought crossed my mind. *What would happen if I walked off the platform and onto the track? I wonder if the train would stop in time, or if it would slide over me?* I could feel my body being pulled magnetically. I took a few paces further towards the edge. Curiously, the stiff wind returned for one last push. Before I realised what was happening, I was standing, precariously, with one foot overhanging the depth of Platform 13c. *Go on then you coward – jump.*

'Get out of the way you bloody idiot!' screamed a distraught driver, as the train came to a halt within breathing distance of my face.

Fortunately, I had not plummeted onto the rails, though I had been dangerously close to doing so.

'I am so sorry,' I returned to the driver, who had now sprung from the train and was heading towards me with a look of pure anger in his eyes and a tirade of verbal abuse falling, understandably, from his lips.

After many apologetic exclamations, the conductor and driver were persuaded to allow me to board the train. I did so hastily, unnerved by my recent behaviour. To be sure, like many travellers, I had often contemplated my destiny, in the event of hurling myself off the precipice, but, never before had I actually attempted to do so.

I somehow managed to settle myself, as the train slowly made its way out of 13c and onto the modern track that lay beyond. Soon enough, the conductor approached, calling for all passes and tickets to be shown. This provided an opportunity for me to apologize once again and satisfy the man as to my mental stability. I then asked a question, which had troubled me. 'I was told there was an accident further up the line – was it serious?'

'Oh, it's nothing to concern yourself with. Enjoy the rest of your journey.'

With that, the conductor carried on along the carriage asking for fares. *What a futile activity,* I conjectured, given that, apart from myself, there was only one other passenger on the York to Manchester.

He was a stout, elderly, dishevelled gent, with a torn jacket and ruffled hair. A seasoned traveller, I presumed, seeing that, due to his preoccupation with the passing scenery, he failed to present his ticket upon request and continued gazing out of the window. The curious thing was that the conductor didn't seem to mind in the slightest, for, as I settled back on the worn seating, I noticed he had continued on his merry way along the carriage, without a moment's hesitation.

Some 45 minutes later the train pulled up outside Castleton station. I had begun to snooze, and, before I had regained any awareness of my surroundings, a steady stream of commuters had started making their way down the aisle, each loaded with his or her daily necessities. *What. Oh hang on a minute...* I grabbed my briefcase and paper as quickly as I could and headed with all speed to the nearest exit. *Stop pushing, can't you see I need to get off at this station. Wait...*

As it happened, I was just in time. The conductor had carelessly dropped his ticket dispenser, enabling my escape from the crowded York to Manchester.

I decided to complete the remainder of my trek to school on foot, since Oakdale Remington High was merely a few busy streets away. *Why, there's still life left in the old dog,* I deliberated, as I strode along feeling unusually full of energy and not the least bit breathless, which was normally the case following any extended physical activity. Presently, I glanced at my watch as I entered the reception area – *four and a half minutes, why that's a record!*

Inside, Silvia, the administration coordinator, was handling the daily inundation of absence calls.

'You're late, David. You missed briefing. The registers are in the drawer next to the photocopier. Remember, all Year 10s are in the blue file now.'

I simply nodded and made my way to the main office. However, the machine, whose services I needed so desperately that morning, was strangely still. 'Great. Just great...' I sighed and removed the hastily scribbled message that was pinned to its lid; the message that informed all that the contraption was: *'Out of Order.'*

At that moment I knew it was going to turn out to be a bad day, a very bad day. I would have no worksheets to assist the pupils with their studies. This was a teacher's worst nightmare. No preparation, no sense of order, no decorum – period. Chaos would result and there would be absolutely no chance of a drink before dinner.

'Yet another break time to be wasted with the kids in deten-tion. Brilliant! You know, this is the only occupation that I know of, where no one seems to think that the employees are entitled to a rest.'

'Who are you talking to, Mr Lowe?'

Just to put the cherry well and truly on top of the cake, the Headmaster, Mr Finnes, was stood right beside me. I reached into the drawer, hopelessly looking for file 10.3.

'No time for talking, Mr Lowe, the second bell has gone, you'll be late to register.'

Without anymore ado, I made my way quickly to HY6, unlocked the door and released my classroom, as I saw it, to the herd of wildebeest that had congregated outside. The ever so demure Year 10s sloped in, threw an assortment of sports bags across the tables and proceeded to converse with one another over all the gossip that had accumulated over the summer vacation.

'Ok, come on now. Let's have a bit of hush for the register,' I requested, though all but a few continued on with their tittle-tattle. 'Right, come on now. You know the school rule about placing your bags under the tables!' Still there was no response. '*Look,*' my voice was raised almost to its highest level, 'we need to get *this* done or you will be late for your first lesson.' I pointed squarely at the idle register on the desk.

There now being a semblance of decorum, I called the register. Following this, the Year 10s exited, almost as enthusiastically as they had entered the classroom.

Subsequently, the rest of the day was spent in a flurry of History, History and more History. Though, how much anyone actually learned that day I cannot say. For my part, I had begun to wonder if all the hard work was worth it. As far as my own health was concerned, the answer to this question had to lie in the negative. After just one day of the autumn term, I was feeling decidedly sick inside. To be sure, during period four I had prayed for the end of school bell to go and, as soon as it had, I had rushed to the toilets to relieve myself of a churning in my stomach.

What's the matter with you? I had never known my nerves to get the better of me in that way before.

Chapter 2

Platform 13 – Possession

I was very relieved when I boarded the Manchester to York train later that evening. I looked and felt positively dreadful. So, I purchased some antacid tablets at the station and, once onboard the 5:35pm to York, clenched my eyes tight shut – determined that I was going to get some rest on the journey home. I was soon dozing, cosily and continued to do so, until the train pulled up outside Leeds Willston Station.

The unexpected halt of the brakes stirred me from my slumber. I sat bolt upright, in a state of semi-consciousness. On peering out of the window, I noticed that it had started to rain. What was more, as I scanned the compartment I saw that it was now almost empty; empty, except for the scruffy looking gent who had travelled along with me on the train that morning. *Still hasn't changed his clothes, probably can't afford any more,* I presumed, before closing my eyes again.

However, I was not to be left in peace for long. Suddenly, I was startled by an icy touch that sent shudders ricocheting up and down my spine. The old man, who had approached without my noticing, had placed his wrinkled, bony fingers upon my right shoulder.

'I can tell you what happened this morning…If you're interested, that is?'

I scanned the stranger up and down, *Looks like a drunk. Best to indulge him:* 'What? Oh, are you referring to the accident?'

'That's right,' he smiled. Though, there was something creepy and other-worldly about that smile.

'This man went and got himself killed,' he continued. 'Suicide from what I've heard. Threw his body right in front of the train he did.'

Mr Hopline, as he introduced himself, then began to outline all the gory details of the event. 'You should have seen it. It all ended for him in a flash.' He now threw his hands in the air, as though giving a first rate theatrical performance. 'His face hit the window, just over there. They had to stop the train for a time, so that they could clean off all the blood...'

At this point I interrupted, explained that I really wasn't interested in knowing anything further and opened a copy of the *Metro*. I hoped that this would facilitate Mr Hopline's departure. I felt ill at ease, in view of my own experiences that morning. The knowledge that someone else had actually carried out the deed made me nauseous once again.

As providence would have it, the lack of deference I had paid towards Mr Hopline had the desired effect. I cautiously peered over my newspaper and was thankful to see that he had returned to his seat. Once there, he proceeded to rub his withered hands together, most vigorously, apparently in great agitation at my rejection of his attempt at conversation. *Well, what does he expect? Besides, what sort of person would go out dressed like that?* I checked my critical gaze, and watched out of the grubby windows. Meanwhile, the train proceeded on its course again into Leeds Willston station.

Approximately 10 minutes later the train entered platform 13. *What's this? I wonder if there's still a problem on the track...* The temperature in the compartment began to drop, steadily. *Where has the old man gone?* I was all alone now. I shuddered. Someone was walking, dancing even, on my grave. I wrapped my arms around myself, in a rather feeble attempt to keep out the cold air which was crawling along the aisle. *Idiots the lot of them, can't run the trains properly. No one can run anything properly these days.*

As the train continued along the track, I was overwhelmed by feelings of intense depression and despair. I also became aware that someone was looking over my shoulder. This time I dared not look. I did not want to see who or whatever it was. I could faintly see my breath moving cautiously through the air. I wanted to ram open the automatic doors that were holding me. When they finally parted, much too slowly for my liking, I pushed at them. I leapt onto platform 13c, to be greeted by the stale stench of the corroded metal and synthetic surroundings.

Even when I alighted the train, I could not rid myself of pervading feelings of some kind of melancholy presence and imminent, though, as yet, undefined danger ahead. Therefore, I practically ran the length of the platform. I headed straight for the stairs – stairs that would lead me to the busier, brighter, safer section of the station.

However, my escape from Platform 13c was to be prevented. A menacingly sordid event was to occur; an event that was to redirect my life along a devilishly sinister path.

Just as I took hold of the handrails to ascend the stairs, I was forcibly hurled to the ground by an unperceivable force. The sheer velocity of the attack on my being was such that I was left thoroughly winded and bruised on the dusty, dank concrete. Helplessly, I struggled to catch my breath and regain my footing. When, what can only be described as a steam iron began pushing, punching almost, upon my stomach. The last I recall of this incident, was a sudden shot of agony through my solar plexus. I then lost consciousness completely.

For how long the blackout lasted I am unable to recall. The next I knew, I was staring at four white walls and a poster on the performance of various rail networks.

'Oh, he's come to,' a rounded, fair-haired lady indicated to another, as she tried to retain a piece of chewing gum that was about to drop, ungraciously, from her mouth and onto the floor. 'You gave us quite a shock, Sir,' she continued. 'We were about to lock up for the night when we found you. Been out on the tiles, eh? Well, all I can say is, it's lucky for you that we were still around. God knows what state you would have been in by the morning.'

I protested and explained that I had suffered some kind of attack. I was not in the least bit intoxicated, as she had suggested. Regardless, my orations fell on unsympathetic ears.

'Look Sir, apart from the cleaners, you're the only one in the station,' one of the two ladies explained, ushering me firmly towards the automatic doors and the harsh darkness that lay beyond.

All the while, as she pushed, I continued to protest, albeit in a half-hearted, weak-willed, fashion, before informing the two good Samaritans that their employer would be hearing from me the very next morning. With that, I hailed a passing taxi and was on my way home.

Never before had I been so relieved to return home – my simple, uncluttered and trouble-free home. Once inside, I locked the aged oak door firmly behind me. I then made my way to the kitchen, where I proceeded to gorge my way through a host of pastries, cereals and biscuits. These, far from further unsettling my stomach, helped to relieve me of the cramps and tensions, which had been my companions during the day. Consequently, I continued to make my way through the contents of the cupboards and fridge; in the style peculiar to pregnant women eating for two. This continued well into the early hours of the morning, when I finally settled down to sleep on my leather settee, full, bloated, but calmer.

Maybe it was due to the lateness of my rest. Maybe it was because of the fact that my body had sent itself into hibernation, following the incident at the station. Maybe it was just the product of a reluctance to return to school. Whatever the cause, the consequence was that I had failed to set my alarm clock, and had slept right through period one.

'I don't believe it,' I stuttered, through hands clenched before my mouth, 'this is going to look so bad. It's only the second day of term. What about cover? Damn!'

Much perplexed, I shot from the couch to the telephone. I then hesitated, holding the receiver in my hand for some time, before developing the courage to ring Mr Goldberg, the school's cover coordinator and fourth in the chain of command.

'Hello Malcolm… It's David, David Lowe…'

Before I could say anymore, Mr Goldberg had commenced with his lecture: just what had gone on that morning? What did I think I was doing leaving the staff in a situation like that? Never had he had a teacher who had failed to call in within the given time limit. It was just plain lucky that Mr Simmons from the P.E. Department had been available. How would Remington have coped without him?

Eventually, I switched off from the one-way conversation altogether. I then bit back. 'Oh, for God's sake shut up. I'm quite sure the little beggars managed to cope for one bloody lesson without me.'

It was only when the line went dead that I reflected on what I had said. Why on earth had I chosen to speak to him, of all people, in that way? Mr Goldberg, the one person who could ensure that your life was made hell within the school? With my hands fumbling, twirling through the thinned front section of my hair, I restlessly paced the room, conjecturing the fate that awaited me upon returning to school. *Surely I will be called into Mr Finnes' office? What was I thinking?*

Auspiciously, or not, my troublesome thoughts were interrupted when a copy of Lewis Carroll's, *Alice's Adventures in Wonderland,* fell from my crammed bookshelf and onto the floor. It was only when I ventured to return the book to its rightful place that I noticed all the books on the ledges had been rearranged. English literature, Mathematics, History and general interest texts were mingled together upon all four of the bookshelves, whereas, hitherto, they had been assigned to their own levels accordingly.

I could not conceive of how the books had come to be in such a mess. Still, being the perfectionist that I was, I began reordering them immediately. This task continued for some hours, which was fortuitous, as it went some way towards alleviating my worries.

However, as I busied myself in this fashion, inexplicably, *Alice in Wonderland* fell from the shelf again, this time onto my lap. Since the dancing text had gone to such great lengths to catch my attention, I decided I would read its battered and worn pages, which had only really appealed to me as a child.

To further my enjoyment of the text, I made a steaming pot of coffee with fresh cream, lit a cigarette, and relaxed back on my leather recliner. I was thankful to be given the chance to enjoy a good read, which, strangely, my chosen profession rarely allowed.

At this stage in my narrative I must pause to impress upon you the fact that events were beginning to drift out of my control. You have to understand, this pleasant diversion during term time soon turned into something more deplorable.

Uncomfortably, as I read the quaint tale, of a little English girl with long fair locks, I became aroused. Thoroughly ashamed of myself, I placed the book back on the shelf, hopefully to be forgotten for another 30 years.

I was disgruntled, disconcerted. As a result, instead of continuing to read, I resolved to head for the kitchen, for whatever food could be found there. The sickness, with which I had suffered, now returned with wrenching certainty. Unfortunately, the only contents of the dated fridge were a block of mouldy cheese and a pathetic, semi-rotten salad. Still, I ate these ravenously, before returning to the sofa for a rest.

'I don't believe this! What the hell is going on?' I gasped, as I entered the sitting room and nearly tripped over a pile of books which had fallen from the shelves. *How did that happen? I never heard a thing.* Although I was normally a very neat and tidy person, I was inclined to leave the books where they lay. My enjoyment of librarianship had been pushed to its limit.

Eventually, my better judgment won over and I scanned the books in order to categorize them correctly. As I did so, I noticed that the open pages of each one revealed explicit pictures of young women – all such exploitations protected under the umbrella of the illustrious title of 'Literature'. *Why, they're in every single book. I never realised how much smut there was in the world.* Ever so slowly, the aching within my stomach faded and I decided to retire to bed for the rest of the day.

Chapter 3

Scandals

On the morning of Friday the 13th September, I returned to work. The decision to do so had been taken out of necessity. I knew that, if I remained at home much longer, a Doctor's Certificate would be required. Like most put-upon people, I despised the thought of having to lie, for half an hour or more, to a virtual stranger. At the very least, Saltaire station was now in action, so there would be no need to pass through depressing Leeds Willston.

The journey itself was uneventful, and, within 60 minutes of catching the local line to Bradford, I was walking along in the direction of Remington High. It was only then that I began to drag my heels, as I recalled, awkwardly, what had passed between the fourth in command and myself that Tuesday.

At 8:30am, precisely, I entered the school's reception area. Panic stricken Silvia was presently hanging the latest bulletin on the main notice board. I smiled warmly at her, though she only returned my greetings with a cold stare, before promptly turning around, to whisper something in her co-worker's ear. *They've heard then. Well, if I'm in for it they'd better get on with it. I'm in no mood to mess about with cackling hens today.*

True, I know now that such thoughts bordered on the chauvinistic. However, at that time, I failed to notice such changes in my manner. That was, until they were brought to my attention by the Head, who had left a note in my pigeon-hole for a meeting at 12:45pm sharp.

'Look, Mr Lowe,' he began, with an air of superiority, 'I, I mean we, have noticed that your mind is not on the game of late. You look shabby and your teaching is third rate – that is, if Year 11's exercise books are anything to go by. They're an absolute disgrace…'

Just in case I was not aware of the poor effort my pupils put into their work, he held up a specimen copy that had been covered with blue biro love-hearts, offensive language and much more besides.

'This sort of thing should not be tolerated. For heaven's sake, why didn't you make Michael purchase a new one? Well never mind that, for now. What really concerns me is the way you spoke to a very well respected member of the staff team. Luckily, he wants an end to the matter, though I for one think you would benefit from an anger management course. Have you considered one?'

This last remark was hilarious, bearing in mind that for the last 20 years I had played the part of a martyr, and held my tongue, no matter what. Nevertheless, I knew some attempt at an apology was needed.

'Look, Alfred, I'm really sorry, I really don't know what got into me that day. I was just over tired and ill, that's all.'

As I spoke these words, I felt a compelling need to air my feelings. Undeniably, at that moment, there was a battle raging in my mind. My better judgment was telling me to accept my punishment, let him say what he had to say, and get the whole sorry affair over with. However, I was concurrently being overwhelmed by bitter and heated emotions. For some unfathomable reason, I was becoming more irritated and angered, by the Head's condescending speech. Soon, my subservient soul was squashed and I interrupted him mid-sentence, with a verbal attack of my own.

'What the hell are you saying? Have *I* considered help with anger management? Just *what* is that supposed to mean? For the record, no, as a matter of fact I have not considered such a course. What's more, while we're on the subject of performance, perhaps if the past 20 bloody years of trouble and strife had been repaid with a trip through the good old threshold, I would have been more inclined to accept the crap that these kids throw at me. It's so typical, bloody typical of *you*, to bring a Special Educational Needs pupil's book in here, when there are more than 300 presentable examples within my classroom. That's it folks. That's all the thanks you get after working your backside off for more than 20 miserable years!'

At this point, I rose and made my way towards the door, turning only once with a last cutting remark: 'Oh, and you can tell his lordship, he'd better not put me on any cover this week. That is, if he wants me to refrain from pulling another sicky!'

With that I exited the office, walking off in a brisk, determined manner, rubbing my hands together in triumph; much like one famous monarch would have done, after beheading his second troublesome wife.

It should have occurred to me that I was digging my own grave. Mr Finnes was not a man to cross. To be sure, he was the Head and, as such, had multiple ways of disposing of undesirable members of staff. To have spoken to Mr Finnes in that manner was tantamount to giving him a noose; one with which I could later be hanged.

The problem was that I was not affected by such considerations. Rather, I was unconsciously being taken over, consumed even, by negative emotions of anger and hatred – towards everyone and everything. I was also filled with a powerful sense of my own self worth, a feeling of solitude within the world, and an overbearing, self-righteous desire to assert my vengeance on those who wronged me.

More disturbing, that very afternoon, I provided the Head with the very ammunition he was now looking for. Recklessly, during the course of period four History, I had decided to keep the talkative, yet attractive, Melanie Price back for a detention at the end of the school day – entirely on her own.

The usual protocol, covering such events, specified that, in the interest of safety, all doors were to be kept wide open. I decided, rightly or wrongly, to save the rest of the staff from Melanie's banter, by closing the door, firmly, once the rest of the pupils had departed.

Then, not wanting to entirely waste the opportunity I had been given, I resolved to assist Melanie with her latest essay composition. Therefore, I placed her chair directly next to mine at the front desk. Thus, as she slowly wrote a piece on why Dunkirk could be seen as both a triumph and a failure, I periodically indicated the incorrect spellings, punctuation and points, which presented themselves in her work.

Soon the school was empty, except for the cleaners, and even they had moved on up to the Information and Communications Technology suite, so as not to disturb our studies. In time, the room descended into darkness. A single spot-light shone on Melanie's text. Through the deafening stillness I could hear her breathing, calmly and steadily, as her shoulders and chest rose and fell to a comforting, rhythmic beat. True, my hand came into contact with hers. It had to – to facilitate the complete communication of ideas. These ideas were burning in my mind and causing a tense headache to develop. Gently, I began to rub my temples, in a circular motion. For the briefest of moments, I closed my eyes. I was now unaware of any troubles, any stress in my life. Relaxed and free: *free to roam in the shadows.*

When I opened my eyes again Melanie had gone. I put her work with the rest of the Year 11s, grabbed my coat and briefcase and headed, contentedly, for the station.

On the way, to save time spent on cooking later, I bought a beef and horseradish sandwich and a calorie-loaded mug of hot chocolate, covered in fresh cream. *You'll be piling on the pounds at this rate, David. Oh, what the hell – so what if you get fat? Wannabe middle classes, always so fussy over what they eat. One won't do any harm.*

I continued to deliberate my eating habits as I boarded the train for home. It was then I happened to catch my reflection, gawping back at me from the unusually clean windows of the 5:35pm. I was, thereby, able to observe how my trousers were becoming uncomfortably tight, forcing the zip to open slightly. I also noted that my chin and upper lip were not as clean shaven as usual and how a pattern of wrinkles were pushing their way through my forehead. *I don't believe it. You're really starting to look your age now aren't you, David?* I quizzed, referring to myself directly; a peculiar habit that I had recently acquired.

I was tired and drained when I arrived home, and so I went to bed early. Yet, before I felt even the slightest benefit from a weekend's rest, I was again rushing through the creaking doors of Remington, in an effort to avoid the embarrassment of being late.

As is usually the case, when one is in a hurry, one fails to perceive all the incidental particularities of life. So it was that I, in my haste, did not detect the disdain, the utter contempt that was etched into the faces of each and every one of my colleagues as I passed them on the corridor. The indications of some kind of turmoil were apparent. Though I, in my innocence, only discovered later, that I was at the centre of some kind of scandal.

The one enjoyment of my life, the one that made the day, any day, almost bearable, was a visit to the Quagmire, or the staff smoke room to be precise. I was determined that there would be no exception to this rule and, as soon as I had put my lap-top computer in my classroom, I headed for my favourite retreat. Once inside, I lit my cigarette and relaxed back on my favourite faded armchair with a cappuccino. Within moments, Mrs Watson and Mr Hawthorn, Art and Mathematics teachers respectively, entered. They declined to sit on their usual seats, adjacent to mine. Instead, they headed for chairs at the opposite end of the room. At first I presumed that this change of position was owing to the sunlight that was warming the area in which they had chosen to sit. I therefore tried to engage in talk with the two, on the forthcoming governmental SAT, or end of Year nine exams: a topic which often resulted in an in-depth and often heated debate.

'Let's hope this year doesn't present the same fiasco as the last, eh!' I remarked, pointing to a copy of the new assessment guidelines.

Mrs Watson and Mr Hawthorn continued to look at one another, in silence.

'Had a bad week then, Phoebe?'

Still there was no answer. On the contrary, Mrs Watson swivelled on her chair, so that her back was turned towards me.

I gathered that efforts at conversation with Phoebe would be wasted, probably owing to pre-exam stress. Instead I chose to coax Mr Hawthorn into some kind, any kind, of discussion. 'I can't get over the fact that they completely messed up the marking of the Mathematics papers last year. They all had to be re-examined, didn't they, Andrew?'

To my surprise, with a look of what can only be described as a mixture of scorn and superiority, Mr Hawthorn clipped:

'Do you mind? We're trying to have a few minutes peace and quiet.'

There were no further attempts at dialogue, and, as soon as the two had finished their cigarettes, they left the room, even before the bell for period one had tolled.

I don't know who the hell he thinks he is sometimes. Who cares if he's the Head of Mathematics? So what if she's an Advanced Skills teacher? I'm not going to put up with being spoken to like that! To be sure, I was most put-out by the unfriendly, ignorant treatment that the pair had chosen to dish out.

However, as I made my way back to the classroom, I became aware that other members of staff, normally on speaking terms, failed to return my greetings, and, worryingly, cast steely glances my way, before disappearing into their own rooms. At the risk of being paranoid, I began to surmise that it was almost as if they all knew something, something that I did not. *You'd better get used to it David. It's always the same with these people. They don't understand.*

It was then. That single, brief moment I stood motionless. For the very first time, I noted that I was not simply talking to myself. I heard his voice, booming and clear. A stranger's voice was intruding into my once private thoughts.

Deeply troubled, I somehow found my way to MA15 for Mathematics. Admittedly, I was still preoccupied. I was in no mood to fret over whether class 9S2 grasped the concept of algebra, and so set them to work from the text. Some kind of supernatural battle was commencing within my mind that was, consequently, being pulled between two distinct and, to all appearances, spiritually opposed entities.

To be sure, as I mulled over the behaviour of my colleagues that morning, my inner self professed a desire to forgive and forget, and to try to find out just what it was that I had done wrong. Concurrently, another, much more powerful, voice was proclaiming a need to spurn those who had turned their backs on me, and seek vengeance upon my enemies.

Just look at them, David! Why would you bother to trouble yourself over them? I don't just mean your 'friends', David. Why, they look down their noses at you now. I'm more interested in those you waste your time and energy on. Yes, that's right…the little boys and girls. Well, you can afford to forget about the boys. After all, they are of no use to you. It's the girls. Surely you can see that they are worthy of a little more attention?

Suddenly my thoughts were interrupted, when Mr Finnes burst through the door, with supply teacher, Mrs Cooke, in tow.

'My office, *now*,' Mr Finnes grated.

Well, whatever it is that I've done, I'll find out now for certain. This thought brought with it a certain amount of relief. I had begun to surmise that the whole sorry mess bore some relation to my rudeness towards Mr Goldberg earlier that week.

This was the only possible explanation I could find, for the hostile reception I had received that morning. Since, try as I might, I could conceive of no further indiscretion on my part. Quite the reverse: following the unpleasant episode, I had made the profoundest effort to appear more palatable towards all members of staff, that good gentleman in particular, although he, like everyone else, had chosen to spurn my attempts at reconciliation.

That must be it. The others must have heard about the incident and taken his side in the matter. Strange though, he's not exactly Mr

Popular…I suppose I did go too far. But, I fail to see why Mr Finnes had to call me into his office again – maybe he wants to know if I've apologised, personally?

Soon we entered his lair. Mr Finnes shuffled an assortment of papers around on his desk, until he found whatever document he had been looking for. He then placed his oversized glasses firmly up high on his nose, pulled his chair under his huge oak desk and raised his eyes. For the briefest of seconds, they met with my own. I froze.

'Never before, during my time as Headmaster of this school, have I had to deal with a matter of this sort, Mr Lowe, and I can tell you, as a man who has been involved in education for more than 30 years, this leaves you in a very perilous situation. Why, I have known men thrown out of the teaching profession for less.'

At this point he paused, took a sip from a glass of water, rearranged his glasses, which appeared to be causing much irritation, and continued: 'What were you thinking, Mr Lowe? You of all people should have known better. You're not exactly new to the job are you?'

I merely remained silent, as I genuinely had no idea what he was rambling on about, or where the talk was leading.

Mr Finnes perceived that I had failed to understand the '*matter*' to which he referred and so provided a chilling clarification: 'On Friday you kept a pupil, one Melanie Price, back for a detention after school. May I ask, for what reason was she retained?'

'She'd been talking all the way through the lesson. Besides, she's not even attempted to start the coursework I gave them to complete over the holiday. You know…because it's so hard to chase them at the end of Year 11 for every rotten piece. You of all people should certainly know, what pressure we're under I mean, to perform when it comes to the GCSE exams?' I stuttered, with growing desperation.

I was beginning to comprehend the seriousness of my situation. Slowly sweat began to trickle down under my collar, forcing me to pull at the offending material.

Condescendingly, the Head persisted in tightening the lariat.

'It was still a damn stupid thing to do Mr Lowe, especially given Melanie's social welfare background. Indeed, if it were not for the fact that she made a false allegation against a member of staff at Hullby Primary, before joining us, the outcome for you would have been a lot more serious. As it is, I've decided to let the matter lie, for now. Her current boyfriend, Carl Squires...?' he questioned, as he again examined his pile of papers, '...yes, that's it, Carl Squires. He has informed me that he and Melanie had a fight last week, and, as he recalls, he did grab her around the neck – which would account for the bruising.'

'What? Let me get this straight,' I interrupted his tirade, 'have I been accused of attacking Melanie Price? If I have, just come out and say it – I am sure my Union will have a field day with this one.'

'Look here, Mr Lowe,' he exclaimed, fretfully, at the thought of the dreaded Union, 'there's no need to involve any outside agencies. The incident is being dealt with by the school. Mrs Arden, the school Behaviour Mentor, has been talking to Melanie and, it appears, she has decided to retract her statement. Melanie has now confirmed that she was wrong, and that Carl was responsible for the sores on her neck. As for you, all I can say is that you have had a lucky escape. Though I am advising – no, telling you – you are not to keep any children out of school hours unless there is another member of staff present.'

With that I was given leave to go back to my lesson. I exited the room quickly, reeling as I did so from a mixture of frustration, anger and fear.

It had been one of the worst days of my entire life. It was a day when all my studies, all my hard work, might have concluded with a disgraceful dismissal and court appearance. It was also the day on which my feelings towards my pupils took a more malignant turn for the worse.

To say that I was bitter about the whole affair would be a gross understatement. Hence, that very evening, the voices within played out their disagreements, in stereo. I became convinced that children were things that could not to be trusted; they were things that were inherently depraved; things to be despised:

How close was that? Twenty years down the drain, just because of a young lovers' tiff. I just can't believe it. Well, I can actually. That's how it is with those people. A good man's reputation ruined, just because some bint decides to go crying to the Head, or whoever else will listen to her sorry tale. She knew exactly what she was doing, David. She just didn't care about what effect her lies could have on your career. Believe me, the Head was right about one thing – you need to be more careful next time. Remember those children are not to be trusted. It's a wonder you're not driven to beat them at times. What they need is firm discipline – just like in the good old days. As for the liars, I'd give them worse, much worse.

Throughout the remainder of the week at school, it became clear that a few of my 'colleagues' had decided to give me the benefit of the doubt. There were several attempts at conversation on their part and a few smiles were cast my way, particularly as I descended the stairs of the Geography Department. Yet, it was too little too late. The damage had already been done. I felt completely isolated within the institution. If those I had worked with for years were so ready to believe the worst of me, then they could go to the Devil. *To hell with them,* I cursed, as I kept my lips tightly shut, refusing to respond to any salutations.

From Friday the 20th September, I became increasingly insular, avoiding the Quagmire and the main staffroom, even choosing to exit the building from the caretaker's entrance at the back. The more insular I became, the more the two opposing voices raged, ever more sadistically, within the unfathomable recesses of my unconscious. That was, until 'William', as I began to call the invisible intruder, became the most dominant, the most influential force – under whose power my actions and thoughts were swayed.

William's control over my being was to be perceived most savagely on Monday the 30th September, when it resulted in a savage attack on a Year seven pupil, one Scott Leon Micklethwaite.

Scott himself was a typical underprivileged child: overbearing, loud, obnoxious and disruptive – all of these attributes owing to a desperate need for attention from an alcoholic father and an absent mother, who, for the most part, walked the streets of Castleton in search of easy money. As I was well aware of Scott's background, I had always tried to steer his conduct on the correct course, via positive reinforcement techniques, which, on the whole, had served to calm the extremes of his behaviour.

However, throughout period one History, Scott had sorely tried my patience. First, there was the constant tapping of his pen upon the desk, as I tried in vain to explain the reasons why William of Normandy won over the other contenders for the throne of England in 1066.

'Alright, that will do Scott. Put your pen down please,' I requested, firmly.

This was exactly what he did. However, the action was soon to be replaced with another more irksome attempt at attention. He proceeded to push his desk forward slightly, so that his foot could now make contact with the adjacent cupboards. Subsequently, as I poured over the best means of structuring an essay on causation, Scott rocked to and fro on his chair – until, he eventually fell backwards with a thud.

'Can you get back on your chair, please? Everyone else is doing really well this morning, except for you, that is. If you don't want a detention with the History Department at dinner, I suggest you sit quietly for the remainder of the lesson.'

Alas, it was not long before Scott found an even more exasperating means of disrupting the session. Unbeknown to me, Scott had taken to tearing small strips out of his exercise book, which he had then screwed into tiny balls, ready for a chance of attack. The opportunity, for such fun, thus presented itself when I turned to write the title and date on the white board.

'Ok folks, let's get the title and the...' I stopped mid-sentence, as the offending object hit my ear from behind. *That bloody kid. Go on get him. Give him what he's been asking for...*

Before I even knew what I was doing, the board rubber,

which had been lying idle on the desk, was flying from my hand. It did so with such rapidity that when it eventually struck Scott's forehead, the force produced an instantaneous cut. Blood began to sprout profusely from the wound – the wound that I had inflicted.

Silence ensued. The rest of the class was stunned. Silence continued and lasted for an age. Silence ached, even while one pupil showed the good sense to fetch some tissues from the cloakroom, in an attempt to arrest the flow. As for myself, I remained motionless. Watching carefully as the tide oozed down Scott's shirt. Watching as it flowed down the legs of the chair. Watching, as a crimson pool began to congeal on the floor.

'Fetch Helen, the First Aider,' I indicated, numbly, to a reliable girl on the back row. I now fell, utterly defeated, into my chair.

Unfortunately, the full force of my expanding waistline forced the seat to commence swivelling, quite uncontrollably. This occurrence eased the mood of the class somewhat, as a few began to laugh out loud. The rest stared. Stared dumbfounded at their awesome teacher; stared worryingly at Mr Lowe, who was now an unknown quantity; stared at Mr Lowe who had now become a God to be revered.

As I expected, I was not allowed to teach any further that day. At the end of the lesson Sheila, a newly qualified teacher from the History Department, arrived to relieve me. I was then summoned to the Deputy Head's office. During this 'meeting' I was informed that, forthwith, I was suspended from all duties on full pay, pending an investigation into my conduct. Particular emphasis was placed on the incident that had taken place in HY6 period one History, the 30th September, 2004.

'It certainly looks very serious for you, Mr Lowe. Personally, I've never known anything like this happen before. Disgraceful, really...' Wilkinson carried on, and on.

I did not hear his last words. As he uttered them, I grabbed my coat and left his office.

Chapter 4

A Most Vicious Assault

I simply do not know how I managed to make my way home from school that day. After 20 years, one month and 29 days in the teaching profession my career was at an end.

Why? Why did I react that way? I can't seem to keep it together anymore. I'm going mad. I must be. Whose voice is that? Who is William? What's going to happen to me now? I'll be sacked for sure. There's no way Finnes will let me stay on after this. I'll never find another job – not in teaching, not now.

I cast a truly pathetic sight as I advanced to the kitchen and commenced eating my way through the entire contents of the cupboards. Though that night, no amount of food consumption was able to lighten my mood. Sleep was also beyond my reach. Still, the unstoppable voice reminded me that I had only defended myself: *He was the one who attacked you first David. Remember, even esteemed politicians can't control their actions when they are pelted by the masses. That's it David, don't feel sorry for the brat now, he's cost you your job.*

Whatever justification was offered, the following day, thoroughly drained, I sat caged within the confinement of the four sitting-room walls. I tried all manner of means to divert my attention from my predicament. I flicked my way through the typically poor offerings of each of the main television channels. It was hopeless. Every programme only triggered thoughts of unemployment, late bill payments, public humiliation and, most profoundly, children, innocent children.

Education, Education, Education, was the most important political issue of the day, or so the eloquent politicians would have me believe. 'Good parenting' advice was presented by the, 'I've experienced just about every thing there is to within my life,' troop, who firmly believed, from what I could gather, that they, and no one else, had the good sense to deal with all of life's little problems. The last straw came when a whole bunch of rabble rousers began to debate the would-be fate of an alleged child offender, who was being released, as they saw it, wrongly, into a quaint village community, under the protection of anonymity. I rose from my chair in disgust and grabbed my umbrella. *It's pouring out, but I can't stand much more of this twaddle. Fresh air, that's all I need.*

For over an hour I paced up and down the streets of Bradford. Fortunately, living so far from my place of work had finally brought a certain advantage: there was no need to hide away here; there was no fear of encountering someone even remotely connected with the school.

Eventually, my tour of the great city ended, when I came full circle upon Robert's Park. I decided to find somewhere to sit down, as the skin on my feet was being rubbed right to the bone by my unsuitable choice of footwear.

It had ceased raining. The clouds had dispersed and the sun was shining brighter, more dazzling than before, causing my eyes to squint and squeeze. Fewer people were in the park that day, owing to the uncertain weather conditions. I began to feel freer, safer, within nature's enclosure, and took the opportunity to enjoy the picturesque scenery.

Grandiose, aged oak trees abounded throughout the surrounding woods, and in close proximity were scattered various sycamores, birches and firs. Droplets were descending from the foliage, creating tiny whirlpools where they reached the damp earth. The great design had benefited from a moistening from the crystal skies above. Finally, my eyes settled on a girl. There was a young girl playing merrily with a young Beagle, all the while gently sucking on a sticky toffee apple.

I was genuinely warmed by the touching scene. The solitary confinement of the bench no longer appealed. I craved human contact. I walked towards the innocents. Luckily, the young lady had failed to observe my approach and so I was able to invade her personal play space from behind. 'Why, that's a lovely pup you've got there Miss…'

She turned, startled at my intrusion. Her locks bounced enticingly upon her back and shoulders.

'What's he called then?'

'She's called Embla,' the girl returned, relaxing into her favourite topic. 'My Dad chose the name, it's Norse for Eve.'

'Really, that's unusual isn't it?' I returned, surmising: *the girl's parents are obviously educated, as no one else is dumb enough to give a dog such a pitiable name.* 'So are you in charge of walking her then?'

'Sometimes, like when Dad wants to watch the TV.'

'Where is Dad then, at home?'

She hesitated before answering:

'Eh, yes…I don't live far from here, he might be along soon. He sometimes comes down here when I'm playing. I should be going home now.'

'Wait a minute,' I restrained her gently with my hand. 'You should be in school shouldn't you? A Year Six pupil I'd say.'

'How did you know that?'

'Oh, I'm a teacher.'

Eventually, I persuaded Bethany to let me accompany her home, along the Saltaire-to-Shipley canal path. We walked slowly. I took hold of her hand. After all, she was very close to the edge of the polluted waters and I knew it wouldn't do for me to be mixed up in any more incidents involving children. As for the girl, she was not at all put out by the action. Indeed, she smiled up into my eyes and told me about the various adventures she and Embla had enjoyed during the holidays, up high on Baildon Moor and Shipley Glen.

The intense light was creating a dull pain, a headache. This was most annoying, given that I was benefiting from a reprieve from all the stresses of daily life. *Enjoying yourself at last aren't you, David? Knew you would. Why don't you just leave the rest to me?* Try as I might, I could not prevent the imperious 'William' from taking control of the situation.

'No, not her,' I moaned, as I lost consciousness completely.

The human condition is such that, even when a man considers that he is utterly bereft of self-possession, the determination to recapture the spirit will conquer all. Little by little, the light began to shine again. My eyes opened wide to the scene, a scene painted vividly in all its sordid detail.

Bethany's dress was torn down the middle. My hands were wrapped tightly around her soft white neck. Her face was turning scarlet, as she desperately gasped for breath. Her young life was ebbing away, being choked out from its centre.

'Stop!' I screamed, with all my might. I knew that if I did not fight for this girl, her fate was sealed. 'Get off...get off her.'

So David, you think you can tell old Hopline what to do, eh?

With one final wrench I managed to pull my hands free from her throat.

'Run, get out of here.' To ensure that she did so, I gave her a push. Though, it was with such force that she fell a few metres away. Thank God, she swiftly regained her footing. She then ran, never stopping, never looking back, as Embla yapped, and the tatters of her skirt trailed behind her.

Chapter 5

My Search for Hopline

I'm an animal! I nearly murdered a child. Home was where I had to go. Home was where I had to stay. I had to avoid all contact with children. It was just too dangerous: dangerous for them; more importantly, dangerous for me.

I knew I had to find out more about the entity that had tried to possess me. *Hopline...Hopline...Where have I heard that name before? I know it's familiar. I've got it. So, it was him all along! That scruffy, hideous man...* I halted, for the realization was chilling indeed.

'The spectre on the train, it wanted to tell me about the accident, it was...it was William Hopline.'

This new knowledge, the face behind the voice, also set in motion a growing desire to understand why I had been singled out for possession. Just who was William Hopline? Was there some kind of purpose behind his unwanted intrusion into my life? Was it simply some kind of supernatural fiend's game? What was the significance of Platform 13c, where I had first been accosted by my tormentor?

I knew I needed the answers to all these questions, if I were to regain my sanity. So, I determined to investigate the personage of William Hopline, through whatever means I could. I conjectured that there were several possible ways of acquiring such information: from the phone directory; from a visit to the local library and from the local archive service – which was where I began my quest for the truth.

The following morning I signed in at the visitor's desk, explaining that I was looking for the details of one of my ancestors. I was duly shown to the third floor, where all the parish records were stored. Thankfully, they were in alphabetical order. Thus, it did not take long to find all the 'H's, which were situated in the centre of the room. My very life depended on a fruitful search and so I speedily began pouring through the surnames of all those who had passed away.

'Ah tissue...ah tissue...' The dated dust that covered each registration card hung in the air, causing my nasal passages a certain amount of irritation and forcing my airways to tighten and wheeze. Still, I searched on, undeterred.

I finally found *'Hopline'*, or to be more precise, 30 or more records of various *'Hoplines'* who had lived and died in the locality over the years. *So, where's William? Ah!* At last, I found one *'William Hopline'*:

William Hopline, of the Parish of Bradford
July 1909–August 1963
Son of Mary and Harry Hopline: Weaver
Occupation: Carpenter.

Surely that couldn't be him. He died over 30 years ago.

Frustrated, at the futility of the search, I headed for the main entrance, to enquire whether there any other records, perhaps on a different floor. However, I was to be left thoroughly embarrassed, being a so-called historian, when the lady informed me, with a haughty smile:

'You said you were looking for one of your ancestors! You need to try the Registry Office.'

'Thanks. Will they be able to give me more detailed information?'

The archivist blew her nose, obviously as irritated by the dust particles as I had been, and replied,

'Well no, not really. It depends on what information you require. If you want to access more than births and deaths, the Central Library's newspaper records, held on Microfiche, will provide more in-depth information.'

Consequently, I exited the building quickly and headed for the main library. Uncharacteristically, in my haste, I took a short-cut, through the seedy, dilapidated north-west of the town. This brought me upon a certain greasy-spoon, the likes of which I had never frequented before.

Paint had steadily crumbled away from the main door of the establishment, revealing the bald, rotten surface beneath. A rather pathetic luminous sign hung just above the single bay window of the café, at least three letters of which failed to light, whilst the remainder flickered in sporadic synchronization. Nevertheless, as I entered the café, I noted that, regardless of the worn green velvet dining chairs, and poor food display, the place was full to overflowing with workers of all kinds: from the professional suit sector, to the builder's bottom brigade.

Indeed, Bette's Café was so busy that customers were forced to stand at the counter to finish their fodder. Nevertheless, as I scanned the room, in the hope of finding an available seat, I chanced upon one which had not been taken in the furthest corner. *Best make a dash for it, before someone else does.* With pincer like movements I made my way through the throng and placed myself down on the chair. I felt a great deal of satisfaction, at having outwitted the opposition. I proudly picked up the menu with the tips of my fingers and began to peruse the fare that was on offer. *Egg and chips will do, with lots and lots of bread and brown sauce.*

For more than fifteen minutes I tried in vain to arrest the attention of the waitress, who whizzed in and out of the crowd. The din created by the banter of the men made any chance of calling her over futile. Frustrated, I was set to leave the café, when the overworked and underpaid helper, caught my eye. She began to glare straight at me, across the smoke-filled, heated, hullabaloo of the room.

Moments later, the girl was at my side. I was just about to give her my order, when she proclaimed:

'That's Bastard Bill's chair, Sir. No one ever sits there.'

'Oh, I'm sorry, I didn't realize this seat was taken,' I muttered, much embarrassed and annoyed by the ticking off I had received. 'Is he here then?'

'Is who here?'

'Bill?' I returned, as my left hand tapped the table in exasperation.

'Don't be daft,' the girl looked me over, as if I were the most illiterate and ignorant being on the planet, 'Bill's dead, dead and buried. Thank God.'

Apparently, I was seated in the chair of some notorious 'Bill.' *Surely, it could not be my William, William Hopline?* The girl had aroused my curiosity. I was most intrigued by the disdain with which the customers of Bette's Café viewed the former occupant of this seat of infamy.

'Why did you say, *"Thank God"?*'

'Excuse me?' she replied, taking a notebook from her breast pocket.

'So who is, sorry, was Bill? You said that it was a good job he was dead.'

'No, I said *"Thank God."*' she grinned, and leant over the table to tell me more on a topic which had served to increase the profits of the café no end over the last few months. 'Don't you ever read the papers? Hopline used to sit at this very table. Imagine that. I used to serve him, many times. He always seemed like a nice man to me…you know…friendly, polite. A real weirdo really! What I can't get over is that on the day that little Rebecca, Rebecca Galloway, disappeared, he was in here. He sat just where you are now. Egg and chips was his usual. I even served him. Dirty pig he was. Just to think of it now gives me the creeps.'

'The girl who disappeared, when was it?'

'It was on the 3rd October, 2002,' she stated more seriously, slowly and sadly than she had recounted her tale thus far.

'Just one more question. How did she die? Where did she die?'

'That's *two* questions, Sir,' I was corrected. 'No one knows exactly how she died, or where. Her body has never been found.'

'Well, if there was no body, how were the police able to pin the murder on Hopline?'

'Oh, they knew he'd done it. He was a known paedophile.' She nodded as she uttered this sentence, much impressed by her linguistic acumen. 'Besides, he used to hang around the school gates. They were going to arrest him, but the bloody coward went and killed himself. On the 9th September it was.'

At last, fragments of the Hopline puzzle were being pieced together. At least I now knew on what dates, if the waitress' information was accurate, to analyze the local newspapers for some kind of clue as to Hopline's life. *So he died on the 9th September... the 9th September.*

Ah! That was when it all began! That was when I had to catch the bloody train from Leeds! I understood with greater clarity now that, when Hopline had introduced himself to me on the York to Manchester, he had recently committed suicide. I desperately needed to ascertain the validity of this information and the particulars of Rebecca Galloway's 'disappearance', which could provide answers as to why her killer had been tormenting me.

Suddenly, the thought of eating egg and chips, Hopline's favourite meal, made me feel quite ill. I left the correct money on the table, in addition to a generous tip, and exited Bette's Café.

Within minutes, five and a half to be precise, I was rising in the lift to the fifth floor of the library, where the Local History database files were confined. Providentially, the library was relatively quiet, ensuring that there was no one else waiting for a computer, and that the Librarian, Ethel Smith, could focus all her attention on assisting me with my search. Ethel was only too happy to oblige, as she retrieved the files on the *Bradford Oracle* for September, 2004. I then began the painfully slow task of scanning the material.

I had surmised that, if Hopline had committed suicide on the 9th September, 2004, from the 10th onwards, there was a chance of a headline at best, or at least a mention in the obituaries.

However, a thorough exploration of the 10th September edition proved to be unproductive in my quest. So too did each publication, from the 11th September to the 15th September. Nothing could be found, pertaining to the said William Hopline.

I glanced at my watch, it was 4:30pm. For over two hours I had been sifting through irrelevant garbage on the local Mayor, Town Hall and services. I was extremely hungry, after failing to eat my dinner, and decided to head for the coffee bar for refreshments. While I sat, with hot chocolate in one hand and a muffin in the other, I pondered over whether, perhaps, the waitress had been misinformed. *Surely, if he had died in such circumstances there would have been some mention in the papers before the 16th? Even if it was just a snippet of information, surely something would have been reported?*

My hunger satisfied, I returned to the database. I sat for some time, tapping my index finger on the return key, working my way down through the obituaries. Suddenly, I experienced a flash of inspiration: *What if Hopline died before the deadline for the 9th September edition? It's worth a try.* I laboured backwards through the meaningless texts. I came to the copy for the 9th September. There, staring boldly from the first page of the morning edition, was, *'Rail Tragedy – No Justice for Mr & Mrs Galloway'*. This has got to be it…

Indeed, it was, for, as I read thirstily, the following story was revealed:

> *'Mr William Hopline, who was wanted by the Bradford Metropolitan Police, in connection with the disappearance of 10 year old Rebecca Galloway, was found dead in the early hours of the morning by rail staff.*
>
> *Initial reports have confirmed that Mr Hopline was fleeing from police, when he fell from the notorious Selby Bridge, causing delays for hundreds of commuters. Tragically, the death of Mr Hopline will leave Rebecca's parents, Sue and Brian Galloway, frustrated in their search for justice, as Rebecca's body has never been recovered…'*

I read no further. This article confirmed that Hopline had died on the exact date on which he had appeared to me on the York to Manchester. Moreover, his suicide had enabled me to catch the delayed 6:40am from Leeds Willston to Castleton. However, there was one particular point over which I was confused.

If Hopline had jumped off Selby Bridge, why had he waited to appear before me at Leeds Willston station? There must have been commuters between York and Leeds that morning, why had he not chosen one of them? It just didn't make sense. If he died in Selby, why would he be haunting Leeds Willston? As I recalled, even before I had boarded the train from York I had made some kind of connection with Hopline; there had been the desire to throw myself onto the tracks of Platform 13c. There had also been the savage assault on my being, on the evening of the 9th September, also at Platform 13c, when I presumed the possession began.

Without a doubt, I knew there was some kind of significance to Platform 13c. I just needed to find out what it was. Since no newspaper could provide me with the missing details, I returned home. I was not deflated. Rather, I was apprehensive. You see, in my wisdom, I determined to return to Platform 13c itself – to put an end to Hopline once and for all.

Chapter 6

The Bloodied Coat

As I had vowed to follow a certain course of action, all else paled into insignificance. The conscious ambitions I held even took over in the realms of fantasy. My dreams became nightmares, consumed with flights of fancy down Platform 13c. In short, that night, I was tortured with visions of 13c and my impending doom.

As I slept, I could hear the faint echo of a child. Calling softly, her whispers drifted through the steely surroundings, along the platform and down the tracks. I followed as she beckoned, until I came to the edge of the precipice.

'Down here, it's down here...'

As I leant over the bank, I could just see a flash of white, a piece of fur. The blaze of the train lights forced me to turn. Yet, it was too late. I fell under the steam roller train. Silence...

Early the following morning I awoke, even more resolute that Hopline would burden me no longer. I did not care what I wore that day and so had donned my faded jeans and dismal 1970s paisley sweater. I fumbled through the cupboards for a torch, batteries and a knife, just in case, and set off to catch the local line to Leeds Willston.

I felt quite safe, on board the newly modernised, bright red and yellow locomotive that linked Saltaire to Leeds. A cheery conductor paced the length of the carriages, only stopping for the briefest of moments to observe that I held the correct ticket. He never cast any untoward glances in my direction. He was not aware of the importance of my journey. He did not know my recent crimes.

Minutes later, the train pulled into Leeds Willston 15a. This was it. I knew that something evil waited within 13c: something that wanted to destroy me; a being that could possess my body against my will.

Still, I marched along, staunch in my search for the truth. I only paused momentarily, to see Mrs Coldwhich devouring a doughnut, completely disregarding a jaundiced, anxiety stricken businessman, just trying his best to make his way somewhere. I could not repress a wry smile, as I continued on to the Café Latte. Other commuters busied themselves with their own troubles, gushing past in a multi-coloured haze. At 6:15am I was walking along the old mainline bridge. With each passing step the station became dimmer, colder and creepier. Finally, I descended the rotten stairs of Platform 13c.

I really don't know what I expected, something – anything. There was nothing. A soft current of air was flowing, naturally, through the great archway. Pigeons were diving, intermittently, from nests they had made in the roofing. In turn they carried pitiable fare back to their waiting offspring. Certainly it was dark. *Surely only children are afraid of the dark?*

'What do you want of me?' The shrill vibrations of my voice resounded noisily. There was no response. 'Come on Hopline – you're not picking on a child now.'

I ached in the stillness, an idiotic vision, calling hopelessly to the wind. I was tempted to head for home and concede defeat, when I perceived what looked like a fallen bird, trapped in the ramshackle brickwork at the far end of the tracks. 'Poor thing,' I muttered, as I stepped closer to see if the creature was alive or dead. *What's this?* As I approached the edge of the platform it became clear that the object was no bird. It was a piece of white, dust stained fluff, flapping in the breeze.

'It's down here…' again there were the barely audible murmurs of a young girl, the same young girl who had contacted me during the night.

I knew I had been drawn to 13c for a reason, to find something. I stepped down onto the track. Carefully, I tiptoed over the rails. I was inches away from the cloth.

'Pull it. Pull it.'

I followed the command, and, as I did so, slowly, the insignificant piece of fur revealed itself to be the hood of a child's winter coat. Clearly the coat had been hidden behind the bricks for some time, owing to its tattered and torn condition. Gently I turned it over in my hands. Around the collar could be seen dark maroon, almost black, stains. 'Could it be blood…?'

I began frantically sifting through the contents of the tiny pockets: a discarded mint wrapper, a matted tissue and a diary, complete with the large gold leaf inscription: *'Rebecca Galloway, 2002'*. Finally, deep inside the breast pocket, stored for all posterity, was a small gold pen keyring engraved with the letters *'W.H.'*.

He killed her. The bastard killed her. That must be his keyring. His finger-prints must be all over it. I had found proof of Hopline's guilt. Surely, Rebecca's body would be nearby. I had to inform the police. The Galloways' suffering had to end.

In my haste to leave Platform 13c, I stumbled over the ridges of the track and Hopline's keyring fell from my hands. As I struggled to my feet, I instantly froze with fear. Stood right before me was Hopline.

'You're not going anywhere, David,' he hissed, as he placed two bulky hands around my throat. Helplessly I was forced to the floor.

Once the initial shock had abated, I began kicking, punching, even, insanely, biting my opponent. Still, Hopline kept on. Speckles of purple and white blurred my vision. As abruptly as he had appeared, Hopline was gone. Dizzy, I lay there, motionless. The tracks vibrated. The roar of the approaching engine rapidly increased. The mighty freight train appeared out of the darkness, travelling at a dangerous velocity. With great presence of mind I rolled out of its way before it bulldozed past. My legs went numb. I drifted into a twilight world.

Chapter 7

Trial and Punishment

I returned to reality on the 7th October, 2004 at 9:00pm. I was a patient at Bradley Royal Infirmary. At that point I fully comprehended the seriousness of the event at Platform 13c. My hands passed slowly down my thighs. Lower to my knees. Below there was nothing. Tragically, both my legs had been amputated, as they had been caught and mangled under the full force of the mighty freight train. I stared mutely at the doctor, who had entered to explain the nature of my injuries, which also included two broken ribs.

'Oh, you should know, there are two officers outside who want to talk to you. I can tell them to leave, if you're not feeling up to it?'

I nodded, indicating that I was *'up to it'* and the two detectives, Chandler and Mitchell, entered the room and stood by my bedside. The more senior of the two then began with a trickle of questions, which somehow turned into a downpour.

'So, Mr Lowe, on the morning of the 3rd October, it appears you were involved in an accident at Leeds Willston station?'

I nodded in affirmation and began to explain the incident further, 'There's something you need to know. I found something on the ...'

'Yes, quite,' Chandler interrupted. 'You found a white coat, Sir. One blood-stained coat, belonging to a missing girl, Rebecca Galloway.'

'That's right, it's her coat.'

'I am well aware of that, Sir; it has been confirmed by forensics.' Briefly he paused, scratched his forehead and resumed, 'What we found confusing, Sir, was how you came to be in possession of the garment?'

'I was just trying to tell you, I found it hidden in the wall next to the tracks.'

At this point both officers glanced at one another and Mitchell took over the interview.

'Often in the habit of trespassing on private property are we, Sir?'

'Of course not,' I protested, irritated by the interview which seemed to be turning into an interrogation, 'I had to go on the tracks to retrieve the coat.'

'Ok, sir...And may I ask how you knew the coat was there? *If* indeed it was hidden, how did *you* know where to find it?'

'What is this? I told you I saw it. A piece of material was sticking out of the wall.'

Thankfully, a nurse entered the room. She could clearly see that I was anxious and reminded the officers that they only had a few more minutes before they would have to leave.

Officer Mitchell confirmed that was all the time they needed and took a glass of water. He then stated, calmly, but firmly:

'You should be aware that, when we searched the area behind the tracks, the coat was not all we found. Rebecca Galloway, rather, 10 year old Rebecca Galloway's body, was also '*hidden*', as you put it, behind the wall.'

He took another sip of water and uttered with frosty certainty: 'Fragments of Rebecca's coat and samples of her blood were also found on your clothing. You are under arrest for the murder of Rebecca Galloway. It may harm your defence if you do not mention when questioned something which you later rely on in court. Anything you do say may be given in evidence...'

The rest I did not hear. It was all a misunderstanding. They had to know the truth. Yet, how could I explain, to the two level headed representatives of the law, that I had been drawn to

Platform 13c by a voice in my dreams? How could I prove to them that Hopline was the murderer? They would think I was mad, for sure, but I had to try.

'She wanted me to find the coat. I had a dream you see. She was trying to tell me the coat was there. She wanted to be at rest. She wanted her family to find peace.'

'By *"she"*, I presume you are referring to Rebecca?' Mitchell was clearly not impressed by my version of events, as he smirked into his cup.

'Look, you have to listen to me. I did not kill Rebecca Galloway. It was Hopline. He was under investigation before. You knew him, the paedophile. I found his keyring. It was in her coat pocket. You must have seen it on the track.'

'No, Mr Lowe. There was no keyring, though we did find a knife on your person. The officers originally investigating the case were over zealous. It seems they were after the wrong man – which makes you responsible for at least two deaths now, doesn't it?'

Mitchell and Chandler left without waiting for an answer. A police officer was placed at the door to my room.

'How could they be so stupid? I'm a teacher for God's sake. Everything will be alright,' I muttered. Though, this display of confidence brought little comfort, as I recalled certain unpleasant facts. *What the hell is Finnes going to tell them? I'm already under investigation...*

Sure enough, as soon as news of my arrest hit the headlines, a torrent of 'character' witnesses poured out their trusted opinions on the nature of one David Lowe. First, there was Finnes, who informed the good detectives of a 'violent incident', involving one Special Educational Needs pupil and myself. Suddenly, Melanie Price was struck by the need to tell the truth about an attack on her person on Friday, the 13th September. There was also 10-year-old Bethany Kemp of Shipley, who had been playing in the park on the afternoon of the 1st October, when a man, matching David Lowe's description, had assaulted her. Even the dim-witted waitress, Tracy Lovitt, felt compelled to notify the police of a strange conversation she had endured with David Lowe. One during which he had apparently shown an unhealthy interest in the murder of Rebecca Galloway.

Finally, a whole host of rail workers appeared from the gloom of Leeds Willston, to share their stories of a hostile commuter, who had loitered suspiciously around Platform 13c and had attempted suicide twice – probably due to a guilty conscience.

As a result, even before I stood trial, my name had been blackened. The actual date set for the hearing to commence was the 12th January, 2005. Thanks to the presence of mind of my solicitor, I had been provided with a brand-new black suit and blue tie; it was, after all, important that I displayed a respectable personage: a teacher, who had been misrepresented, indeed, vilified by the press.

However, despite the best efforts of the legal team, *I* was the one who shouldered all the blame for the negative outcome of the case. Once the proceedings had commenced, Hopline returned, more sadistically cruel than ever. You must understand that, even in death, this predator wanted others to suffer. Since he had made up his mind that I was fair game, he set out to possess my body once again, so that, during the trial, verbal abuse poured forth from my lips – towards the jurors, the witnesses and even Judge Duckworth herself.

I, or to be more precise, Hopline, also provided the prosecution with all the evidence they needed to confirm my guilt. I confessed to the crimes and even admitted exactly where the infamous noose was hidden: along the rocky towpath that linked Salt's Mill and Shipley Square.

I could not, still cannot, remember exactly what took place in that courtroom. Most of the particulars were brought to my attention by Dr Croft, of H.M. Prison, Bradshaw. At his request, I was later transferred to Hollbury Psychiatric Unit, which is, for want of a better word, a 'madhouse'. I became an inmate here on the 3rd October, 2005, three years, to the day, after Rebecca Galloway's death.

I have tried to appeal. Though it seems no one in this immaculate prison wants to listen to what I have to say. No one will read my story. Only one learned inmate, the rounded Dr Salopek, has shown any interest in my predicament. He too has been touched by a dweller of another sphere; a lady who performs miracles. A lady whom he chanced to meet one cold winter's day, the same day his wife discovered an indiscretion on his part, with a more than helpful trainee nurse.

Mr D. Lowe, April, 2006.

Dr Salopek on Mrs Clarke

Dr Milner's diary entry: 7th March, 2006

There is nothing truer than the statement that doctors make the worst patients. Dr John Lee Salopek is no exception to this rule. Repeatedly, during his interview, earlier this morning, he highlighted how he had been a well respected Oncologist at Belle Cross Memorial. He even had the audacity to refute the mini mental state examination, which had revealed problems with prospective memory and orientation, stating that it was, 'modern fangled hogwash'.

I had to laugh really. In reality, he cast a pathetic figure as his pear-shaped form flopped onto a chair that swallowed him. To note that he was dishevelled in appearance would be a gross understatement. Rather than presenting an aura of respectability, he looked akin to any of the regular tramps one sees frequenting the city's great station. Still, he spoke with an eloquence that was wholly out of place under the circumstances.

Indeed, he insisted on detailing the events of his 'wonderful' life: which had included a close attachment to supportive parents; wild enjoyment at a top private school in Derbyshire and the highest academic accolades from Cambridge University.

You would not have known, during the first 20 minutes of the session, that Dr Salopek was in fact a depressive. The evidence of this facet of his persona only became perceptible when he touched on the subject of his wife, with whom, up until recently, he had maintained a good relationship. The stressors he did identify commenced with his separation from bubbly Mrs Alice Salopek.

Crucially, he confessed to believing that, as a result of an extra-marital affair, a monstrous female spectre, one that frequented the Belle Cross Memorial, was persecuting him. Moreover, he stated, categorically, that this apparition was responsible for weakening his resolve and wreaking havoc with his terminal cancer patients, who were somehow being miraculously cured.

Despite reasoned argument, on my part, Dr Salopek retained his implausible explanations for events at the hospital. So, tiring of his company, I signed the Psychiatric Report as follows: 'Depression with Psychotic features', and sent him on his sluggish way to Ward nine: Acute Psychiatric Unit.

Note on the text: Unfortunately, Dr Salopek was uncooperative during Narrative Therapy. He has written about supernatural occurrences, however, he has chosen to focus his attentions on a former patient, Mrs Clarke. In this instance he has taken on the role of omnipresent narrator to recount her, not his, experiences.

Dr Milner, Psychiatric Registrar.

Chapter 1

The Belle Cross Memorial

The Belle Cross Memorial was constructed when England's thirst for power had reached its crescendo, and, consequently, the nation's world domination was reflected in its imposing brick work, now just a musty shade of brown. In stark contrast, over the years extensions had been made to the Memorial, in order to accommodate the growing numbers of sick amongst the population. Unfortunately, these had taken the form of modern and post-modern designs. Thus, the exterior of the Belle Cross was a curious patch-work of old and new architecture, which had a depressing effect on visitors, who preferred a structure to follow one particular design pattern or another.

Nevertheless, on entering the establishment on a fine, crisp, spring morning, the senses were immediately overwhelmed by the sickeningly sweet, unnaturally clean aroma of the contemporary interior.

As was the custom, in all institutions of modern medicine, the walls and equipment were of unfriendly white or grey and the remnants of anti-bacterial potions filtered through the air. Though, not even these were potent enough to dispel the smell of death that hung over the inhabitants of the Belle Cross – particularly Mrs Clarke.

For her, this was just one in a series of visits, which was determined to be of longer duration than those hitherto. She was, after-all, suffering from terminal cancer, which had already worked incessantly upon her small frame, until she was virtually unrecognisable. Indeed, in her youth Mrs Clarke had been considered by many as quite a catch, possessing, as she did, large, dark brown, almost black, Boleyn eyes, long lashes, a feline shaped face and a slight, though curvaceous figure.

Now, she only inspired pity, looking a truly sorry sight as she struggled to make the short journey from the departing taxi into a wheelchair that awaited her at the entrance. Regrettably, such an aid was an absolute necessity, enabling her to make the difficult expedition to her private room: Ward 15, number 18.

As was usually the case, Mrs Clarke arrived alone, ate a small, insignificant meal and then read. She always chose some work of romantic fiction, while she awaited the late arrival of her dear husband, Mr Clarke.

Yet, as always, Mr Clarke stayed briefly, too briefly. All the while he watched the passing of time on the over-sized clock placed high upon the pristine wall. Once he had endured what he considered to be a socially acceptable length of time by his wife's side, he muttered, 'I'll see you tomorrow then?' He then left, taking his daily paper and old flat-cap with him before any answer could be returned.

Thus left alone, Mrs Clarke began to ponder over her seemingly Christian marriage to Mr Clarke; a marriage based on the time-honoured promise that they would remain together until death. It was not that she thought there was anything unusual about Mr Clarke's behaviour; on the contrary, she believed that it was quite normal for husbands to be independent and detached. Nonetheless, as she did possess a much more generous heart and spirit than those owned by her partner, she was troubled by the gradual decay of amorous activity on the part of Mr Clarke. Since displays of love had been replaced and surpassed by demonstrations of anger, ill-will and, sometimes, downright contempt.

Certainly, it was upon one such incident that the lady in question currently dwelt, as she looked out, somewhat hopelessly, from the frosted glass of number 18 and onto the artificial garden that lay beyond.

It had been Mrs Clarke's 30th Birthday, which also happened to be the 10th anniversary of her marriage. As the occasion deserved, Mrs Clarke had gone to a great deal of trouble and expense: firstly, to make sure that she would be ready for the evening out, which Mr Clarke must surely have planned, and, secondly, to ensure that the particular gift that she had bought for her beloved would be exactly to his liking.

Therefore, she had paid a little more than usual to have her hair styled at Xavier, and had procured some sophisticated black satin trousers and a matching beaded blouse. Finally, she had spent the remainder of the day hunting within Salt's Antiques, intent on finding the finest Half-Hunter that money could buy, and had only left the establishment when her search had ended most successfully.

All in all, when Mrs Clarke finally arrived home, she was thoroughly pleased with all her purchases. More importantly, she looked forward to the coming evening with eager anticipation – so much so, that, as soon as the grandfather clock on the mantle struck 5:00pm, she ran a luxurious bath, overflowing with orange oil and strawberry salts. Soon enough, steam dispersed through the entire terraced house, filling the interior with fruitful, misty vapour. Mrs Clarke's soul was lifted and, to add a touch of decadence to her toilette, she opened a bottle of Merlot that had been cooling in the fridge. She then poured herself a large glass, and proceeded to slide slowly into the rising bubbles, which instantly warmed her aching bones.

She was thus engaged when she heard Mr Clarke return home; a fact easily ascertained by the noise from the television, which was instantly discernable. 'I am upstairs dear, do come on up,' called Mrs Clarke, rather excitedly.

'The news has just started,' was the only reply she received.

Mrs Clarke continued to bathe and, regardless of her husband's lukewarm reception, she positively glowed; though whether this was a consequence of the perfumed water, Merlot, or fond thoughts, it was impossible to say.

Subsequently, once Mrs Clarke had finished her ablutions, she carefully applied her powder and paint, donned her new purchases and descended the stairs, harbouring the vain hope that all her efforts would achieve the desired result – a positive response from Mr Clarke.

Yet, alas, Mr Clarke failed entirely to notice his wife's attire, being too engrossed in the larger events of the day.

'Edward,' Mrs Clarke cooed, 'Edward...Edward...*look,*' she persisted.

Finally, much irritated by the interruption, Mr Clarke turned to behold his wife; 'See you've been spending money again,' he clipped, through lips pressed almost into a sneer.

'Do you think my clothes look nice, Edward?'

'*Passable!*' the gent replied, and with that brusque oration, resumed his aforesaid occupation.

This was clearly not the reaction that Mrs Clarke desired and she now struggled to find the correct introduction to the main question that had been plaguing her mind. You see, she was rather beginning to wonder if Mr Clarke had really forgotten the significance of the 13th October. After some deliberation she broached the topic: 'Edward, do you know what day it is today?'

'What a stupid question,' Mr Clarke grunted, as he tried to keep all his attention focused on the screen.

'Well, I was just wondering, have you made any plans? ... For tonight I mean?'

At last, Mr Clarke noticed his wife and, as he turned to stare at her directly, a smile seemingly pulling at the corners of his mouth, he stated, quite plainly: 'It looks as if you have spent enough today – let's give the meal a miss.'

It was true, at first Mrs Clarke believed that Mr Clarke was fooling her; there really was a meal booked in a plush restaurant for that very evening and, any minute, he would reveal some carefully hidden gift which he had taken pains to acquire. However, as she laboriously watched the clock, she realised that all her eager preparations for the celebration had been for nothing. To be sure, unbeknown to Mrs Clarke, Mr Clarke, a novice historian, had previously decided upon his plans for the 13th October. He would, of course, be watching *A History of Britain,* followed by his second favourite choice of viewing: a thoroughly modern film composed of a predictable plot pattern, and played out by third-rate actresses, who needed only the promise of financial gain in order to unveil the young female form.

That evening, Mrs Clarke watched in subservient silence as Mr Clarke offered his most reliable opinion on the attributes of various unknown 'actresses'. She neither tried to agree nor disagree with her husband, since she had long since given up the 'great debate', that had always ended in her being accused of jealousy. More to the point, as she still felt a deep and unbending loyalty and devotion towards her husband, she was truly hurt by his unfeeling and callous remarks; and as everyone knows, when one suffers genuine heartache, this most powerful of all muscles has the ability to hold the tongue itself within a painful grip.

It was, therefore, much later, during the twilight hours, when Mrs Clarke was able to reflect calmly and retrospectively on the evening. It was only then that she began to forgive Mr Clarke, who had been rather busy at work of late, and who had never before neglected to partake in the niceties of present swapping.

Still, in time, Mrs Clarke came to see that this was just the first in a catalogue of similar lapses in romantic ardour, with the succession of passing birthdays and anniversaries being equally laid to rest by her husband. She realised that he increasingly chose to retain all his wealth for better things: like nights out with his work colleagues; modern gadgetry; fishing tackle for the weekends and new and improved means of conveyance, which somehow always managed to reflect the very latest models of the market.

Gradually, Mrs Clarke was stirred from such morose musings by the constant patter of rain upon the windowsill. It was only now that she began to feel the dull ache that had been developing within her groin, and was currently moving slowly upwards towards her abdomen. As the throbbing increased, she rang for one of the nurses, who swiftly entered the room with a measure of morphine. Once this had been administered, Mrs Clarke, thank-fully, felt the pain ebb away and once more resumed her reading of *The Lovers*. She hoped that this would transfer her attentions to much more pleasant thoughts and, eventually, much needed sleep, which it did.

Chapter 2

No One Called Mrs O'Grady Indeed!

On waking the following day Mrs Clarke beheld Mr Clarke, who had entered the room some 15 minutes earlier and was now scanning the morning papers which had been left on the bedside-table.

'Hello, dear. Sorry, I didn't hear you come in. Have you been here long?' she smiled, grateful for company at last.

'What? Emm, yes, some time', Mr Clarke replied, his eyes still drawn to something of great importance in the entertainment section.

'What's going on in the world then, Eddy? I wish I was out and about. It's so monotonous in here…'

Mrs Clarke paused, as she could now clearly see that Mr Clarke's attention was centred on some lovely lady pictured provocatively on the third page.

Then, whether it was due to incessant physical suffering, or the fact that she had placidly endured years of emotional neglect, Mrs Clarke uncharacteristically glared straight at Eddy and protested: 'Oh, for goodness sake, can't you put the damn paper down for one minute. You make me feel completely worthless sometimes!'

Quite taken aback, Mr Clarke placed the paper on the table. Perhaps some effort to make conversation was in order. Mrs

Clarke was not herself. Therefore, removing his faithful cap, Mr Clarke started to outline the main events of the day to his wife, whom he believed would be much diverted by such current affairs. Unfortunately, the list of topics covered by the tabloids was somewhat disheartening: a murder investigation and council tax rise being the only pieces of information Mr Clarke had to offer. Yet, in all fairness, he was making a profound effort to settle and comfort his spouse.

Having amused Mrs Clarke in this manner for some 20 minutes, Mr Clarke considered that he had fulfilled his duties for the day and rose to leave. However, just as he was about to don his jacket, his wife held him back.

'Oh, Eddy, please don't go…Not just yet,' she pleaded. 'I feel so low today. Maybe it's due to all this rain. You've only been here such a short time. Besides, there's not much for you to do at home.'

'Ah, but you forget Mrs Clarke, there's Sheba to take out. I can't leave her all day,' Mr Clarke returned, as he proceeded to leave.

'Please Edward, just another 15 minutes. That won't make all that much difference, will it? You seem to spend more time with that Pug than you do with me!'

Well, that was the last straw for Mr Clarke, who had been dividing his precious time between obligations at home and never-ending hospital visits. Why, even due to this one excursion he had forgone the chance to watch a particularly interesting episode of *The World at War,* just so that he could make his daily visit to his sick lady, and even that was not enough for her! Besides, did Mrs Clarke not realise that it was hard for him too – having to watch someone slowly die by inches?

'Listen here,' he began, 'I'm going. You have to realise I need some time on my own, to look after myself and the house.'

Mrs Clarke merely shook her head sadly, not entirely convinced that the other 23 hours of the day were not sufficient enough for such matters. Unfortunately, her actions greatly irritated Mr Clarke, who stated categorically: 'Don't try that on me Mrs! It's not my fault you're ill. You should be grateful I'm not in here as well. Who would look after everything then?'

Alas, Mr Clarke's egocentric ponderings set in motion further negative thoughts. Crucially, at that very moment, he committed a gross cardinal sin. He actually wished it was all over. He prayed that his nagging wife would soon be dead and buried.

What was worse, this desire was not borne from any consideration towards Mrs Clarke. Oh, no. Conversely, it sprouted from the more righteous belief that he, Mr Clarke, was suffering most terribly: from the monotony of having to undergo tortuous infirmary visits; from the requisition that he watch death's inevitable approach; from the fact that he had to forgo his favourite pursuits and, finally, that he had to pander to the wants and whims of someone who now only repulsed him.

Callously, Mr Clarke deliberated what life would be like when he could choose when and where to go, and with whom. Eventually, he realised that he had been offering his conjectures orally.

'What would you be glad about, Edward?' Mrs Clarke questioned. 'You said that something would be great, when something else had ended.'

'Nothing, nothing at all,' Mr Clarke muttered testily, whilst exiting the room. 'I am just glad that it's you and not me.'

It was fortunate that Mrs Clarke had not been able to hear Mr Clarke's words. Nor had she understood what thoughts had passed through his mind. She was, though, more than a little depressed at the prospect of having to spend the rest of the day entirely on her own, and was about to look for an occupation of some kind, when something quite extraordinary caught her eye.

As she gazed at a small bookshelf in the corner of the room, she saw a small green light that appeared to be moving very swiftly, in a circular motion, across the front of the display. Believing that her eyes were simply tired from reading, Mrs Clarke squeezed them shut and rubbed the lids firmly, before opening them. Yet, there it was again. Only, this time the orb was slightly larger and travelling in the pattern of a figure-of-eight.

'How bizarre,' she exclaimed.

For some time Mrs Clarke stared, transfixed. Nevertheless, she shook herself from this preoccupation. She became quite worried that perhaps her illness was beginning to work itself upon her senses. For this reason, she quickly lay down and closed her eyes, trying to give sleep at least a chance of success. However, through the darkness, she heard a calm and clear Irish voice proclaim: 'Don't *you* fear my dear, Mrs O'Grady is here.'

As is often the case, when one really experiences something of the seemingly supernatural, Mrs Clarke decided to pay no attention to the voice she had heard; choosing, wisely, to dismiss the occurrence either as one of imagination, or a fault of her senses themselves. She, thereby, continued to seek peaceful rest. In due course this came, bringing with it the strangest dream this good woman had ever known.

In the deepest of sleeps Mrs Clarke envisioned herself walking naked and barefoot upon powdery white sands, surrounded by humongous rocky crags. So overhung were these boulders, with moss and a mass of seaweed, that they were more emerald than grey in hue. Undeterred, she walked along, thoroughly chilled by ferocious winds that were pushing against her and the waters. Abruptly she halted, as she heard a shrill howl that appeared to be coming from some distance. Instinctively, she turned to behold who, or what, was making the incredible din. She saw nothing. Yet, she still heard the piercing cries – which seemed to be growing louder with every passing second.

Suddenly, she saw it. She jumped back in alarm. Mrs Clarke distinguished a black cloaked figure, travelling at great speed along the beach. It was making its way directly towards her. All the while it yelled, as yet, incomprehensible terms. Mrs Clarke was filled with terror. She realised her vulnerable position, and swiftly twisted, to run in the opposite direction.

What was this though? Her escape was prevented by the sodden sand beneath, as it cruelly dragged her feet and legs into its dense surface. Desperately trying to wrench her body from the pit into which she was sinking, Mrs Clarke screamed out with all her might: 'God, help me!'

In the event, this oration was barely audible amidst the crescendo of the storm; that had developed with the sole intent of drowning out the lady's urgent pleas.

Ultimately, the situation was hopeless – as the form that had been so persistently pursuing Mrs Clarke came menacingly before her.

The poor lady had neither the strength nor the inclination to face her tormentor. He now remained quiet and still, upon the same spot. Ever so slowly, Mrs Clarke forced her eyes to look upwards. Yet, she instantly regretted that she had done so.

A monstrous face came into view: hideously pock-marked, wrinkled, wretched and withered, as though battered for many years under the precarious weather conditions. Further, this most callous of spectres proceeded to increase its hold over the lady's senses, when the already inhuman facial features it possessed contorted into a sinister sneer, and a deep, grating voice murmured:

'So you are the one she has chosen? You're all the same; you sap the strength from godly men. You, inevitably lead to their damnation…Curse you, *both* of you.'

For a second, Mrs Clarke's whole body was frozen. It took all her powers of self-composure to close her eyes once more and pray: 'Get me away from here, far away…Oh please, help me…Help me!'

'That's what I am here for dear.' A faint echo resounded through Mrs Clarke's mind. She struggled to regain complete consciousness. Subsequently, she felt firm hands placed upon her shoulders, gently shaking her from her nightmarish slumber.

On opening her reluctant eyes, Mrs Clarke was struck by the marked difference in appearance between the repugnant vision she had encountered in her dreams and the person now before her. For, standing right by her bedside, was a lady of some years, dressed in a neatly pressed nurse's uniform – a lady who was the essence of matronly respectability, wearing a pattern of wise creases upon the forehead and a warm smile that stretched from ear to ear.

'Perhaps I should introduce myself. My name is Mrs O'Grady.'

Some minutes later, having calmed herself, Mrs Clarke glanced at the clock. The display established the time as 12:00 midnight. Slightly shocked by this discovery, she looked out of the window. The oppressive blackness beyond confirmed that she had slept through the evening meal and supper. Oh dear. This was an awkward position for Mrs Clarke to be in. She was not used to asking others for help, especially the nursing staff, whom she did not like to trouble beyond their normal daily duties, unless pain made this an absolute necessity.

Yet, she did begin to wonder, why the nurses had not attempted to wake her. Would she have to wait until breakfast the next day for a bite to eat? Had the water on the bedside cabinet been changed, or had it been festering all day? Finally, the pangs of extreme hunger and thirst overwhelmed Mrs Clarke, to such an extent that she determined to ask her matronly visitor, if it were not possible to satisfy her cravings.

This was precisely what she was about to do, when the welcome intruder interjected: 'They didn't want to disturb you... the nurses I mean. You were sound asleep. It's just not like it was in my day you know. When I did my training you put the patient's health first. Yes, I could see you needed a good wholesome meal down you. Ah, well, we can't have you waiting all night for something to eat. Besides, your water needs changing. You know Caroline, you are going to have to take more care of yourself – than you have been doing, lately I mean.'

Well, Mrs Clarke was quite taken aback. It was almost as if Mrs O'Grady had read her thoughts completely. She was also intrigued. How did this nurse, who she was certain she had never met before, know her Christian name? No one had called her Caroline since she was a little girl, when her forename had been changed to Kim by an impetuous and head-strong mother. Still, the overall effect of hearing her long-rejected title brought a smile to Mrs Clarke's face, as it was associated with much happier and healthier times.

'I always preferred Caroline. Tell me, how did you know my name, my childhood name?' Mrs Clarke asked.

At first, Mrs O'Grady seemed to struggle to find an answer to this question, before stating rationally, 'It was in your medical records, my dear. They keep all the facts, even when names have been changed. It's the only way to gain access to a patient's medical history, for inherited conditions and the like.'

After this Mrs Clarke felt rather silly. Well *of course* doctors and nurses would have to know about childhood illnesses. *It stood to reason,* or they would not be able to carry out their duties properly. So, with her mind put at ease, she settled back against the freshly ruffled pillows. Meanwhile, the good nurse exited the room, explaining profusely that food was what Caroline needed.

In no time at all, Mrs O'Grady returned with tea and muffins oozing with dripping. Mrs Clarke began to devour the fare with relish, as she watched her very own Florence Nightingale performing her other duties: like folding freshly washed white towels, which were placed over a heater; straightening the sheets of the bed, so that not a single crease was in sight; turning the television, so that the best possible view could be obtained, and arranging flowers that had been provided by a local charity.

Gradually, Mrs Clarke began to feel a growing warmth and admiration towards Mrs O'Grady. How, she wondered, did some people end up being so sensitive, caring for the sick, whilst others could think of nothing better than to please themselves? Furthermore, why did she feel that, for the first time in her adult life, she had been provided with someone who took her needs and requirements as her primary concern? To be sure, Mrs Clarke contemplated, rather fancifully, that she had been sent her own guardian angel. Though she was not sure why, since, at this stage in her life, there appeared to be so little time left.

Gracefully the mists of dream sleep overtook Mrs Clarke once more. This was most welcome, as now the lady pictured herself amongst the fields of Hopwood Farm, North Bradford – a place where she had spent many boisterous days as a fledgling, tending to the horses and other livestock.

Radar, a chestnut colt that Mrs Clarke had ridden until the saddle slipped from side to side with the bounding creature's perspiration, was romping through the open grassland, kicking his hooves back in excitement. A gentle summer breeze was wafting fairy seeds across the fields. All the vibrant shades of a rainbow were pleasantly represented in the various fresh flowers, which were sprouting underneath the buttermilk sun.

With a youthful burst of energy Mrs Clarke approached her childhood friend and proceeded to mount the animal with equestrian skill long forgotten. Her objective was easily achieved and, soon after, the pair travelled off at high speed, clearing bracken, fences and walls which lay in their path. Empowered and exhilarated, Mrs Clarke crossed field after field, only hesitating for an instant when a large partition wall, perhaps over six-feet high, came into view on the horizon. Surely, she and Radar could conquer this obstacle? She had certainly cleared many a hurdle, such as this, when she was a young girl. So, in preparation for the feat, she gently increased the pressure on the stirrups and the pace accelerated.

They were presently travelling at what would have been a dangerous velocity, for any but a seasoned rider. Rapidly they came upon the barrier. When, unexpectedly, the colt reared, threw its forelegs and head into the air, and neighed in frightful terror. As for Mrs Clarke, she was thrown, violently, some distance. Thus, she found herself in a sorry heap on the ground.

'Stupid, stupid... Radar, Radar...,' she called, as her mount sped off in the opposite direction.

'What, what's this?' she stammered, whilst pulling herself upwards. Mrs Clarke gazed through misty eyes at the black bricks of the wall. They seemed to be swaying in the wind. She shook her head, in an attempt to correct her vision. She then watched the partition, more closely. She could now see that someone was clambering over it. It was someone who looked vaguely familiar.

'No. Not here. It's not possible,' she cried, as the hooded spectre of her nightmare returned.

What was more, as she had discovered during her previous encounter with the evil emanation, any attempt at escape was futile. Try as she might, her legs refused to run, contrary to her mind's command to do so. The only option open to Mrs Clarke was to wait – wait to find out what this fiend wanted to say or do. These questions were answered, all too quickly.

'Don't even think about rising above your station in life, Mrs Edward Clarke. So, you have some help now, do you? Ha. Well if that is the case, you will also have to deal with the good doctor. What a stupid, feeble woman you are. Rest assured, as long as she stays, I stay. I say to you, are you going to give her up?' growled the hooded fiend, in anger, stating the last remark as a command, a threat, and certainly not as a question.

As for Mrs Clarke, she was scarcely able to respond. She was numbed into silence.

'What's wrong? Cat got your tongue? Speak now you fool! Give up your ghost, or, I swear, this year you will breathe your last.'

As one usually finds under such circumstances, when one is being asked to speak against one's will, the result of further implorations to do so, is the exact opposite to that required. So it was with Mrs Clarke, who remained mute. She was simply dumbfounded, as to why this ghoul was hounding her. Still, she had to compose herself. Then, with surprising bravery, she turned the process of interrogation upon itself.

'Who are you? Tell me, what is it that you want of me?'

'So you can speak. Who or what I am is no concern of yours,' the tormentor hissed, all the while, pointing a warty finger at his victim. 'All you really need to know is that, if you do not do what I command, you shall never be rid of me. That, Mrs Edward Clarke, is a promise.'

To the great irritation of the unwanted companion, rational objections, which can intrude into the shadowy depths of the unconscious, did so within Mrs Clarke's twilight world, and she called out: 'Wait a minute, this is just a dream. All I have to do is wish and you will disappear. Who's the fool now?'

With this the spectre's facial features contorted, in a murderous fashion, and he proceeded to stamp his foot, almost as a small child would do, in reaction to her pretty speech. All the same, Mrs Clarke closed her eyes tight shut and made her wish. Thankfully, when she opened them again he was gone.

The remainder of the night was spent in truly peaceful slumber, disturbed only in the morning with the call that breakfast was ready. Miss Partridge, an experienced nurse of Belle Cross, had sorted a tray of toast and jam, bran flakes and orange, which, although nutritionally more substantial than Mrs Clarke's midnight feast, was far less enjoyable.

'Where's Mrs O'Grady this morning?' enquired Mrs Clarke, certainly not prepared for the strange expression of disbelief upon Miss Partridge's face that her question provoked.

'Who…? What? What did you just say?' the normally steadfast nurse enquired, hesitantly.

'Mrs O'Grady, where is she today? I was kind of hoping for some more dripping. Haven't had any quite like it for years.'

With that statement the poor nurse's complexion turned sickly pale. She explained, sincerely, that there was no such person employed at the hospital, not to the best of her knowledge. Also, that perhaps Mrs Clarke was mistaken: she had been attended by Nurse Grattan, a trainee on the ward with little experience. Yes, that must be it. It simply was not good enough. Dripping's so bad for the arteries!

Swiftly the nurse exited the room, barely pausing to hear her patient offering her thanks for breakfast.

As for Mrs Clarke, she was left slightly amused and somewhat irritated by the nurse's bizarre behaviour. No one called Mrs O'Grady indeed!

Chapter 3

The Hospital's Haunted...?

Mrs Clarke was still out of sorts, as Mr Clarke arrived for his customary visit.

'Thought I would come early today, Manchester are going to be playing Bradford tonight. It's on the box.'

Preoccupied with her recent experiences, Mrs Clarke ignored Mr Clarke's initial remarks and commenced a narrative on the events of the previous night, focusing on the strange nightmares that had been disturbing her sleep.

Eventually, she looked at Mr Clarke for a response, yet gasped, when she saw his dishevelled appearance. Large patches of midnight blue circled his eyes, his hair was unkempt, whiskers were on his upper lip and chin, which were normally kept strictly shaven, and his shirt was hanging out from his brown cords. 'Eddy, are you feeling alright? Is something wrong?'

Mr Clarke explained that he too had not slept well. All the hospital visits had really been getting to him. Why, he was even beginning to have nightmares about confounded nurses. As if he did not see enough of them during the day. 'It's always the same. There's this old woman, a nurse. She's a really bad sort, bad tempered and that. Every time I look around she's there. Has an Irish name...that's it, Grady, O'Grady.'

Mrs Clarke could not help but grin, 'Oh Edward, you must

have seen her here. She works here, and what do you mean she's a bad sort? She's lovely.'

No, that was not the case, Mr Clarke was adamant, he had never met the woman before. He knew most of the nurses on the ward and was on first name terms with them. So Mrs Clarke, not wanting to push the subject, as it seemed to be one that made Mr Clarke disconcerted, tried to choose another topic to discuss. Just at that moment, the said Mrs O'Grady entered the room.

The nurse displayed the same smile and friendly manner that had previously impressed Mrs Clarke. To the good nurse's credit, she also took the time to comment on how well her patient looked and suggested that Mrs Clarke should take a walk in the garden. However, within moments, the lady's eyes caught sight of Mr Clarke, sat in his usual slouching manner on the chair.

'Oh *he's* here is he?' she stated, as Mrs Clarke observed, quite brusquely. 'How *long* are you going to stay today Mr Clarke? Ten minutes?'

Taking off his faithful cap, Mr Clarke's complexion grew even pastier. Initially, this was due to the shock of being proved wrong, about the existence of the nurse. Next, it was in anger, as he prepared to offer his reflections on the nurse's attitude and comments. Mrs Clarke, perceiving that a heated debate was about to ensue, asked Mrs O'Grady, politely, if she would not mind fetching another jug of water, since she was feeling rather parched. As always, Mrs O'Grady complied with Mrs Clarke's wishes, leaving the husband and wife alone for some minutes to converse.

'Well, I can't explain it. I can't understand it, Eddy, she's always nice to me.'

'To you maybe, but I can tell – she's one of *those* feminist types,' Mr Clarke retorted.

'What? Oh, Eddy, what are you talking about now? She's just an old woman. Maybe she's just tired today?'

'Never, not *that type*, men-haters the lot of them. Think they know everything. The problem is they just want to be men.'

Mr Clarke continued in this way, quite put out by the old woman who had dared to question him. Just who did she think she was?

Unfortunately, the presence of Mrs O'Grady curtailed the length of Mr Clarke's visit. When the nurse re-entered the room with the water jug, he put on his cap, grabbed his paper and headed for the door. He muttered, grumpily, that he would be back the next day, when they could have some privacy.

However, this event set a precedent. As the weeks passed, the privacy that Mr Clarke craved was not forthcoming. Eventually, even Mrs Clarke began to wonder how Nurse O'Grady managed to time her entrances and exits exactly to the rhythm of her husband's daily visits. The length of these visits, therefore, diminished even further, with the shortest being a mere miserly four minutes.

Mrs Clarke worried. She worried about her marriage. She worried about the lack of civility between the nurse and her husband. Most importantly, she worried about Eddy's shattered, insalubrious looking countenance.

More than ever before, she had noticed the criss-cross creases that marked his forehead and aged him well beyond his current years. She had also been struck by the condition of his skin, which virtually hung down, as if forcibly shaken from the surface of the muscles beneath. Finally, she had perceived a dull, sallow, yellow tint that clung to the delicate area around his eyes, and accentuated the dark circles already nestled there.

Often she had ignored her concerns in this area, concluding that Eddy's appearance was a result of the nightmares, which he had claimed interrupted his sleep. Yet, the good wife soon surmised that this was not reason enough for the sickly hue that surrounded Mr Clarke on his visits to the Belle Cross.

Mrs Clarke was so anxious about Mr Clarke, that she carefully broached the subject of his health on his next visit to the hospital. At first she stated tentatively: 'Is everything alright at home, Eddy?'

Mr Clarke, in a fashion peculiar to himself, grunted in the affirmative, asserting that everything was just as it always was, except, of course, for the damn bed, which needed a new mattress.

'Not been sleeping too well then?'

'No,' Mr Clarke snapped, harshly. 'Where's she today? I was beginning to think that you two were joined at the hip.'

Mrs Clarke explained that she had asked Mrs O'Grady not to bother her, as she wanted to spend some time alone with her husband.

'Well, that's how it should be!' Mr Clarke asserted, somewhat defiantly, as if arguing his case before judge and jury.

Now, one would have thought that the two lovers left with so little time together would have made the most of it, but this was not to be. The fact remained that, although they had spent so many years together, they had very little to say to one another. What was more, although Mr Clarke resented his wife wanting anyone's company but his own, he still wished to be free of her. For this reason, he urged her to try a short walk to the television room, where at least some human voices would be discernable in the cold silence.

With very little fuss, Mrs Clarke gathered her red velvet dressing gown. She was about to call for assistance, when she made a surprise decision: to attempt the journey on her own.

Initially her steps were hesitant and small, but, within moments, she was striding along the corridor, for the first time since she had entered the Belle Cross. Occasionally she reached out for Mr Clarke, who was walking a few feet in front of her. Though, when he swiftly removed his arm from her touch, she made do the best she could. Her best was certainly impressive. To be sure, as they entered the rest room, where other patients were gathered around the television, Mrs Clarke had actually overtaken her husband.

Now conversation was even harder to achieve. Mr Clarke proceeded to watch a gardening programme, not that this particular brand of entertainment was to his liking. All the same, Mrs Clarke was in high spirits, and turned to converse with a stout elderly lady, who sat on a dated leather chair beside her.

'I was never into gardening. We only have a small brick backyard. It's just as well. Whenever we've kept plants they have always died,' Mrs Clarke laughed, oblivious to the objections that the use of the d-word roused amongst such company.

'*Really?*' Miss Cheswick replied, quite sourly, as she turned to commence a tête-à-tête with Mrs Grinnsburgh.

The nature of this particular conversation caught Mrs Clarke's attention and greatly fascinated her.

'Do you remember the murder I told you about? I told you last week, when *The Sound of Music* was on,' Miss Cheswick questioned her neighbour.

'Yes, about that nurse. Wasn't she murdered or something? What was that doctor's name?'

'Never mind that for now, that's not important,' Miss Cheswick interrupted her companion, rather rudely, and continued: 'Well haven't you heard about all the fuss? It's got Miss Partridge all worked up, and I thought she was such a sensible woman.'

Miss Cheswick cunningly paused at this crucial moment, in order to heighten the tension for the listener, poured herself a glass of orange and recommenced. 'It seems that Ward 15 has its own ghost! Really, I am not making this up – the whole story was told to me as gospel.'

Mrs Clarke listened intently to the rest of the conversation, during which Miss Cheswick described how Miss Partridge had been given quite a scare by one of the other patients, who had claimed not only to have seen, but also to have spoken to the ghost of Ward 15.

Finally, being unable to resist the temptation to join the discussion, Mrs Clarke interjected, 'Which patient...? Which room has the ghost been seen in?'

Annoyed at the intrusion into what was, after all, a private conversation, Miss Cheswick turned on Mrs Clarke and declared coolly, 'Why the patient in room 18. It's haunted. Surely everybody knows that. Now if you don't mind...'

Mrs Clarke replied, quietly, that she did not mind in the slightest, being as she was deeply troubled, and feeling something akin to an icy trickle of rain, running up, then down, her spine. Not normally a person given to superstitious inclinations, she was rather disturbed that someone, like the hitherto calm and collected Miss Partridge, had seen a presence in her very own room. Mrs Clarke actually began to wonder whether a transfer was in order; as she certainly did not want to encounter a ghostly apparition when she was on her own, especially in the middle of the night.

Oh don't be so stupid. It's only some story they have made up to pass the time, she eventually chastised herself, almost aloud. Within seconds she had regained her collected composure. Still, story or not, she was eager to question Mrs O'Grady on the matter – for, who else was sure to know all the particulars of the case than someone who had been an employee of the hospital for many years?

Unfortunately, Mrs Clarke was to be frustrated in this quest for knowledge for some time. Over the next few days Mrs O'Grady was nowhere to be seen in the Belle Cross. Concluding that she had taken some leave, Mrs Clarke was left more wearied and bored than ever. Unwisely, perhaps, she had come to overly rely on this larger than life character, who knew just what she wanted and when.

Consequently, Mrs Clarke became restless. Even her books were no longer of interest to her, being as they were too steeped in a romantic ideology reminiscent of much earlier times. Mrs Clarke was also more agitated than usual, owing to certain miraculous physiological changes taking place within. With each passing day she began to feel the strength of life's blood flowing back through her veins. She, thus, wanted and needed more exercise and over the next couple of days made frequent trips to the TV suite and outdoor garden. These 'outings' became a noticeable part of her routine, much to the bewilderment of the medical staff who had consigned her to the grave.

To be sure, if one had observed Mr and Mrs Clarke on the 14th June, one would have been at a loss to determine which one of the pair was at death's door. For, to the exact degree, as pronounced as were the positive changes in Mrs Clarke's physique, Mr Clarke's had been affected negatively.

Indeed, as Mr and Mrs Clarke walked around the rather

pathetic fauna and flora provided in the small outdoor clearing, a trainee and a qualified nurse, looking on from their desks, could be heard remarking to one another upon this very subject.

'Look there…you see, just there…Who are they? They don't look very close…See, he keeps pulling his arm away from her.'

'Oh, that's Mr and Mrs Clarke. Poor woman, been in and out of here for years. She's terminal you know.'

'What, don't you mean he is?'

'No,' the nurse replied sternly, not appreciating the fact that a trainee was choosing to question her in an impertinent manner.

'So, she's the one with stomach cancer?'

'Yes, as I said, she's had it for years, can't seem to get the better of it. The prognosis certainly doesn't look good. She's due for more chemotherapy next week. It's awful, makes her terribly sick.'

'Well it's strange…'

'What?'

'Life and death, I mean. To look at them you would think she would outlive him by 10 years, at the very least.'

So the conversation continued, with its subjects being completely oblivious. Although it was true, such thoughts had been running through Mr Clarke's mind. He had discovered, that very morning, that the clothes hung from him as they did from the clothes hook. As a result, he had weighed himself, and could not quite believe what the scales revealed: he had lost over 13 pounds in less than a week. He was also extremely concerned about the constant ache in his groin, which had been disrupting his sleep and was now making him wince in pain, as he paced around the garden. Crucially, there had been the nightmares, those awful nightmares, during which his pursuer, Mrs O'Grady, had promised death would befall him.

So much had Mr Clarke been troubled by these factors that he had called Dr Harrison, much to that gentleman's surprise, since Mr Clarke had not attended his surgery in over 15 years. He had, therefore, been given a cancellation for the next day. All that remained now was for Mr Clarke to tell his wife why he would not be visiting her as usual.

'I won't be coming tomorrow,' he commenced, '… actually,

I've got an appointment.'

Mrs Clarke stopped walking and turned to look at Mr Clarke. There was a peculiar tone and pitch to his voice.

'Where...? The doctor's...? What's the matter Edward? Have you got a bug or something? I am not surprised, really. You don't have a good diet Edward – all that junk food you eat.'

'Well I hope a bug is all I have,' Mr Clarke sighed, looking even more downcast.

Mrs Clarke became anxious. She had not been blind to the changes in her husband, but she had repressed her instincts; she could not allow herself to conceive that anything serious might afflict her Mr Clarke. The mere thought of the possible diagnosis, given the symptoms he displayed, made her bite her lip, in a vain attempt to hold back tears that were threatening to overflow.

Mr Clarke could perceive her inner struggle, and, not being a man given to emotional outbursts, made his excuses and left for a tortuous 48 hours.

Although these hours passed excruciatingly slowly, Mr Clarke did return. Yet, his visit was to be of little comfort to Mrs Clarke. The only information he could provide was that the doctor had completed a thorough examination and was sending him for an x-ray and scan. This made her even more fretful.

'So, he thinks it's something serious then? I mean, he wouldn't be sending you to the hospital otherwise, would he?'

'Thanks a lot. That's just what I needed to hear,' Mr Clarke complained. 'Let's talk about something else.'

Fittingly, the conversation was quickly dropped by Mrs Clarke. She realised that she was being somewhat inconsiderate. After all, when she had been waiting for news on her illness, the last thing she wanted was to have the prognosis conjectured by those close to her. Instead, Mrs Clarke focused on examining the latest scandal in the *Daily Royal,* regarding the rights and wrongs of the coming war in Iraq.

Whilst Mrs Clarke rambled on endlessly, knowing very little about the topic of conversation which she had chosen, for the first time, in more years than he could remember, Mr Clarke began to appreciate his wife, whom he could see still loved him deeply. What was more, as he gazed into her eyes, he was again mesmerised by their dark beauty. They looked almost as enchanting as they had done when Mrs Clarke had caught his attention at the postal workers' annual Christmas dinner and dance celebration.

At that moment he felt a sudden pang of guilt, for the harshness of his temper, and his own lack of sensitivity towards her, as she had battled bravely through her own illness. Duly he said, softly, 'Perhaps we should go for a walk, if you're feeling up to it? It's not a bad day outside, it would be a shame to miss it, Caroline.'

Mrs Clarke, for her part, almost jumped from her comfy chair, on hearing Mr Clarke talk to her so gently. She smiled in a demure fashion, like a schoolgirl on a first date and got ready for what would, hopefully, be an enjoyable release from room 18. This it certainly proved to be.

The sky was clear blue, the air crisp and the sun streaming, as the pair circled the garden many times. Their conversation was at first stilted, confined as it was to current affairs but, within minutes, the tête-à-tête veered towards pleasant trivialities, and onto jovialities. Before long, Mr and Mrs Clarke were laughing together, as they wondered over the strange follies of the past. They could be seen walking ever closer together. Mr Clarke eventually placed his hand within his wife's. A long-lost warmth was returning to their personal lives.

That evening Mrs Clarke sat bolt upright in bed. A beam of smug self-satisfaction crept across her face, as she thought of Mr Clarke. Then Mrs O'Grady, quite unexpectedly, breezed into the room looking rather flustered.

'There just aren't enough hours in the day my dear...' she complained, as she took to watering the plants and straightening the sheets before turning to leave.

'Mrs O'Grady wait, please,' Mrs Clarke requested. 'There's something I really need to ask you, it's been bothering me for ages.'

Halted by the sudden imploration, Mrs O'Grady returned to her patient's side.

'What is it, Caroline?'

Momentarily Mrs Clarke remained mute, as she struggled to conquer her own feelings of stupidity over the question that had been plaguing her since she had overheard the gossip of the two ladies in the television room.

'Well,' she began, 'I don't really know why it has upset me so much, but,' she paused again, 'it's all over the hospital. Well you have probably heard yourself. Everyone is saying that there is a ghost in my room. I know it's ridiculous, but have you heard anything about it? It's just Miss Partridge, she's seen or heard of it, or something, and she's normally so straight and sensible. This room isn't haunted, is it?'

In an instant, Mrs O'Grady's countenance plunged, her eyes glazed over and she stared rigid at the wall. In this manner she remained for some moments.

Mrs Clarke, feeling rather perturbed, conjectured, 'It's probably stuff and nonsense. They've nothing better to talk about.'

As if awoken suddenly from a hypnotic trance, Mrs O'Grady's facial features twitched, and she returned to the world of the living with a start.

'That's right, Caroline, stuff and nonsense is what it is.' That being said, the conversation was dropped and Mrs O'Grady again attempted to leave.

Yet, Mrs Clarke's curiosity threw upon the lady another question: 'Just one thing, did you enjoy your holiday?'

'It was no holiday my dear. I had a lot of work to do elsewhere. I sometimes do home visits,' she returned, before finally exiting.

Chapter 4

Miracles

The following day Mrs Clarke rose in fine spirits, from which even the prospect of a thorough examination and scan did not detract. She prepared for the indignities of the day with speed and waited, quite contentedly, for the customary wheelchair to arrive. In due course it did. Hurriedly she was whisked along the corridors of the Belle Cross Memorial and deposited, in an unchivalrous manner, at the Radiography Department on the first floor.

Soon enough Dr Salopek, freckled and pear-shaped, appeared with his faithful medical records in hand. Taking hold of the chair, in a firm and ever so swaggering a way, he wheeled his patient into the examination room, where his able assistants were eagerly waiting to unceremoniously drop Mrs Clarke onto the ultimate diagnostic device.

Before long, Mrs Clarke was completely swallowed inside the rotating tomb of bad-tidings and, some time later, was churned out again, to be reunited with her nightdress and gown.

Although Mrs Clarke was quite used to the procedures involved in such affairs, and readied herself for the post-scan pronouncement, she was certainly not prepared for the look of sheer bewilderment on the face of the self-assured Dr Salopek. He had now taken to pacing around the room, excitedly removing his glasses one moment, only to replace them the next, stating with some trepidation: that of course something must be wrong, ever so wrong with the equipment. He had never in all his days seen anything like this before.

'What is it? Tell me, is it much worse? How long do you think I have?'

Mrs Clarke's endless stream of questions fell on deaf ears, until the held back gent of yester-year turned towards her, placing a strangely reassuring hand on her shoulder and proclaimed: 'It's a medical miracle. Naturally we will have to do further tests...You see, I have *never* known someone to make such a recovery, not when the cancer was so far advanced...but, Mrs Clarke, it's clear, never mind in remission, there is not a trace of it – you are completely in the clear!'

Of course when mere mortals are given such unexpected news it can take some time to digest, and so it did with Mrs Clarke. She felt numb, completely numb: from all the years of worry, anger, and then final resignation to her lot in the scheme of life – a life which now promised to be of a much longer duration than she had been led to expect.

Mrs Clarke's mind was positively spinning when Mr Clarke pushed open the door of room number 18. She did not know quite how to tell her husband the strange but wonderful news. So, she quickly rushed into a brief oration of how her life expectancy had risen dramatically within the last 24 hours,

'...Well that's it, Eddy. I don't really know what to think. We can plan the rest of our lives together.'

For his part Mr Clarke simply smiled hesitantly, both shaken and relieved that his wife's suffering was finally at an end.

He then recalled, to himself, the many occasions on which the two of them had shared bad news and felt oddly uncomfortable, suspicious that the diagnosis was an illusion and any minute someone would call to apologise and explain that certain records had been confused.

Of course, the real reason for Mr Clarke's uncertainty was a depression, a depression brought on by a tragic discovery made earlier that morning. He, Mr Clarke, was living under the shadow of a malignant cloud – cancer. If only he could tell his wife and share his concerns, but now really didn't seem to be an appropriate moment. A burden was being lifted from Mrs Clarke's shoulders and the prospect of replacing it with another weight seemed wholly unfair.

Still, it was perhaps naïve of Mr Clarke to think that his wife was unaware of his worried brow. She had witnessed his reaction to her news and knew well enough that something profound was troubling her husband, that 'something' being all too obvious under the given circumstances. All the same, her thoughts remained distinctly positive. It seemed to be a time for miracles. If she had been a lucky recipient, there was no logical reason why Mr Clarke should not be. She thus steadied herself and stated plainly; 'It's alright Eddy, it really is. Don't worry love. We will get through this, we've done it before.'

With that the two held each other, in a loving embrace.

Subsequently, the following week proved to be a crammed one. In order to set the records straight, Dr Salopek carried out further tests. At long last, he was more than satisfied that Mrs Clarke should be allowed home. This release being under the strict proviso that if there were any additional symptoms, Mrs Clarke would return to the Belle Cross at the earliest opportunity. Mrs Clarke agreed to do so, and was discharged from the hospital on Friday the 13th July.

So it was that, as the season finally turned warmly into summer, Mrs Clarke packed her toiletries, gown and nightdress into a small tweed bag. She was all ready for the amazing journey home. Faithful Mr Clarke arrived to assist his wife and, despite the fact that she was probably the stronger of the partnership, he insisted on stacking her belongings in the car, before returning to accompany her down the stairs.

However, Mrs Clarke would not hear of leaving the hospital without, at the very least, thanking the nursing staff who, as she claimed, had restored her to good health.

There was a buzz of excitement at the nurses' station that day.

All those who had met Mrs Clarke gathered to bid her a fond farewell and wish her all the best for the future. She returned the adieux with thanks, a bunch of flowers and a donation, for the patients' charity appeal. The whole event was uplifting for Mrs Clarke. Regretfully, there was one problem – despite her best efforts to ascertain the whereabouts of Nurse O'Grady, no one seemed to know who or where she was.

'But surely one of you must know her. She must have worked here for years,' Mrs Clarke maintained.

Even this was not enough to receive an answer in the affirmative and seemed in itself to provoke feelings of unease within Nurse Partridge, who busied herself filing records. Mrs Clarke was, therefore, obliged to leave the establishment with a slightly heavy heart, at not seeing her guardian angel one last time.

Later that day Mr and Mrs Clarke pulled up outside their Victorian terrace. The squashed face of an old companion waited to greet them at the door.

'Come on now Sheba, get down girl,' Mrs Clarke pleaded.

The excitement was so great for the little creature that a puddle was left on the floor. This was swiftly removed and Mrs Clarke's bag unpacked. At long last, the couple were able to relax in their own home, with a hot mug of coffee apiece.

Left alone, in silence they both scanned their surroundings: patches of frayed carpet scattered randomly around the room; flaking white paint from the window sill that revealed the cracked wooden frame beneath; a truly worn out sofa, the original grey velour covers of which were now completely flat and bald, and a curious mismatch of mahogany, pine and oak wall units. All of these objects were a decade past their prime. For the first time in years, Mr and Mrs Clarke noticed just how neglected and gloomy the house had become.

'I say Eddy, this place looks awfully dark. It's dusty too, I'll give it a good clean this week and maybe a lick of paint, to cheer it up again,' Mrs Clarke began.

'Yes, that's right, Caroline. We need a fresh start. This place has a lot of good memories for me, but there's a lot of bad too.'

'What do you mean, Edward?' Mrs Clarke questioned, whilst stirring the coffee with her little finger.

'God knows, Caroline. I swear, if I have the time, I will make it all up to you. You're like this house, you see. If I hadn't been caught up in myself for so many years, I would have seen how I have neglected you. It's high time we turned this shell into a home,' Mr Clarke promised. He reached out to Mrs Clarke, taking her hand in his, and completed the touching scene by proclaiming, 'I love you Caroline…I know it now.'

Rudely the chimes of the rusty doorbell rang out. At first, Mr Clarke was quite inclined to ignore the unwelcome visitor, yet decided to see exactly who had precipitated this untimely intrusion. He rose, placed his mug on the mantle and went to open the door. Initially, it jammed over the musty carpet that was being forced onwards and upwards by the rotten boards beneath. Following much pushing and pulling the door finally opened with a squeak.

A smartly dressed stranger was revealed, clothed in a black pin-stripe suit, finest blue silk shirt, a chequered black and white tie and highly glossed gents' leather shoes. 'Hello. You must be Mr Clarke,' the man began, 'I know you are probably very busy, but I wondered if I might have a few moments of your time.'

'I am not interested. Whatever it is you're selling.' Mr Clarke nodded to the gentleman in good humour and turned to close the door.

However, the intruder placed his foot squarely and firmly inside, so that the door could not be locked.

'Look here…' Mr Clarke began, before the stranger apologised and passed him his identity card, which read:

'Mr Philip Grimshaw (M.A.)
Journalist for: Bradford Local Gazette
Tel: 01274 …

Chapter 5

Revelations

Mr Clarke welcomed Mr Grimshaw who, as it turned out, had heard of Mrs Clarke's miraculous recovery with some interest. He had taken it upon himself to investigate the particulars of the case, which he wanted to report in the local paper as a feel-good story.

'It's just, our Gazette all too often reports on the negative aspects of life – crimes and the like. I just thought it was high time we covered a story from a positive angle. You know, to give some people out there some hope. Your story, Mrs Clarke, does just that, it will give other sufferers a ray of light.'

He then settled down in a chair and noted down the important facts of Mrs Clarke's medical history, as best as she could remember them. His jottings came to a halt when Mrs Clarke touched on the matronly assistance of Mrs O'Grady.

'Are you sure the nurse was called "O'Grady"?' he questioned cautiously, to which Mrs Clarke nodded.

'The room you stayed in, it was number 18?'

'That's right, number 18,' Mrs Clarke stated, curious to know why the interviewer's tone had become more serious.

'You say she helped you more than the others?'

'Yes, it seems quite silly now but…well, at the time, I felt that as soon as she arrived my recovery began.'

At this point Mr Grimshaw took a handkerchief from his

jacket pocket and wiped his brow, before continuing; 'Did any of the other nurses *see* her?'

'Why, no… That's strange isn't it? No one in the hospital seemed to know who she was, or, for that matter, where she disappeared to half the time.'

Mr Grimshaw suggested that he was not at all surprised that the others in the hospital knew very little about Nurse O'Grady. He asked for a glass of water. Then, he began to relate to the couple how he had covered a tragic story on that very lady many years before; a story that Mr and Mrs Clarke would never forget:

'Nurse O'Grady, or Mary McBride, as she was known before her marriage, started working at the Belle Cross Memorial when she was just 19 years of age. She dedicated all her life to the hospital and worked there for over 30 years. She was liked by all her colleagues, even the doctors, who tended to keep themselves aloof in those days.

'Well, later in life, she inherited a large sum of money, I can't remember all the facts now, but she was certainly a very wealthy lady. Naturally, this made her even more interesting to many of the male members of staff and one Dr O'Grady – a real charmer if ever there was one. If memory serves, he had relations with a number of young trainees and got himself quite a reputation.

'Still, the couple married, and, for a time, lived contentedly. But, it didn't last. The good doctor soon became bored with married life and she, regretfully, became seriously ill. Stomach cancer they said it was. She ended up being a patient at the hospital herself, on Ward 15, room number 18. Within a year, Mrs O'Grady was dead.

'Now that would have been the end of it, but, one of the nurses, a young friend of Mrs O'Grady's – Miss Partridge was her name – insisted on a post-mortem examination. She wasn't at all happy about the diagnostic procedures that had been used to confirm Mrs O'Grady's illness – all carried out and signed by her husband, of course. And, now we get to the shocking part of the story, and where I come into it. The post-mortem revealed that Mrs O'Grady did not and had never had cancer. The real reason for her ill health was a steady dose of poisoning – arsenic acid – administered on a weekly basis by Dr O'Grady. You see, no one had ever suspected him, regardless of his adulterous affairs.

'It caused a real stir at the time – hit the local and national headlines. Who would have thought a respected doctor could kill his wife in so callous and cruel a fashion? In any event, he was tried and hung for murder in 1958.

'He never showed any remorse. He only admitted his guilt the day before his execution, when it is claimed by the warders that he screamed from his cell: *"Damn her! Damn the lot of them! I am glad I killed her, I wished her dead often enough – don't all married men wish the same?"'*

As you would imagine, Mr and Mrs Clarke listened intently to this horrible tale. Somehow it seemed to make sense of their own recent experiences, which they shared, in detail, with Mr Grimshaw over the next few days.

Sure enough, Mr Grimshaw subsequently passed this information onto me. Indeed, he was to become a frequent visitor to the Memorial, owing to the numerous spectral sightings and miracles that have occurred there.

Understandably, I have taken on the role of omnipresent narrator, to tell the tale of Mr and Mrs Clarke. Admittedly, some of the events have been portrayed in a vivid form, obviously not available to anyone other than those involved.

However, you must appreciate that many of the particulars outlined within this narrative were given to Mr Grimshaw by the Clarkes themselves. Later this information was given to me. Not that I agreed with everything the good journalist chose to tell me, especially the derogatory references to one Dr Salopek – freckled and pear-shaped indeed!

Now, I realise that, as interesting as all this may be, what you really want to know is how I came to be a patient at this fine institution on the 7th March, 2006. Suffice it to say that, after years of witnessing varied supernatural phenomena at the Belle Cross, phenomena which I as a scientist could not explain, the panel decided that I was no longer fit to be a member of its staff. Moreover, I too have been hounded by Mrs O'Grady, albeit following one foolish indiscretion on my part.

Thus, I have been forced to endure the humiliation of being referred for treatment by a doctor of lower standing and qualifications than myself. What's more, I have been consigned to Hollbury for 'recuperation and rest'.

Yet, what you people don't seem to understand is that, until the wolf in sheep's clothing decides enough is enough, that is, until she has finished with me, and I have shown her sufficient penitence for my *crime*, I am doomed to remain here – whilst the pain of insomnia eats away at my sanity.

Dr Salopek, April, 2006.

Mr Dylan Holt

Dr Milner's diary entry: 11th March, 2006

Mr Dylan Holt. What can I say? He is an archetypal 1970s child who has curiously never advanced into adulthood. This lager-lout made his acquaintance with Hollbury today.

Strange as it may seem, Dr Blackwood has informed me that Holt has no history of mental illness. I found this hard to believe earlier this morning, when the tattooed skin-head pronounced that he has attended countless séances, during which he has discovered that he is indeed a grandiose reincarnation of a personage of some importance!

Apparently, poor Holt has also endured difficulties in coping with the activities of daily living. Well, I for one am stunned that such a thug manages to crawl out of bed in time to see the passing of the daylight hours.

Maybe I am being a little too harsh on the man. After all, he was polite and attentive during the session. Though I am not so sure that he would have been, had my skirt been longer and my blouse not so tight.

In any event, given that Mr Dylan Holt showed a lack of intrinsic motivation and clear signs of Major Depression, medication was prescribed and he was sent to his new quarters on Ward nine: Acute Psychiatric Unit.

Note on the text: Fortunately, for once, Mr Dylan Holt cooperated fully with the Narrative Therapy. Consequently, what follows is a faithful transcript. Though, I have to admit to diminishing the number of expletives in the tale!

Dr Milner, Psychiatric Registrar.

Chapter 1

The Cattle Market

'Oh, come on for fuck's sake. Just let me in,' I spat at the obese doorman.

He didn't move, not one inch.

I must have reeked of vomit, since I had just left a mound of it down an alleyway that ran alongside *The Cattle Market*. Still, I had to get inside. I had to. I tried to push past Tony again.

'Look man, you've had enough. Just go home will you, before there's any more trouble,' he warned, as he held both of his hands hard against my shoulders.

I was too sick to fight. So, fuming, I stumbled into a waiting black cab.

'Stupid bastards,' I called out of the window, 'I'll be back tomorrow. You…you stupid sods, I can tell you that!'

The driver looked in his rear-view mirror but said nothing; he too was sick, sick and tired of cleaning up after all the drunks who were ruining his car.

The following morning I felt worse, much worse. I had downed over 13 pints the previous evening, as *The Cattle Market* had been holding a 50p-a-pint night.

'Are you going to stay up there all day?' Salina bellowed, at the top of her voice.

I didn't answer her. I made my way to the bathroom. I had to dispose of the fur on the inside of my mouth, which was throbbing and in desperate need of a powerful mouthwash. Eventually, I found a bottle of the liquid in the battered wall cabinet and swished and gargled no fewer than five capfuls. Then, wearing the same faded jeans and t-shirt I had worn all week, I crept down the stairs and deposited myself at the breakfast table.

Bacon, eggs and fried bread were sizzling in a blackened pan, producing a soothingly greasy aroma that went some way towards relieving my hangover. Salina frowned, as she poured a treacle-thick, black coffee.

'So, will you be going to the Job Centre today, Dylan?' she quizzed, running her tongue around the inside of her mouth, so that she looked almost Boxer-like.

'Yeah, I guess so,' I retorted.

'Surely there *must* be some job you could do. You know your father would turn in his grave. He was such a proud man. *He* never had to sponge off the State.'

I slammed my plate down. Why couldn't the old battleaxe give it a rest? It wasn't like I hadn't heard it all before. She never tired of reminding me just how great my parents had been. How different it was in *'those days'*. How *'hard'* they had worked to build a home. How much they had *'struggled'* to keep a roof over all our heads. I couldn't remember either of them. Both had died shortly after I was born.

Of course, my tantrum didn't stop her. She managed to scorn and criticise for a further 10 minutes. It was time for the morning lecture on my dissipated lifestyle. How could I hope to find employment, if I was out all hours of the day and night? Why would any decent businessman want to employ someone who looked like a thug? The crew cut and tattoos had to go or, at the very least, I had to cover them up for my next interview. Most importantly, I had to watch the amount of alcohol I was consuming.

'You've already got shadows and wrinkles and your eyes are always bloodshot. You mark my words, young man, if you don't sort your life out you're heading for an early grave.'

'Bye Salina,' I muttered, grabbing my wallet as I headed for the door.

'It's Aunt Salina to you,' she called.

I was gone.

Regardless of my present condition, I headed for the local bar, *The Crown*. Leon and Karl were already inside playing pool. They too were 'job-seekers' who spent most days idling away the hours. Leon was in his fifties, a semi-skilled weaver who had been made redundant in the early 1970s. He had never really attempted to find any other kind of employment. His side-kick, Karl, was game-for-a-laugh, and had tried his hand at just about every type of unskilled occupation.

In comparison, I was lazier than either of those two. I had only held down two jobs in my life: one at a local supermarket, stacking shelves, and the other packing boxes at a large card company. Neither had lasted longer than a year. I was untrained. I was also unwilling to lower myself to earning a crust. You see, I figured that the State would always be there with handouts. Failing that, Salina's house was worth a bob or two. After all, she was an old woman, and I was bound to get her place when she was no longer around.

The date was Monday the 12th May, 2005 and I was in my 31st year of being a sap. All day I sat supping ale, gambling on the fruit machine and testing my skills at the pool table. I hardly spoke to Leon and Karl. I rarely did. Even then, it was only to comment on how the area was turning into a shit-hole, or where the attributes of any given female belonged on a scale of one to 10.

At 5:00pm I left the pub for home. Waiting there, as usual, was a well-cooked meal, after which I showered and shaved, for a night on the town.

Subsequently, two hours later, Karl and I were heading for the city centre. It didn't seem to matter that we were both broke, it being the day before our benefits were due. In total, between us, we only had 20 pounds. With the costs of a taxi, this meant that we only had enough for four pints each. This was nowhere near enough, not to get plastered. There was nothing else for it, but a trip to *The Cattle Market* – the seediest of nightclubs, where the beer was cheap, albeit watered-down, and a little rancid.

As luck would have it, when we arrived, the doorman I had jostled with the previous evening was not there. In his place was another hard head in a tuxedo, who simply stepped aside as we entered.

Inside, disco lights and lasers flashed across the club's mirrored walls. As you would probably expect, Karl and I were not into boogying. We, therefore, passed quickly along the dance area, and made our way to the darker second floor. This was where all the heavy drinkers hung out. This was where the sexes met briefly at the end of the evening, to impress each other with their sexual prowess, and 'score' before time was called. However, it was now deserted. The only people in the building, aside from ourselves, were the bar staff and one tatty looking old man.

'I just don't get it Dylan,' Karl said, as he broke from his refreshment for a moment.

'What?' I questioned.

'Why the hell do they let him bring that mutt into the club?'

Sure enough, Karl was right. I wasn't normally in the habit of paying much attention to my surroundings, not when I was on a 'bender', but there, sat at the old man's feet, was a scruffy Scottie dog.

'God knows, silly old sod,' I quipped, as I tried to continue with my drink.

However, it was then that I paused and placed my glass slowly on the table.

The doors to the VIP suite on the top floor had opened. Ms Hampton, or the *She Devil,* as we preferred to call her, walked through them. She was the not-too-friendly owner of the establishment; a dominant figure, who was always seen with a lengthy cocktail cigarette protruding from her overly red, glossed lips. Directly behind her followed the strangest quartet I had ever observed. There was just something very peculiar about them. All were certainly out of place in *The Cattle Market*. Moreover, all were agitated, anxious, as they made their way, hastily, to the old man perched at the end of the bar.

On closer inspection, I could tell that the group were up to something. Crucially, as one spoke to another, his or her eyes darted this way and that. They didn't want anyone to hear what they were saying. They also, apparently, did not want to be seen, since, minutes later, the group disappeared again, up into the VIP lounge.

'Well, I guess it takes all sorts,' Karl noted.

'Yeah, I guess so,' I agreed.

Our in-depth conversation over, we continued to consume our beverages.

It was a further six pints later, just before midnight, when the lights around the club were dimmed, to signal time.

'Bloody licensing laws,' I grunted, adding that they should be changed and opening hours extended during the week.

Nonetheless, we were asked, politely, to drink-up and leave. Obstinately, we disregarded this request, and it was more than 15 minutes later that we staggered from the building and into a taxi.

It was the perfect end to, what we considered to be, a perfect evening; we sang *New York, New York*, all the way home, and woke Salina for the fare – the fare we had already spent.

I suppose I can appreciate why she was furious the next day.

'That's the last time Dylan. I'm just not having it any more,' Salina warned, shaking her bony finger at me as she did so, 'You've got your benefits, make them last.'

For my part, I promised that, from then onwards, I would be much more careful with my finances. Hence, I determined to spend more and more evenings at *The Cattle Market*, instead of the other more expensive clubs scattered around the town. I had no intention whatsoever of curbing my cravings for alcohol. Drinking was my life.

Accordingly, on Friday the 23rd May, I could be found leaning against the 'Lagoon' bar, on *The Cattle Market's* second floor. I was on my own that particular evening, because Karl had somehow found a part-time Saturday job and didn't want to sleep in on his first day. It didn't bother me in the slightest. I often went to town alone. I liked it that way. It meant I didn't have to try to make conversation with anyone, save any pretty barmaid who caught my eye.

Unfortunately, that Friday, 'Curly Mel', a podgy, plain chatter box with two blackened front teeth, was serving at the bar. I certainly wasn't interested in anything she had to say. So, I sat glaring at the dance floor below, just in case any talent came in.

Intermittently I glanced at my watch. Soon it was 11:30pm and the club was heaving with sweaty bodies and foggy mists. I had been mixing my drinks, alternating between beer, whiskey and vodka, and my head was starting to whirl a little. These symptoms worsened, as I watched the blue lasers move to the rhythm of the music, Seal's *Crazy*. I closed my eyes for a moment, to quell the sickly feeling inside.

However, I opened them suddenly. The party animals of *The Cattle Market* were screaming. I couldn't see a thing. I closed and opened my eyes once again, to check that I had done so before. It was still pitch-dark.

'It's all right ladies and gents. Just stay where you are, the lights will be back on in a minute,' the DJ settled the crowd, which was becoming disconcerted.

I think it must have been some five minutes before the lights flashed once again. It was definitely longer than a minute. Still, the revellers below carried on undeterred, as if nothing untoward had happened. But, something had happened, something strange.

The odd group that I had seen emerge from the VIP suite once before, had done so again. They were in a state of sheer panic. The old man was clutching his dog so tightly that it struggled to be free. One of the women had clearly been crying, as streaks of mascara ran down her cheeks. I was only a few metres away from the troop, and could faintly hear their high-pitched tones, even over the booming beats of The Farm's, *All Together Now*. This was exactly what they said, word for word:

'For God's sake Esther, maybe we should leave well alone? What's going to happen next? I, for one, have all the information I need to write my thesis. Besides, we can't keep on holding our meetings in a crowded place like this. Someone's going to get hurt, if we're not careful.'

'Look Heather,' a pale faced, older woman in gothic dress replied, 'it has to be here, don't you see that? It won't work anywhere else. This is where it all happened in the first...' She stopped short, as she caught my eye. 'Let's go back upstairs and discuss this up there.'

With that, she left and the others obediently followed. The 'entertainment' over, I turned my attention back to my pint. It was empty.

'Fill her up,' I instructed Mel, who was sitting on a stool polishing her nails.

She shrugged, none too pleased that she was being torn away from her little preoccupation to do some work.

'That's one pound,' she stated, holding out her hand for the money.

'No chance, look at the size of the head on that.' I pointed to a three-inch layer of froth at the top of my glass.

Mel, who was loosing her patience, snatched the pot and filled it right up to the rim. Only then did I hand over my hard-earned cash and allow Mel to go back to her perch.

I gulped down the bitter-sweet beverage, pausing just twice to catch my breath. Gradually, the liquid bloated my stomach and my jeans grew tighter. I jumped off the chair and headed for the toilets, which were situated, inconveniently, on the first floor.

However, as I descended the precarious spiral stairs, the club fell into darkness once more.

Unfortunately, at the precise moment that the lights went out, I was about to place my sole onto the next step. Consequently, I lost my footing, dropped to my knees with a crack, and slipped, head first, down a further four steps.

'Shitting hell!' I cursed, as I tried to get my bearings. Then, as quickly as the lights had failed, they returned. 'That does it! I'm not bloody having this!' I informed a passing male on his way somewhere. I clambered to my feet and examined my jeans, carefully. They were covered with grime and the knees were torn. Somehow, I still managed to get to the toilet in time. I then hobbled as swiftly as I could back upstairs – to find the owner of the dump.

She and her bizarre pose were at the doors to the VIP lounge. Like before, they looked strained, stressed. I didn't care. They now had something else to worry about. I limped over to them, perhaps in exaggeration of my injuries.

'Look lady,' I interjected, tapping Ms Hampton on the shoulder. 'Is this place of yours some sort of joke? I've just gone for a burton on your damn stairs. I've a good mind to sue. Look at my bloody jeans!'

This outburst caught her attention and she turned around with indignation furrowed into her brow.

'Sorry, were you talking to me?'

She knew very well that I was.

'Yes who else? You are the owner of this shit-hole aren't you?'

At this point in our conversation two doormen appeared from the shadows. Ms Hampton called off her 'dogs', and indicated that there was no problem. Nothing she couldn't handle anyway.

'I do apologise, Mr…?'

'Mr Dylan Holt.'

'We'll discuss this upstairs shall we, Mr Holt?' She pointed to the entry, much to the surprise of her companions. Apparently, I had been causing a scene and a few punters were watching.

I nodded and followed her up to the VIP suite – the VIP suite where my tale of horror and personal discovery truly begins.

Chapter 2

Twilight Séance

What I found in the VIP lounge was weird in the extreme. The suite itself was immaculate. The walls were pure white, where they could be seen behind all the hanging mirrors. There was also a bar, constructed of speckled cream marble with a stainless steel trim. The finery was completed with the flooring, which was made of toughened glass, so that one could view the revellers dancing below.

Sure, it was an elegant room, where all the most important visitors to the club could hang out. Yet, those who now hid there were not interested in showing off their elevated status to others. They had far more disturbing things to do. For, placed over a glass table, surrounded by chairs, was an ominous looking board.

'I don't believe this! Is that one of those Ouija boards?'

The group turned to me then looked at one another. It was obvious that I was right.

I had to laugh. They took my discovery so seriously. The straight, auburn-haired Goth, chastised Ms Hampton for allowing me access to their secret world. Another man, with silver whiskers, was forced to agree. However, a pretty woman with large, dark brown eyes, sprang to my defence. She tried to settle the group, by insisting that, it really didn't matter if someone had found out what they did. It wasn't like they were breaking the law or anything like that. Her arguments were seconded by a balding, scrawny fellow, who kept gawping at her chest. As for the old man, he remained quiet, which was more than could be said for the snarling Scottie at his side.

'Well, Mr Holt, you must think all this is very strange, yes? Let me introduce you to the members of our group. My name's Cynthia,' she stated.

Next she gave a few words, outlining the particulars of each person in her little sect. The old man, whom I was accustomed to seeing at the bar, was Reginald Wilkes, an amateur studier of the paranormal. Next, there was Heather Riucous, a lecturer on local history at the city's university. Jacques Russell worked alongside her. He was a professor of historical studies, with an M.A. in Local Myths and Legends, from McMighten University. In addition, there was Brian Fowler, a promising student in his early twenties, whom I guessed was attending the 'sessions', more because of Heather, than any actual interest in the supernatural. Finally, the last member of the sextet was Esther Brewster, a spiritual medium and clairvoyant.

From the first moment our eyes met, I knew there was something inherently hostile about Esther. Whilst all the others had smiled as they had been introduced to me, she did not. Her eyes were a frosty, ice-blue. They were quite menacing against the black of her attire and make-up.

'We are currently investigating paranormal activity at *The Cattle Market,* Mr Holt,' Cynthia explained. 'It all began, for me anyway, when I bought this place four years ago. Do you know why it is called *The Cattle Market?*'

'Because it is, isn't it?'

'Oh no, Mr Holt, it has nothing to do with *that.'* She paused to light a pink cigarette. 'This place was built on the site of a cattle market and slaughter house.'

'Really…?' I tried to sound interested, but my leg was starting to throb.

'Yes, *"really"* – local legend has it that the blood of hundreds, possibly thousands, of animals has formed a river, one that flows beneath the foundations of the building.'

'Oh, I see, so you're trying to make contact with a dead cow then?'

My sarcasm was not appreciated and Cynthia continued. 'Long before this area was used for the mass slaughter of animals, it was used to dispose of human undesirables.'

'What do you mean?'

'In the 1600s a building stood just below where we are now. It was used as a primitive courthouse. At the back of *The Cattle Market*, there once stood the gallows.'

'That's pleasant.'

'Well, Mr Holt, scores of miscreants met their maker on that site. Many of them were women. Most were hung as heretics.'

To be perfectly honest, I did not know what a heretic was and my ignorance was clear for all to see. Cynthia thus took it upon herself to set me straight, with a short history of heresy and witchcraft.

According to her, a belief in the existence of witches was acknowledged in the Bible. For example, in Exodus it was, and is, stated, *'Thou shall not suffer a witch to live.'* Or, in other words, witches should be put to death. Nonetheless, Cynthia went on to outline that, for centuries, 'witches' were allowed to practise their arts, and were considered by many to be useful old hags. They were responsible for healing the sick amongst the poorer sections of society: by providing nettle presses for backache; worm stews for weakness or simply by using a bowl of water to tell one's fortune. No one in Medieval Britain seemed to mind them, and they were, by and large, an accepted part of life throughout Europe.

However, this period of tolerance came to an abrupt end. The first seeds of rejection were sown with the formation of the Cathar religion: a sect that rejected vital segments of both the Old and New Testaments. For instance, they claimed that, whilst the heavens and soul were created by God, the body and Earth were the Devil's handiwork. Their renunciation of certain Christian beliefs was unacceptable to the Papal authorities, who set out to eliminate support for them.

It followed that, for many years, this particular religious group was harassed and persecuted. Though, things were to become worse; much worse. In 1208, a papal legate was killed as he slept in his bed. His murderers were claimed to be representatives of an extremist Cathar sect in the Toulouse region of France. As you would probably expect, the Pope was outraged. Henceforth he vowed that all heretics would be hunted down and severely punished. Thus, the Papal Inquisition was formed, expressly to dispose of heretics (those persons who did not follow the strict teachings of the established Catholic Church).

So, the bloody rampage for religious purity was initiated. Now anyone who failed to follow the exact doctrines of the Church was accused of being in league with the Devil. Wise women thereafter became 'witches'; treacherous, venomous vipers, who could only be dealt with utilising the stake or the gallows.

Though, Cynthia explained, '...it wasn't until 1604, that England caught up with the rest of Europe and witchcraft became a crime punishable by death.'

'Let me get this straight,' I collected my thoughts, 'you lot disappear up here to contact witches?'

'Yes, we call to the souls of those who perished on the gallows.'

'Well have you? Have you managed to 'contact' anyone?' I began to smirk. What an absolute joke they were.

'Actually we have,' chipped in the disgruntled Esther, 'the twisted souls of the heretics have come through for us many times.'

'You can't take all this crap seriously? You don't *really* believe in witches do you?' I glanced at each member of the group, then back to Esther.

'Yes, I, I mean we, do. Perhaps, if you are a non-believer, you wouldn't mind staying for the rest of tonight's session?'

I simply couldn't resist. I had to see them all make complete and utter fools of themselves. Besides, Heather was rather easy on the eyes, and Cynthia had also offered free refreshments, if I stayed as her new VIP guest. You see, the way she figured it, I would be of benefit to the group. By having a detached observer attend their meetings, their *scientific* study would be all the more grounded in reality.

Subsequently, a couple of pints later, half way through the 'witching hour', the troop sat down around their precious board. I had never seen an object like the Ouija board up close before, and took a minute to examine it. It was made of wood, painted white. Carved into it were the letters of the alphabet, all in black. In one corner of the board was the word 'No' and in the opposite corner was the word 'Yes'. In addition, the numbers zero to nine were inscribed across its base. Finally, placed in the centre, there was an opaque, heart-shaped article, which the others explained was a planchette. Carefully, each member of the group placed a finger upon it. The attempt to contact those on the 'other side' now began.

'Hello, is there anybody there?' Esther asked, seriously. Nothing happened, so she repeated her question, a little louder. Again, there was nothing.

'Is that it then? I'm really convinced,' I mumbled, over my pint.

'Why don't you join us Mr Holt?' Esther suggested, nodding her head in the direction of the table. 'Just so you can see that there's no trickery involved.'

'Why not?!' I slumped over to the table and pulled up a chair.

Esther called to the spirits once more. Only this time, the planchette went wild. With arrow swiftness it shot to 'Yes'.

Esther hesitated and removed her finger. She seemed genuinely surprised.

'Is anyone pushing it?' She assessed the response of each member of the group. After composing herself, she placed her little finger back on the object.

At this stage in the séance, Ms Hampton took the lead. First of all, she wanted to know the name of the presence.

This was spelt out with lightening speed, 'Helen Wilkes'.

This time Reginald shot to his feet.

'Look, are any of you pushing the damn thing?'

He was reassured by the others that they were not. Even I was forced to admit that I found it difficult to keep my finger on the planchette, since it was moving so quickly. Reg took a swig of his whiskey and sat back down.

What now occurred defies any rational explanation; none that I could provide. Our 'visitor' was able to provide personal information on two members of the group. The first was Esther, whose name the planchette found with ease. As if to verify that the sprit was in fact contacting the right person, Helen indicated: 'Aunt Carmel hairdresser'.

I glanced at Esther. It was strange that this simple snippet of trivia brought such an ashen appearance to the addressee. Esther was clearly distressed that someone, or something, from the 'other side' was singling her out for attention. I found this odd. Had she not told me earlier that the group had made contact many times? Why all the fuss now? I turned my gaze back to the board. There was movement again. Helen's message now took a sinister turn.

The information included the following: 'Why murder the innocents?', 'evil', 'witches' and 'Peter Mason'.

The planchette came to a standstill. It seemed that the séance was over. Yet, this was not the case.

You must understand, out of all those attending the session, I would have said that I was the most calm; the non-believer, the one who thought such things were a bit of a laugh and nothing more. Though, I certainly wasn't laughing when my name was spelt out on the Ouija board.

'Come on, you all knew that,' I claimed, implying the others were colluding in a pathetic joke.

However, I knew that this was not so when, 'Aunt Salina slave', was the next message that we received.

How could they have known that? I don't know these people from Adam. My thoughts raced, and so did the cursor. This is what else it had to say: '1624', 'murder', 'Salt', '1d' and 'witchcraft'.

I was stunned. What on earth did all that mumbo-jumbo mean? I was sure it meant nothing to me. The board fell silent. Helen was no longer with us.

'God I could use a drink. Who wants one?' Brian had gone to the bar, where he proceeded to play host. With shaking hands, he poured the liquors, which each of us required. Understandably, we all opted for spirits, since beer just wouldn't cut it, not after what we had been through. I held the brandy in my hand as though it were a precious jewel. Each sup brought me back to my sceptical senses.

'There must be some explanation,' I stated. Though, what that was, I did not know. The only plausible reason for the message I had received was that I was pushing the planchette myself. I was adamant that I had not done so, both to myself and to the others.

'It seems that we're *really* onto something,' Ms Hampton exclaimed. She was aglow with excitement after recovering from the initial shock. 'Well, couldn't you feel the difference?'

'What do you mean, Cynthia?' Esther enquired, pointedly.

'You have to admit, the planchette has never moved like that before. It was virtually hovering over the board,' Heather interjected, and carried on, nervously sipping her soothing drink.

'It was faster, that was all.' Esther seemed to be sulking over the changes the others had noticed.

Even the distant Jacques chose to join in with the conversation. 'Look, ladies,' he slurped, condescendingly, 'I for one am certain that tonight we made a real breakthrough. You could feel the very presence in the room. At one point I could have sworn Helen was standing behind me.'

Unfortunately, this was the last thing that the group wanted to hear. It made the VIP lounge creepier and crowded with spectres.

Although the chill was now lifting, we still wanted to be out. So much so, that Cynthia suggested that we all take a breather downstairs in the club. We were all glad to oblige and, minutes later, we were surrounded by the booming beats and flashing lights of *The Cattle Market*. It was there that Cynthia commented on another strange anomaly: during this particular séance there had been none of the typical negative effects upon the electrics.

The time was 2:10am and there were only a few awkward punters left, trying desperately to get just one more pint from the bar. Everyone was tired. I felt positively dreadful. I must have, since I left half of my drink on the bar.

'I've got to go,' I told Cynthia, as I struggled to put my jacket on.

'You will be back won't you, Mr Holt?' She enquired, 'I'd really appreciate it if you would attend more of our meetings.'

Of course I would, I told her, as long as the beer was free. She agreed and I left for home.

Chapter 3

A Quest at the Library

I awoke the next day sluggishly squinting at the sunlight that was streaming through my bedroom windows. I closed my eyes tightly, to keep out the intense rays. With them still sealed, I somehow made my way to the stairs and slouched down them to the front room, where Salina was watching *Breakfast TV*.

Regardless of the warmth outside, the room was frosty. I glared into the fire, which was on low. Then I began to reflect on what had happened the previous evening. In the stark daylight, events appeared to be much more palatable. How stupid had I been? To have thought that what occurred was real. There was nothing 'real' about it. I had just had one too many, and, without knowing it, had pushed the planchette on its psychic way. In light of this, I concluded I was onto a good thing. The galley of fools could believe what they liked. I would participate in any future meetings, only on the proviso that intoxicating refreshments were provided free of charge.

'What's with you this morning?' Salina asked, turning her eyes my way just long enough to cast a reproachful glance.

'Nothing,' I muttered, refusing to take her bait. I then did something that I hadn't done for ages: I decided that a conversation with Salina might be remotely interesting, and proceeded to ascertain what her feelings were on the topic of séances.

'Salina…'

She frowned.

'Aunt Salina, have you ever used one of those Ouija boards?'

She was taken aback and nearly choked on the black liquid in her mouth.

'What on earth are you talking about now?' Salina laughed openly, and took a chocolate biscuit from a tin on the table.

'I was at a séance last night.'

'What?'

'I was at a séance. There's a group of oddballs who hold them at *The Cattle Market*.'

'Oh I see, *The Cattle Market*, eh?' She understood everything now. 'Well, I can appreciate why twisted souls would see fit to visit that place. After a pint are they?'

It was no use. Salina was as sceptical as I was. Though I had to wonder why I had broached the subject at all. Yes, I was cynical, but I was also curious. I wanted to know more about the use of devices such as the Ouija board to make contact with the 'other side'.

Therefore, I surprised even myself when I passed by *The Crown* later that lunchtime, and headed instead for the local library in the Old Mill, on Bottle Road. That was certainly a place that I, in my infinite wisdom, had never required before.

At 12:30pm I entered the Old Mill. A straight-laced, grey haired old lady immediately approached me, as if she too knew that I was out of place.

'Can I help you?' she questioned.

I presumed that she could and explained exactly what type of text I was searching for. Jane, as she introduced herself, informed me that there were several works on different aspects of the paranormal, supernatural and so forth. Next, with her assistance, I completed the required membership forms. It was all very easy, and once I had shown her my Driving License, I was permitted to take a total of six texts of my choice.

However, this task was not that simple. When I started to sift through the contents of various forgotten shelves, I found only one offering that seemed to promise answers to at least some of the questions I had. This was *Ouija Boards – The Serious Practitioner,* by Collin Grahams, 1972. It was not the most well thumbed publication in the world, and its 400 pages were damp, due to its long life on the library shelf.

Even the librarian herself thought I, and it – a skinhead and a spiritual work – were oddly matched. So, I held my head down and averted my eyes, as the book was stamped. Shortly afterwards I left the library, calling briefly at a local store on the way to Salina's. This detour was an absolute necessity, not that I particularly wanted to buy anything, but, rather, I needed a plastic bag – just in case I bumped into any old friends on my way home.

Fortunately, I arrived home undetected and ascended the stairs to the sanctity of my bedroom. There, I became immersed in the text. Though, I have to say, it was something of a let down. What it really contained, within its covers, were the findings of various investigations. Naturally, these would have been of great interest to Heather and Jacques, but not to me. What I wanted was hard evidence, facts on the validity of such research. These could not and, perhaps, may never be given.

Subsequently, the only pieces of information which I found to be of any use were outlined in the introduction itself. This covered a mere four pages, on which the author hinted at the dangers inherent in the use of the Ouija board. In short, if one genuinely believed in the existence of demons, the Ouija board should be approached with caution – since, by definition, such a device could potentially offer evil entities an easy means of gaining access to one's soul. More importantly, Grahams warned that the device should never be misused by those under the influence of alcohol, as this could leave them open to attack.

I placed the book on my bedside cabinet. It was 7:30pm and growing dark outside.

'Bloody hell, I'd better get a move on!' I barked, shooting for the bathroom for a quick shower. Saturday at *The Cattle Market* was never a night to be missed, certainly not Saturday the 24th May, 2005.

Chapter 4

Tortured Souls

I arrived shortly after 9:00pm, and was greeted by the aroma of stale beer escaping from the interior. If that were not bad enough, once I entered, the spillages on the carpets stuck to the soles of my shoes. As a result, I squelched my way up the grand stairs to the Lagoon bar. Ms Hampton was there, waiting.

'Mr Holt, it's good to see you again. I was a little worried that you wouldn't turn up tonight. Let's go and see the others shall we?'

Without wasting any time, we made our way to the VIP suite. The group were already poised, eager for the séance to begin.

'Where do you want me?' I directed my question to Heather.

'Anywhere,' she replied, confused by the emphasis I had placed on the words and a certain glint in my eye.

In the event, she had failed to receive my signals, and I settled for a place next to Brian, where there was a small space.

'Beer?' I indicated to Cynthia, who obliged with a pint. I was ready for the games to begin – they did in earnest.

When all fingers were placed on the planchette, Esther asked if there was anyone present.

In an instant, the instrument sped to 'Yes'.

'Who are you, a witch?' She questioned our guest.

The cursor circled the board and returned to 'Yes'.

'Why do you come?' Esther enquired.

All the assembled group held their breaths, till the visitor gave this incoherent answer: 'Sarah Mason killed here, evil needs humour'.

'This is certainly a troubled spirit, I can feel its power,' Esther expressed her higher understanding and perceptual feelings. 'Can you show us a sign?' The leader continued, as we fell quieter, stiller, than we had been. The whole group was tense with anticipation. Esther paused and scanned the room.

We waited for what seemed like an age. Esther was becoming impatient. 'Show us a sign,' she repeated.

No glasses floated, no table rocked, no lights flickered. We were all disappointed. We all wanted something to happen. I glanced at Esther. Her reaction was different. She appeared to be quite angry, agitated. From what I could tell, she genuinely expected that something would happen, and bit her lip in frustration when it did not.

'We're not getting that much through. We should have a break and continue in a little while.' Esther stated, then stood quickly and left the suite.

We were all a little surprised by her sudden exit, though her absence did allow the rest of the group to help themselves to refreshments. We also took the opportunity to debate what we thought about the night's meeting, so far.

To begin with I listened as the others prattled on. Clearly, each member of our secret society was excited about the amount of information they had received from an old inhabitant of *The Cattle Market*, one who had already graced their sessions on a number of occasions. In contrast, I was unimpressed. The simple truth was I couldn't quite shake the feeling that someone in the group was not being completely honest. Surely, one of them was helping the planchette on its way. What was more, I couldn't adapt my beliefs to fit correctly with the current events; I had never believed in witches, witchcraft or demons for that matter. That is not to say that I completely rejected the possibility of troubled spirits making contact with the living. Rather, I believed that such tortured souls made contact for a reason.

'We have to find out what that *reason* is,' I told the others, who seemed to find the idea of being investigators appealing.

Not so Esther, who re-entered the room a few minutes later. She objected to Cynthia's suggestions that more probing questions be asked of the visiting spectres. She also rejected the very idea that any demon spirit would have a noble reason for making contact with the living.

'You're treading on very dangerous ground,' she warned, 'you can't afford to be taken in by these evil entities.'

However, regardless of her protestations, the group's will was to prevail. It was settled that, for the remainder of the evening, the remaining sextet would take on the roles of assistors and harmless inquisitors.

As for Esther, she was left to sulk in the corner; having decided not to sit in on the final attempt at connection.

So it was that, for the first time, I was chosen to lead a session. To begin with it was an honour I tried to wiggle my way out of, but the group was having none of it. I have to confess that, initially, I tasted feelings of self-consciousness, stupidity even, as I found myself asking questions to the air. Nevertheless, once a series of enlightening rapid responses were given to my questions, my embarrassment abated. A fresh invigoration overtook my mind and body. Beyond any doubt, on Saturday, the 24th May, 2005, I became convinced that the Ouija board was an undeniable practical device for contacting the dead.

You see, at first, I adopted the same questioning techniques that I had seen the others display. Hence, I had asked if there was a presence and then requested her name. This was duly given as Helen Wilkes, the same *lady* who had visited the suite the previous evening. Then, I changed my tone; 'Look Helen, this kind of thing, I'm still not completely convinced. During the last meeting, you provided facts on certain members of the group. Could you tell us something else, something concrete, something that no one could guess?'

Unfortunately, the message that came through was the same as that we had received before: '1d...Salt...witchcraft.'

'I don't understand, Helen. Could you tell me something about myself, my birthday perhaps?'

This was quickly given as, '14 November 1973.'

'Is that right?' Heather enquired, looking intently into my eyes. I nodded. The group was stunned.

'Ok, so you know my birthday. What about my father's?'

For a while the planchette was still. I was about to go on with the next question when Helen revealed: '13 May dead now'.

Of course the date was correct. My sceptical side was squashed. One accurate guess was possibly acceptable to the cynic, but not two; not when coupled with the knowledge of my father's passing. We were communicating with a being of another realm. That was now an established fact. The main question was, from the multitude of those who had died – why had this particular spirit chosen to make contact with us?

This was what I set out to discover with the next question. However, I found the reply both strange and disturbing. Helen was unwavering in her determination, as she repeated, over and over: 'Matthew Salt…1d…witch finder'. To which she eventually added: 'Look inside Dylan remember the dreams', and finally, 'murderer'.

I left the table. I was confused, sick inside. The 'meeting' had been so personal. As far as Helen was concerned, we had a history. At some point in time, our lives had interlocked in a story of witchcraft and murder.

'What's all this about dreams?' Brian encroached upon my thoughts.

I rummaged around in my mind, but found only a void; I could remember nothing.

I told the group a complete lie: Salina had been ill that day and I wanted to check that she was feeling better. At 11:30pm I left for home; an unheard of conclusion to a Saturday night that even surprised the sickly Salina, who was still watching a thriller when I flopped down on an adjacent chair.

'Want some supper?' She offered.

I accepted. I was ravenous, and devoured the six hot buttered crumpets with ease. Then, with a heavily laden stomach, I retired to bed – for what I thought would be a peaceful night's rest.

Chapter 5

Witch Finder

In the event, sleep came quickly. More or less, as soon as I nuzzled my head into the duck down pillow, I was oblivious to the current world. In contrast, the dreams that accompanied my slumber were anything but serene. The first, and most memorable of the fragments that unfolded, told of a time long gone, during the reign of James I, in the early 1600s. The setting was a place called Broadford, a small town community.

For some reason, an old man was in a great hurry to reach this town – since he raced along the rugged, muddy highways which led to it at perilous speed. Eventually, the foul-faced reptilian arrived at his destination, and his carriage came to an abrupt halt. That instant, men, women and children flocked to his side. He was obviously a personage of some importance, as all the villagers who thronged the streets bowed or curtsied as he passed by. However, his business there did not abide with the bustle of the crowd.

His head was held high with arrogance. He simply ignored them all, whilst they praised God for his swift reaction to their cries for help. This man was on a mission, one which took him straight to the grand doors of a church. There, he was greeted by one Reverend Moore, a pasty faced specimen of frailty, who grinned profusely in the old man's direction, sickeningly revealing the rotten yellow teeth behind his lips.

'Oh, Sire, we must give thanks for your safe journey. Please come inside the Lord's temple.' Moore looked about him and gestured that the others should keep their distance from the revered visitor.

'...As you are well aware Master Salt, there is much to fear in the town at present. I for one believe that *such matters* must be spoken of in private.'

With that, the two entered the cold confines of the church, to discuss Broad-ford's blighted future.

As it transpired, a respected landowner, one Lord Peter Mason, had watched helplessly as a whole herd of his cattle had been overtaken by a mysterious affliction. The beasts had suffered for two days or more, and in the final stages of the 'disease,' had struggled to even stand on their own four feet. They had died in agony, twisting, rolling and gasping for air, over the green fields that surrounded Brookbank Hall. According to Reverend Moore, these strange events had transpired shortly after a row between Lord Mason and a young girl, one Mary Illingsworth.

'Mary Illingsworth,' the Reverend sighed, 'an angel on the outside, but as the Lord has said; the Devil himself can appear as an angel of light. I'm sure you must know how these girls are these days – shrewish, headstrong. Naturally, I'm certain your eminence will be wishing to *interview* Miss Illingsworth. I shall take you to her – the residence is but 10 minutes from here.'

'In good time Reverend Moore,' Salt clipped briskly, brushing the dust from his black overcoat. 'You mustn't fear; if there is witchcraft in Broad-ford, I will find it.'

Though, he had no intention of doing so until he had consumed a great feast in his honour at the vicarage.

The next scene in the nightmare was set in a worker's cottage: a pitifully flea-ridden, habitation that reeked of cow dung and dogs. In total there were five long-toothed brutes that snarled and spat menacingly as the good Reverend and his visitor entered.

'Familiars?' Moore indicated.

'Possibly,' Salt agreed, 'remove the hounds will you.' He gestured to a pretty cow maid, with blue-grey eyes and long brown hair.

She immediately complied, first calling to them from the doorway, then forcing them through it when they failed to follow her instructions. The girl was nervous. Salt could tell, after years of experience, and he passed his observations onto the young lady.

'You have nothing to hide have you, Miss Illingsworth?'

She shook her head vigorously, 'No sir, nothing at all.'

He rejected her reply, it was clear that she was scared of something. So, Salt ordered a physical examination of the accused, before proceedings could be taken any further.

The 'examination' itself was degrading and vicious. The girl, Mary, stood motionless as the clothes were torn from her back. The only objection made was done so via her crimson cheeks and flashing eyes. Master Salt seemed to care nothing for her personal embarrassment, which was, he suggested, further evidence of her reluctance to allow a proper investigation.

'Ah ah, Reverend Moore, will you look here...'

He crept over to the body, slowly. Salt's index finger pointed straight to the incriminating brown mole on Mary's back. Initially Moore did not know what to make of it, but the crinkled old man set him straight; 'This mark shows that this girl has allowed the Devil to suck the very blood from her. This is how they keep the familiars alive. Do you understand Moore? All witches have familiars, like those foul smelling dogs, it is through them that contact with the Devil is made. As our noble King James himself has written, such beasts feed on human blood, and when they suck it leaves an imprint, such as this one, upon the witch.'

Salt grinned, bursting with superiority. He had found the proof of heresy in Broad-ford, and all that remained was to set a trial date for Mary. This was to take place on the 16th May, 1624, in the old barn at the end of Cattle Street.

Subsequently, it was to this trial that my reveries flowed. A 'trial' with all the trimmings of a huge wooden table, instead of a judge's elevated bench, and one where the six judges themselves were dressed in foreboding black and ridiculous yellow-grey wigs.

Proceedings commenced when Mary was dragged into the 'court'. She was, to the modern eye, a vision of innocence. Her eyes were as wide as the lids would allow. Her hair was tangled, matted, through want of washing and a sleepless night. Droplets of perspiration intermittently wetted her worried brow. Her hands were kept to her sides, tightly clenched. She was clearly terrified of the so-called justice she was about to receive – and, as it turned out, she had very good reason to be.

For hours the young girl was interrogated, or questioned, as the judges preferred to call it. Her whole life's history was open to suggestion. Her relationships with men in particular, were twisted into the sordid tale of a whore and temptress. Then, the judges focused their attentions on the matter of Lord Peter Mason's cattle. First, there was the issue of the altercation that had taken place between Mary and the landowner, shortly before his cattle became ill. To ascertain the particulars of this incident Lord Mason himself was called as a witness into the courtroom.

From the moment he entered the room, there was something about this man that I despised. He was a perfect caricature of landed-gentry decadence. His costume was grossly colourful and extravagant, whilst his tights were a bawdy joke. Only his eyes were hard to fathom, since he averted them from all but the judges themselves. Not once did he glance at the girl he was condemning. For some reason, he could not bring himself to look at the witch who had tormented him.

Oh, and who could forget his voice, what a voice: croaky; high-pitched and pleading, to the point of annoyance. Nevertheless, the evidence of this fool in tights was enough to ensure that Mary's fate was sealed. This is the conclusive proof he had to offer the judges:

'Lords, it was on the 2nd February of this year, near Fuller Way, that I was approached by Miss Illingsworth. Her father was recently deceased and she was in need of money. However, one cannot go on giving charity forever, can one? She had troubled me already for the sum of three shillings, so, I simply refused her last request. Well, that was when the snarling began. Such foul words I will not repeat! Then there was the curse itself – she said I would be sorry for turning her away. The very next day my cattle were afflicted with a strange disease and all were dead within two days. If that is not sorcery, can you tell me what is?'

For a while the judges whispered amongst themselves, every so often nodding their ancient heads in ascent. Next they glared at Mary. It was obvious that they had already reached a decision, whatever she had to say in her defence. All the same, Salt gave her the opportunity to clear her name.

'Miss Illingsworth, you have listened to the grave charges levelled against you. What do you have to say?'

'I am innocent, Sir, you must believe me.'

'So, you still persist in hiding your sins? You refuse to renounce the Devil's work?'

'I do not know the Devil, Sir.'

'If that is true Miss Illingsworth, can you tell me why Lord Mason would make such an accusation?'

Mary hesitated to answer as tears were flowing down her filthy cheeks. 'No Sir, I cannot,' she said, softly.

Now, that would have been an end to the matter. The godly patriarchs were already gathering their papers and preparing to give judgement, when, suddenly, a lowly young woman burst through the doors of the old barn.

'Please, I must be heard,' she called, waving her hands in the air.

What Helen had to say was news indeed to the court. According to her version of events, Lord Mason had made unwanted advances towards Mary, who no longer enjoyed the protection of her parents. So forward had been his advances that Helen had advised her friend to avoid his company altogether. Yet, this was a very difficult thing for Mary to do, since Mason was the Lord of the Manor and owned the land upon which she worked.

More or less everyday, Mason had made some excuse or another to visit Mary's cottage, and it was at the cottage that Helen came upon them both, on the 2nd February.

As Helen explained, she had arranged to help Mary take the day's milk into the town. However, when she had arrived at Mary's home, she had heard cries from inside. Without knocking at the door, she had entered the cottage and found Lord Mason in the process of, *'deflowering'*, as she described it, the accused.

'That's why he wants her dead, he wants to silence her.' Helen finished her account and collapsed onto a chair with her hands in the prayer position.

The court was silent. However, you must remember this was an establishment of the 1600s, presided over by the most misogynistic 'religious' gents in the land. The grand judges were not quiet for long.

'Do you realise the severity of what you have said young lady?' Salt, the chief witch finder, grated, 'You have charged into this court and disturbed its proceedings.'

He then expressed his doubts, on why such a fine gentlemen would risk his honour, in the pursuit of someone of much lower social standing. Helen could give no sufficient reason to that effect, only that the girl in question was pretty. This was not enough for the judges. At any event, this would seem to implicate Mary further, as she had thus used witches' arts to captivate her Lord.

Fortunately for Lord Mason, his convenient memory was to be given a second wind. Of course, the morning of the argument, there was someone else on Fuller Way. Someone had been hanging around behind the old oak tree.

'Yes, I'm certain it was her, she too had called out that I would pay. They are great friends you see,' he explained, in such assured tones that the judges were compelled to surmise that both girls were involved in the practise of witchcraft.

The story of rape was just that, a story; one concocted by Helen in an attempt to save her accomplice from justice. That justice was to be sought after swimming the girls – the final test of a person's innocence of witchcraft.

The remainder of my nightmare was given in flashes. My subconscious soul was unsettled. One instant Helen and Mary, with right thumbs bound to left toes and left to right, were tossed into the nearby River Aire. After a couple of minutes both were brought back to the surface. They were still alive and screaming wildly.

'Do you confess you sorceresses?'

They did not. Not even to relieve themselves of their current torment.

Then the final grisly vision unfolded. It was the following morning, the 17th May, 1624, and all the town's men and women surrounded the gallows, at the bottom of Cattle Street. Mary and Helen, weakened and pale, with their heads crudely shaved, were dragged to the scaffold. Both prayed and sobbed, as they were lifted onto buckets and nooses were placed around their necks. The crowd went still. Savagely the executioner kicked their supports and the crowd let up a tremendous cheer. The nooses tightened and the girls wriggled, kicked and choked. Death came slowly to the Broad-ford 'witches', who were left to swing stiffly in the winds for some time to come. They were eventually taken down, after all the vultures assembled had been truly satisfied with the day's entertainment.

I woke uncomfortable within my sheets and saturated with sweat. As I opened my eyes, the last images I had witnessed stayed with me for a time. Whilst the girls had swayed too and fro, Salt's carriage could be seen heading out of the town. In his hands he clutched a bag of gold coins, which he persisted in counting over and over. There was so much gold, and all from the good Lord Mason, in gratitude for Salt's insightful services. It was obvious that Salt felt no compassion, no pity, for those he had condemned. He smiled, contentedly, as the rugged moors passed by. He smiled as his features faded and were replaced with someone else's – that someone was Dylan Holt. I was Master Salt.

Chapter 6

The Final Meeting

My past life as a grasping, merciless witch finder had been revealed. *Surely*, this could not be true? Admittedly, I was a lazy bum, a drunk, but not a killer. However, if I really was the reincarnation of one Master Matthew Salt, how on earth could I atone for my past actions? How could I clean away the murders I had carried out in the name of religion? How could I settle Helen's soul?

I had to find out for sure if my visions were grounded in a sordid reality and the only way to do that was to return to Cattle Street. I did so on Sunday the 25th May, 2005. There, I attended the last séance ever held by Cynthia's illustrious team in the confines of the VIP suite.

Given that it was a Sunday, and licensed premises were bound to shut earlier, I set off for the town shortly after tea. I arrived at the club at 7:10pm and banged at the doors, which were still closed to the public. For several minutes there was no answer and I began to feel quite self-conscious.

What a pathetically desperate character I must have presented to the people on the street. Indeed, one group of young louts, on their way somewhere, shouted, 'piss-head,' as they passed by.

Instinctively, I hurled an expletive at them and carried on knocking, harder and harder.

'Alright, alright,' a frustrated Ms Hampton repeated from inside, as she struggled to release the lock.

When she eventually managed to do so, and the door creaked open to a dishevelled Mr Holt, she started. 'Well, Mr Holt,' she faltered, 'I wasn't expecting you so early, come in.'

I followed her through the club and up the stairs to our retreat. The other members of the group had not yet arrived, and the lounge was in the process of being cleaned by a scrawny, aged, underpaid immigrant. Almost immediately, my head started to ache, due to the incessant buzz and squeal of the industrial-strength vacuum.

'You've done that bit already haven't you?' I complained to the insignificant man, who was about to go backwards and forwards over an area of carpet he had already covered three times.

The man, whoever he was, muttered a curse under his breath, pulled the plug from the socket and left.

For once the VIP suite was calm. Perhaps in my current frame of mind, I would have suggested it was eerily quiet. Cynthia had scurried away, to replace the empty bottles at the various bars scattered throughout *The Cattle Market*. It was more than an hour later when she burst into the room again, short of breath and holding several ties. I glanced at her curiously.

'Oh, these are for the staff. You can guarantee at least one of the lads will have forgotten his.'

She placed the objects on the bar and poured herself a double scotch. Yet, her moment of peace was to be disturbed, when Mel popped her head around the door and moaned that there were no pound coins in her till.

'No peace for the wicked!' Cynthia commented, disappearing into her adjacent office to fetch a cluster of coins.

I was getting impatient. The others were really late and I wondered if they were going to turn up at all. It took an age for them to appear, one by one, each taking a tipple from behind the bar.

'Are we going to get started?' I couldn't stop my question sounding like a command.

The others complied and gathered around the table. Cynthia dimmed the lights and took the lead in calling any spirits present to reply. The planchette was still. I joined in her request that any unearthly visitor make his or herself known. Sure enough, Helen was with us again. I turned to the group. 'Look, there's something I need to ask her, if none of you mind?'

Since no one objected, I took the opportunity to quiz Helen on my nightmare.

'Helen, who is Matthew Salt?'

The answer was clear enough: 'You witch finder'.

I dropped my head in shame. Heather peered at Brian, who simply shrugged his shoulders.

'What do you want from me, Helen? What do you want me to do?'

There was no answer.

'I'm sorry for what I have done. There's nothing more I can say. I'm truly sorry for what happened to you.'

The planchette moved to the 'Yes' position and one could faintly feel the table shifting, lifting a little, from the floor.

'Stop, stop this.' Esther pushed the cursor so that no one could reach it. 'Just what the hell do you think you are playing at? What are you trying to achieve?' She croaked out the words, her eyes filled with hatred.

I deduced that she was seething from the fact that it was I, and not her, who the spirits sought to address.

We then paused from our supernatural game, long enough for a blazing row to ensue, between Esther and myself. From the very first moment we had met, there had been a thinly veiled layer of antagonism between us. Now we could contain our contempt no longer.

'Who the hell do you think you are Holt?' She screeched.

She turned to the others to outline her objections against me: why was it that Helen had only made an appearance when Mr Holt had been admitted to their sessions? No one knew who this intruder was. No one knew if he had some sort of hidden agenda. How could the group be sure that it was not Mr Holt himself who was 'making contact' and not some spirit from the otherworld? She even went as far as to claim that I had instigated the supernatural movements of the table.

Well, that was enough to trigger my temper. As I explained to the rest of the group, the ridiculous light displays, which used to accompany their 'séances', had ended the night I joined the group. Besides, I was not the one interested in uncovering the existence of a sinister witches' coven, one that waited in the wings of *The Cattle Market* ready to pounce on any unsuspecting clairvoyants. That role had been left to the singular Esther, who found devils where others found lost souls. I also told the others certain particulars of my dream, and how, in essence, the messages that the group were now receiving were coming close to the truth, the truth about the Broad-ford witches: that they were ordinary women; women murdered by men like Peter Mason, for ulterior motives.

The more modern-minded clan had to agree. After all, as Russell suggested: the reality of witchcraft lay more in male dominance, social change and financial gain, than in any authentic demonic power. Meanwhile, Esther squirmed, silently livid, as she was finally loosing her hold over the others in the group. For sure, it took much cajoling on Cynthia's part, to persuade Esther to rejoin us all at the table. 'It's only nerves dear, let's keep calm.' She patted Esther's shoulder and the séance resumed.

It sickened me, but to keep Esther quiet, she was given control of the meeting. She repeated her mundane and inane addresses to her captive audience. However, her 'moment' was to be short-lived. Our guest refused to respond to any of the questions she put forward, bar one: when she asked who Peter Mason was. The answer that Esther was to receive was shocking indeed, devastating for her.

Slowly and precisely the word 'You' appeared.

Instantaneously, Esther protested that someone in the group was pushing the planchette; it wasn't a very funny joke, it wasn't a joke at all. However, I knew, the group knew, that no one was trying to have fun at Esther's expense. I stared at her in disgust. Of course it made sense now. Her unwavering insistence on the existence of witches was a cover for guilt, a guilty secret that spanned centuries. It sounded crazy, when I expressed my beliefs orally. Maybe I had simply lost the plot. Yet, the most staggering indictment of Esther was to come from her own lips: when she insisted that witches like Helen Wilkes and Mary Illingsworth would say anything, anything at all to save themselves from death;

'They would even claim that an accuser had attacked or raped them.'

Right there was the proof: the proof that Esther had been present during the trial and murders of the two girls; the proof that she was the reincarnation of Lord Peter Mason. For, at no point during my account of the nightmare, had I mentioned the nature of Helen's evidence – that her friend was the victim of rape. More importantly, neither during this meeting, nor any that had gone before, had I, or anyone else for that matter, uttered the name of Mary Illingsworth. No one, save a contemporary witness, could possibly have known the name of the second 'witch' in the unrecorded trials of 1624.

As you would probably expect, that night Esther left *The Cattle Market* in a state of heightened agitation and terror. Anguish heightened all the more, in light of the fact that I threw further accusations her way as she stumbled down the stairs. After all, if one rejected her claims of demons, one also had to question the sinister light displays that had accompanied her séances. Although I have never found hard evidence to support my conjectures, I am still certain that Esther utilised something as simple as a circuit breaker to achieve the desired effects.

So, my bizarre tale of self-realisation, set amidst the stench of stale beer, has finally been put to paper. The mismatched seven, who had dabbled in the realms of the supernatural, never met again. We had looked for a demon and had encountered a young girl's cries from the grave. It was a simple story, but one that marked a turning point in my life. It was a critical moment, after which my own personal trials began. After a year, these are still far from over.

Naturally, the debt I had to pay for the murder of the two

girls, and scores of other unfortunates whom my persona, Salt, chose to eradicate in his lust for violence and gold, was not cleared with one heartfelt apology. Universal justice, what some would perhaps know as Karma, henceforth dictated that I should suffocate under a cloud of depression and sink into a sea of alcohol. I feel for frail Salina, who worries that my 'illness' will hasten my maker. Though, I hold no such fears. You understand, I am doomed to suffer and, the greater my grief, the more intense my pain, the better chance I have of escaping an eternity in the hell fire of unquenched guilt.

Mr D. Holt, May, 2006.

Miss Catherine Stanley

Dr Milner's diary entry: 15th July, 2006

In my position at the unit I have learnt to maintain a certain distance between myself and the patients. However, occasionally, even I can feel compassion and sympathy for certain individuals who, through no fault of their own, suffer traumatic life events that hold them back from an otherwise promising future. Miss Catherine Stanley, who I met this morning, is surely one of those people.

Miss Catherine Stanley's parents died in a car accident, when she was only two years old. The only living relative left in England was one aunt, named Phoebe. She was an aged lady, much too old to take in Miss Catherine Stanley and look after her. All the same, Phoebe's home provided Miss Catherine Stanley with a retreat, as she was passed through various state and private homes, where love and encouragement were sadly lacking.

Nevertheless, Miss Catherine Stanley did try to better herself, by undertaking a part-time degree course in Collective Studies, at McMighten University. However, as her history was hardly one to inspire confidence in her own abilities, she became anxious about her studies, to such a degree that she could no longer put pen to paper. Admittedly, Miss Catherine Stanley's explanation for her withdrawal from McMighten and consequential suicidal ideation was to confess to a bizarre delusion:

that her soul was fractured. Again, this was merely an attempt to make sense of her thwarted intelligence.

Regardless, apart from the pitiful life events I have described, Miss Catherine Stanley showed no signs of depression or affective disorder. Therefore, the preliminary diagnosis of 'Schizophrenia' had to be forwarded. Further, she was given the appropriate medication and placed on the female wing of Ward nine: Acute Psychiatric Unit. All I can say is tragic, truly tragic.

Note on the text: Miss Catherine Stanley had some difficulties with writing. Still, with assistance, she did cooperate with the therapy and the following is an authentic account of the text I received from her.

Dr Milner, Psychiatric Registrar.

Chapter 1

My Only Way Out of a Pointless Life

Pointless, the endless process of sorting the white, yellow and lime green invoices was completely pointless. I never thought, for one minute, that anyone ever bothered to check the countless mistakes I made within the filing system. In truth, I really didn't care. For the most part, I spent each working day dreaming of better things: a little more responsibility, and a lot more respect. After all, the position of Administration Assistant at Calderbrooke Cards was scarcely the most sought after post in the scheme of things. In reality, they paid me for nothing. A nothing job, with no purpose and no prospects.

As if work was not bad enough, my home life was also dull in the extreme. I had met Marko in a nightclub, where I had previously worked, and, at first, he had seemed to be a great catch: game for a laugh; considerate and handsome – though the latter was more owing to his illustrious, romantic origins, rather than his actual facial features. Eventually, a little too late, I had discovered the real Marko: the wordless, hopeless lover; football fanatic and typical chauvinist of our time. I say too late, because, as a foolish, headstrong teen, I had moved in with my dark aficionado; much to the dismay of my aunt, who had anticipated much greater things for my future.

I was thus trapped in a world of half realizations. Sure, I was surviving, but the reality of my life was only a shadow of what it could have been. The studious star pupil of Moor View High Secondary School had surprised everyone and accomplished nothing. I am certain it was this feeling of being ensnared in an eternity of underachievement that finally drove me back to Valerie Street, back to face the demons of my youth, who were now preventing my success.

My journey of discovery began with a chance encounter. It took someone else, someone more self-assured, to point out my quandary, before I could challenge it myself. That interloper came in the form of Mr McIntosh, a former Biology teacher at Moor View, where I had studied as a girl.

It was the 6th May, 2003. I had been shopping at the local market for the usual Friday night treats: a video; a bottle of wine; chocolate and 20 cigarettes, when the bearded botanist caught my eye.

'I say, hello Catherine,' he called, whilst he scratched his nose in a most undignified manner. 'So, what are you doing with yourself these days?'

I hesitated, a little surprised that I had been recognized. Then I wanted to lie and exaggerate the importance of my 'career'. Instead I told the truth, 'Oh, I work for a greeting card company, in the Administration Department.'

'Good...*good*...' he repeated, though with each utterance the opposite sentiment could be deduced, 'And how did you end up doing that, Catherine?'

'Well, it wasn't that difficult,' I stressed, uncomfortably. 'When I left school I started on a Youth Training Scheme at a local firm and it progressed from there.'

Mr McIntosh tweaked his whiskers and nodded. 'You know, Catherine, you should be an employer, not an employee. You sold yourself short. I'm not trying to get at you,' he stressed, noticing that I had lowered my eyes, 'It's just that it's such a disappointment, when you have a clever pupil who doesn't quite find their true calling in life. Why, you should be a doctor, not a nurse, a dentist, not a dental assistant, you see...?'

The strange thing was I did see. I knew I was worth more,

could achieve more, and would be the happier for it. I had to turn my life around, before it was too late. So, the helpful Mr McIntosh duly provided me with the names and numbers of those who could help me do just that. I was going to return to school, or to be more precise, night-school. I would study a part-time degree, composed of a number of subjects, given that I was unsure of which profession I wanted to pursue. Within a matter of months I was enlisted on a course at McMighten University.

However, the early gusto with which I attacked my new venture soon dwindled. I found the pressures of working all day and studying all evening, often into the early hours, emotionally and physically draining. The tight deadlines required for each essay resulted in an almost conveyor belt-like form of dissertation production. Yet, the more I grew accustomed to the banality of the thesis, anti-thesis structure, of each and every piece, the less I felt I understood. I became perplexingly uncertain about my capabilities and my future.

Maybe, if I had been struggling, this self-doubt would have been justifiable. Conversely, in light of the highest accolades I had received from the tutors, it was inexplicable. Still, I struggled on, battling the nagging doubts within. This continued until I came to the very last composition of the course.

For weeks I had been gathering primary sources from the local archive on sewer construction in the 19th century. From this information, which amounted to more than 100 accounts (from the local Bradford Sanitary Act, 1804, to the design plans for the Esholt Sewage Works, 1909), I had to write not less than 15,000 words – explaining why it had taken so long for the local authority to address the sanitary needs of the Borough of Bradford.

Night after night I sat down at my PC to commence the introduction of the essay. I never got past the first sentence. Each time my fingers touched the keys, I could remember nothing of the notes I had made from the countless papers I had read. I would just sit gazing at the screen, hoping that some kind of inspiration would sprout forth. Yet, it did not. I became desperate; desperate not to replicate the failures of my youth. Finally, just days before the final deadline, of the 14th June, 2006, complete impotence set in.

Although I was well aware that Marko had never shown the slightest interest in my studies, the situation was so hopeless I even turned to the one I knew never would, or could, help me. Teary eyed, after another evening of fruitless study, I returned to the sitting room, where Marko was watching the 'Big Match'.

'I can't do it,' I mumbled, hoarsely.

He continued to watch the game, gurgling crudely on the vat of beer in his hand. At last he responded, 'What?'

'I can't write the essay. It's got to be handed in on Friday. I can't do it.'

'Don't be daft. Of course you can. You've written hundreds of the bloody things. What do you mean you can't do it?'

'My mind goes blank, every time I try to write. There's something wrong with me.' Deflated and defeated I began to cry, again.

Marko sat, awkwardly staring at the screen. He was never one for sharing his problems, and he really did not care for others to do so. He reiterated that I was being 'daft', and explained that, for my benefit, he would go to the pub – just so as to provide me with the peace I needed to complete my studies. Minutes later the door closed behind him.

Left alone, I returned to my work. However, I still could not write and so found another use for my busy fingers. I began twirling my hair, at first slowly, and then in a frenzied fashion. Eventually, I noticed that warped clumps of my mane were scattered across my lap. *God, you'll go bald,* I surmised, as I attempted to prevent any further occurrence of this peculiar form of self-harm, by sitting on both hands. Yet, the fingers proceeded to wriggle about in frustration and, in due course, freed themselves from the given restraint and found their way back to the locks; locks which were periodically wrenched from their origins.

By the morning of the 14th June, sure enough, the only thing I had managed to create was a circular area of exposed skin underneath my fringe, which could be seen no matter how I tried to disguise it. At 10:00am, I headed for Mrs Piece's office, genuinely dreading the forthcoming interview, for I knew others had been thrown off the course for the non-completion of set assignments.

In the event, Mrs Piece M.A. was more approachable than I had been led to expect, and I was given a formal extension of slightly over two weeks. Nonetheless, even this was wasted time, for those two weeks turned out to be just as unproductive as the last. Finally, on the 30th June, 2006, I withdrew from the degree course − my only way out of a dead-end job and a dead-end life.

There was one tiny ray of light at the end of the tumultuous tunnel. I was suspended from studies on the grounds of ill-health, as Mrs Piece was convinced that I was suffering from some form of depression. She did not, after all, want to loose her star pupil, who held the promise of acquiring a special commendation from the Board of Examiners. So, she recommended that I seek professional help. This was to involve a thorough assessment of my person by the college counsellor.

'You see, Catherine, in most cases, problems like these are often caused by psychological and social problems,' she explained.

I was then ushered from her office and into the reception area, where I was given assistance with my completion of a Health Declaration Form.

Depression − the word conjured in my mind visions of helpless, over-emotional individuals, who never attempted to pull themselves out of the doldrums. Yet, I too had to accept this unflattering title, if I were ever to be allowed back into my studies. I, therefore, left the college embarrassed, discomfited, and self-conscious, complete with a 9:00am appointment for the following morning, with one Mrs Judy Freshfield of the University Counselling Service. This I kept hidden deep within my breast pocket.

Chapter 2

13 Valerie Street

I rose earlier than usual the next day, which allowed plenty of time to take a refreshingly cool shower, iron a flattering pin-stripe suit, apply a little more make-up than was customarily the case and eat a full English breakfast. You see, I wanted to appear professional: a woman in full possession of all her faculties; a woman not given to self-pity; a woman who could very well sort her own problems. Accordingly, I sprayed an expensive eau de toilette liberally over my attire, rang the office with a feeble excuse for my absence and set off for my appointment.

Not knowing what to expect, from the forthcoming session, I entered Mrs Freshfield's headquarters diffidently. A sour-faced lady, with grossly enlarged facial features, frequented the reception area. She enquired, insensitively, after my name and told me, quite rudely, to sit on a white synthetic seat in the corner. The warm welcome I had received left me even more apprehensive about the whole counselling process: *I haven't come here to be insulted. If she thinks that I am just going to sit there and be patronised she's quite wrong. Maybe I should just forget the whole thing?*

I was about to leave, when a much more jovial woman popped her head out of a nearby door and called, 'Catherine Stanley? Would you like to come in please?'

I wanted to run. I didn't need a counsellor. Nevertheless, I conformed, following Mrs Freshfield into her den. It was surprisingly warm and inviting, complete with comfy chairs, a coffee maker and tissues on the table – should they be necessary.

For a few minutes Mrs Freshfield sat mutely smiling, whilst she fidgeted with a pen between her index and middle fingers. It was almost as if she expected me to lead the session; she was waiting for me to open up and pour out all my troubles.

'Look, I've never been to a counsellor. I don't really understand what it is that you actually *do*.'

'Well, Catherine, what we *try to do* is find out exactly what is troubling *you*. Why is it that you are here?'

'I was hoping you could tell me that,' I laughed, nervously. 'Mrs Piece recommended that I attend these sessions, you see. I couldn't write an essay.'

'Yes. When you say you couldn't write it, what precisely do you mean?'

'I don't know. Every time I sat down to write, my mind went blank. I never got past the first line.'

'And how did that make you feel, Catherine?'

'I suppose I felt frustrated, angry, hopeless, confused. It just didn't make sense. I'd spent over six weeks in the archive and probably knew a lot more than all the other students.'

At this stage in the proceedings I began to laugh out loud, at the absurdity of it all. Here was I, a 24-year-old woman, seeking psychological assistance to complete an essay on the sewers of Bradford! For her part, Mrs Freshfield continued with her probing: probing into my present home life; probing into my non-existent relationship with my parents; probing into the nature of my liaisons with others.

True, I had suffered more than most. Further, I had engaged in excessive sibling rivalry with my foster brothers and sisters in various 'homes'. Though there had always been my aunt, with whom I had remained on friendly terms throughout my teens. Nothing in my past could explain, to my satisfaction anyway, why I had failed, failed yet again, to achieve the academic adoration I so desperately required.

I concluded the whole exercise was completely futile, so I started to watch the minutes tick away on a cheap and tacky digital clock. Eventually, the timepiece revealed that there were only five minutes remaining, of this most exquisite torture.

It was then that Mrs Freshfield stumbled upon a series of questions, questions that would trigger a chain reaction in my psyche, and eventually lead to an explanation of my defeatist attitude.

'You were saying you didn't have many friends at Holton Middle School. Why was that? Were you ever bullied at school Catherine?'

'Yes, I was.'

'What happened to you?'

'There was this girl, Georgiana Baker,' I paused for a moment, as I had *successfully* erased all thoughts of her from my mind for over 14 years, 'She used to live on my street.'

'She was the one who bullied you?'

'Yes. But it wasn't just her. You see, she used to tell the others lies about me. For over a year I was picked on by a whole year group. Everyone joined in, even the lads. One boy, Syed Ahmed, gave me a black-eye, as I was just walking down the corridor to P.E.'

Mrs Freshfield shook her head in sympathy.

I carried on. 'Everyone goes on about how bullies are a product of their home environment. That's just bull-shit. Georgiana had everything: affluent parents; a good home; everything. She was just a spoilt, manipulative bitch – who ruined my childhood.'

'So, how did you cope with the bullying?'

'Cope? I wouldn't put it quite like that...' I stopped and glanced at the clock, again. My one hour was thankfully over and I rose to leave.

'Wait a moment, Catherine. You really need to talk about this...'

The stunned Mrs Freshfield was left to talk to the wind; wind created by my coat tails, as I rushed past her and out of the room.

Once I was safely outside the building a torrent of tears flowed freely down my cheeks. I could see Georgiana who, in my mind, had not aged one day. She was still the freckled, pout-lipped, obnoxious character who possessed all the confidence in the world, concerning her own attributes and abilities. Fortunately, under closer adult inspection her features now left little to be desired, and her grating voice, under whose commands the whole peer group swayed, was less than melodic to the ears.

Next I recalled, all too clearly, the days of loneliness and isolation. Endless holidays, spent within the confines of a flagged back garden, so as to avoid all contact with my persecutors. There I was, playing against the old red-brick wall, with my two faithful childhood friends, a tennis ball and a Boxer called Rocky. There I was, just a young girl whiling away the hours. There I was, a young girl internally wishing away the days in fear, and watching helplessly as a part of her soul was dying – the innocent child who had enjoyed life to the full and excelled at everything.

I wanted to yell at my oppressors. I wanted them to understand the repercussions of their actions. I wanted them to know that the hurt was not only instantaneous, but also lasting. Well into adulthood, this victim of the constant verbal and physical abuse had experienced pain in a million different guises. This was why I always failed – I never wanted to shine. This was what had drawn Georgiana's attention to me in the first place. This was why I had always been singled out for *special treatment*.

Consequently, I had turned my back on school and a promising future. Instead, I had veered towards a glittering career in the numerous nightclubs dotted throughout the city. Eventually, I had ended up in the position of the lowest of all office workers and glued to a man who barely knew I existed; all because of a bossy, overindulged child.

'I say, are you alright dear?' An old lady was comfortingly holding my hand in hers.

For over half an hour I had been stood in the middle of Bradford city centre crying into a sodden tissue. Highly embarrassed, I explained to her that I was fine, even though my sore eyes and red nose said otherwise, and set off for the Interchange to catch the next bus home.

When I arrived home Marko was slouched on the settee. An assortment of trainers, sweaty clothing and weight training equipment were scattered around the living room, which I had left typically tidy that morning.

'Where've you been?' he queried, without taking his eyes off the paper for an instant.

'Oh, nowhere. Have the office called?'

He nodded, 'Rochelle wanted to know where to find a sales invoice. She couldn't find it in the files, apparently.'

'Oh, I'll ring her in a minute,' I replied, as I passed through the clutter and into the kitchen to feed Bonbon, my sable Collie.

Marko carried on reading the sports section, utterly oblivious to the fact that I had been crying. In all fairness, though, I had not told him about the counselling sessions. I couldn't face the incessant jibes and jokes that would result if I did. Being a great man of the world, he simply would not understand. In his eyes I was already 'daft', 'stupid' and even 'idiotic'. I, therefore, did not want to provide him with anymore justification for categorising my behaviour in that way.

Accordingly, after satisfying the dog's hunger, I returned to the lounge, and, instead of discussing my problems with my partner, I determined to call Rochelle, my supervisor: a woman who always seemed to struggle with searches when I was absent from work.

'Hello Leeds 545...,' her dulcet tones resounded, with disdain, down the line.

'Hi Rochelle, it's Catherine. Marko said you called this afternoon?'

'Hello Catherine, I'm sorry to bother you, it's just that I couldn't find the yellow copy of Parkinson's sales invoice for January, 2006. It's all sorted out now, it turned up later in your sorting tray, so no need to worry. How are you anyway?'

I knew this was the real reason why she had called. Rochelle was the notorious office gossip, who was enticed by any kind of tittle-tattle. You see, her own life was both dull and uninspiring; that was why she had to squeeze the sap from the lives of others. Thus, I gave her as little information as I could, for the following morning's tête-à-têtes. 'Just a stomach bug,' I stated, being more than economical with the truth, 'the doc says I'll be fine in a couple of days.'

As Rochelle's thirst for knowledge remained unquenched, throughout the rest of the conversation, she soon tired and explained that she had to go. I was thereby freed to begin preparations for the evening meal.

Sausages, chips, sweet corn and onion gravy was the feast I eventually provided. After the meal, since Marko was determined to remain in the front room, I decided to settle down before the television. For the first time in months I enjoyed the various quiz delights on a BBC channel. Not that I could answer more than a third of the questions asked. Long past midnight I retired, sleepy, though more content than I had been of late.

Indeed, in light of my journey of self-discovery that day, I wondered if there would be any improvement in my linguistic acumen. Undoubtedly, I was no longer under the pressure of having to write to a strict deadline, and was at will to sleep in the following morning. So, before undressing for bed, I made one last attempt to finish the introduction that had caused so much upset.

I turned on the PC, as quietly as I could, for Marko was snoring soundly in the adjacent room. My fingers then hovered, expectantly, over the keyboard, as I waited patiently for ideas to flow. *Come on, you can do it.* No I could not. After two hours, one sentence of the long-awaited essay was closed down in its file. I decided to call it a day.

I quickly undressed, carefully pulled back the covers and slithered into bed. The air was too dense, too humid. That night my skin clung to my oversized, dated nylon nightdress, which would have been more at home in my late great aunt's wardrobe.

Intermittently grunts were audible from the other side of the bed. I began to toss and turn and kick the covers. Still, I could not find a comfortable position. I sighed deeply and turned onto my back.

As I lay there, in the dead of the night, a peculiar feeling began to make its way slowly up through my stomach. Suddenly, with a rush, I was taken hold of by a most exhilarating and liberating phenomenon. A sensation, akin to the tickle one feels when descending down the drop of a mighty roller coaster, gripped hold of my whole being. Its intensity increased. I closed my eyes. I wanted to laugh out loud. I was strangely excited, out of control. It stopped.

When I opened my eyes again I was dumbfounded by what I saw. I was looking down, looking down at my body sleeping, peacefully, below. Weightlessly I hovered, watching my chest rise and fall. Soon I floated from the room. My soul was free: free from all earthly considerations; free to explore at will in the deserted night sky. Oh, the beautiful night sky, so dazzlingly lit by the moon and stars, which were now at their brightest.

Higher than the lampposts, I travelled down the patchwork lanes of the city. I was heading somewhere. In what must have been a matter of minutes, I approached the old, derelict bridge at Shipley Square. I drifted down the stairs and along the route of the canal. Gentle ripples now followed my path, as I made my way along the only blot on the pleasant landscape: a grey and red-brick industrial estate.

Here and there, rusty boats were anchored along the banks of the waterway. I gazed as they currently bobbed up and down in the breeze. Ducks were also busy diving in and out of the water, interrupting the serene silence of the night. Every so often, I was brushed by erratic bats, as they sporadically darted in one direction and then the next, not seeming to comprehend where they were heading or why.

Eventually I arrived at Salt's Mill: a fine remnant of Bradford's industrial past that had been transformed into an apartment block, crammed with wealthy occupants. At present the whole building was shrouded in darkness, save for a hallway lamp that had been left on to light my way. At this point, I exited the canal and mounted the steep incline which led to Saltaire. Seconds later I was floating outside 13 Valerie Street, the former address of my late Great Aunt Phoebe.

The cathartic journey now became a nightmare. I had been magnetically drawn towards this address. It was certainly not one I would have consciously chosen to visit. Indeed, I had not called at 13 Valerie Street in over 14 years. I hated this place, a place that had been my dismal retreat, during all the years of torment at school. This had been the one place to which Rocky and I had ventured, beyond my involuntary incarceration at my fourth foster home. Consequently, many unhappy hours had been spent crying, secluded within the old, damp walls of the back bedroom. Hence, there were just too many unpleasant memories associated with this location.

Deep within, I was uncomfortable, fearful of entering this weather-beaten house. I wanted to turn back. I wanted to return to my new life, no matter how dull it was. Yet, I could not.

Against my will, I could still feel my soul being pulled towards my old haunt. The force of the tempest rose and I was swept across the threshold. I squirmed and attempted to twist myself around. I was restrained. An overpowering feeling of extreme invigoration lifted me even higher and I ascended the stairs. 'No, I can't go in there…I can't go in there,' I repeated.

Regardless, I drew closer and closer to the dreaded door. An intense battle for my survival ensued. I knew that something, something unspeakably horrible, awaited me in that room. The struggle continued. Gradually, I won over. The force of the feelings subsided. I floated back – back to my body and back to the reality of my everyday life.

Chapter 3

A Time to Talk

At 6:00am I sprang from my bed. I needed to tell someone about my experience. Marko was the only person available. Thus, I proceeded to accost him in the kitchen, where he was currently packing his lunch for work.

'Listen Marko,' I stuttered, as he lifted his eyebrows, puzzled by the unusually excited tone of my voice, 'the weirdest thing happened to me last night.' I paused for effect.

He nodded, indicating that I continue with my tale.

'You know the programme we saw a few weeks ago on out-of-body experiences. You must remember it. It was that one with the girl who does the coffee commercials?'

Marko looked even more bewildered. 'Yes,' he drawled, very slowly.

'I think I had one last night. It was bizarre. I woke up in the middle of the night and I was looking down at myself sleeping!'

'Oh, really,' he smirked and, with that, he grabbed his coat and set off for the construction site.

I was left alone, with a great deal of time to think about what had happened. I was so consumed by my thoughts that I forgot to make the daily absence call to the office. Though, this was perhaps justifiable; I had experienced a supernatural phenomenon first-hand. A supernatural phenomenon! My soul had been set free.

Yet, why, in view of the fact that I had the whole world in which to wander, had my soul taken that most unwelcome course to Valerie Street? In the cold light of day, I also speculated on why I had been so horrified, at the mere thought of entering that room? It was, after all, only a space, regardless of whether it was crammed with best forgotten memories.

That must be it, I thought naively. *I can't write because of what happened in that house, all those years ago.* I determined to open-up to Mrs Freshfield, during my next appointment. I was going to tell her all there was to know about the bullying; all there was to know about the room at the head of the stairs. *I must face my past, if I am ever to have a future,* I concluded.

Soon enough, the next session arrived. As before, I was very particular concerning my attire, which consisted of a purple satin blouse, black trousers and smart high-heeled, crocodile skin boots. Unfortunately, the receptionist at the college was as impressed with this effort as she had been with the last, and I was marshalled to the corner like a pathetic schoolgirl, badly in need of a sharp shake or some form of electric-shock treatment.

Once inside Mrs Freshfield's office she immediately broached the topic of bullying, for this had resulted in my hasty exit from the last session.

'Well, Catherine, why don't you tell me more about your experiences at Holton Middle School. You've already stated that you were bullied, by Georgiana Baker, as I recall. You also mentioned feelings of frustration and anger, which resulted from your alienation. How did you manage to cope with those feelings at that time?'

'I used to go somewhere,' I faltered, as I resisted revealing intensely private information, 'to 13 Valerie Street, where my great aunt used to live.'

'You felt safe there?'

'Yes.'

'Why do you think that was?'

'No one from school knew I was there.'

'So you felt more in control of the situation at your auntie's house?'

'Great aunt's,' I corrected, deciding that now was the time to relay to my therapist the details of the bizarre supernatural occurrence that had disturbed my sleep just a few days before. 'I've been back there, recently.'

'Back where, to your auntie's house?' She questioned.

'Yes. Well, not quite, she died two years ago and the house now belongs to someone else, but I have been back there.'

'When was that Catherine?'

'Last week, after my first session here,' I informed her, quite innocently.

For a few moments Mrs Freshfield looked puzzled. She began to fidget with her pen before asking, 'Did you go into the house?'

'Yes.'

'And, did the new owners not mind your visit?'

She didn't understand, so I had to explain the event in more detail. 'When I said that I had *"been"* to the house, I meant that I had been back there – but not necessarily in body.'

Mrs Freshfield relaxed and smiled, 'I see, in your dreams you went into the house…'

'No,' I interrupted, forcefully, causing her to start, 'that's not what I said. I was very upset when I left here last week, but I was not dreaming when I went back to the house, back to Valerie Street. You see, I think I had one of those out-of-body experiences.'

The same as anyone, anyone who has had to explain the ways of the supernatural, I was irritated by the pathetic attempt at mock appreciation that Mrs Freshfield now displayed. She nodded knowingly, somehow managing to restrain her grin, and explained, ever so politely, how she had heard much on the topic. All this, before she tried to restate my own experiences as some form of self-inflicted therapy for repressed emotions.

'You understand Catherine that, when someone is reluctant to face certain painful memories from his or her past, he or she will subconsciously be driven back in an attempt to deal with them.

You told me earlier that the bullying was a result, as you saw it, of your academic success at school. Now, here you are at college. You need to succeed. You need to write. However, the bullies from the past have come back to haunt you – to make you afraid of your own achievements. So, you have a dream, a dream in which you go back to 13 Valerie Street: the one place where you felt in control as a child, the only place where you felt safe from the bullying.'

I was far from convinced by the good counsellor's theorizing. Her ideas failed to explain one important fact:

'...But, it doesn't make sense. I know I felt safe there. So, why in my dream, as you put it, did I feel so afraid of entering that room, the room at the head of the stairs?'

Mrs Freshfield pondered over this perplexing point, before finishing the session.

'You may have felt safe there Catherine, but you still suffered in that house. You experienced feelings of rejection, isolation and loneliness in that room. When you were inside those four walls you were also shutting out the bullies, shutting out your troubles. As an adult you know this, and you know if you return to that room, you are turning your back on your problems today.'

True, Mrs Freshfield's views echoed those of my own a few days earlier. Nonetheless, I still left the university feeling less than satisfied with this explanation of events.

There is, after all, a world of difference between uncomfortable anxiety and terror – and it was pure, unadulterated terror that I felt when I neared the old rotten door at the head of the stairs.

Chapter 4

The Eager Half

Disappointed, I returned home, only stopping once on the high street, to collect a suit from the dry cleaners. When I arrived, I pushed open the front door, sluggishly, to reveal Marko, home early from work.

'Would you like a coffee?' he enquired.

I was stunned, not being used to any consideration on his part.

'No thanks,' I replied, as we both settled down on the unbalanced chairs which surrounded the self-assembled dining table.

Initial pleasantries over, we sat mutely, not really sharing any mutual interests or experiences we could communicate to one another.

Occasionally, I raised my eyes across the table. That was, until I realised there was no glint in the eye, no reciprocal attraction – that had dissipated years before. I was discontented, fundamentally unfulfilled. I could not stay with him, even if that meant finding a place of my own.

'Look, I've been thinking,' I began.

'Yes,' he grunted, 'what?'

'Oh, it's nothing.'

No matter how many times he implored that it was better to share whatever was on my mind, I remained quiet. I was not ready; I was still too scared to branch out on my own.

That night I went to bed at 10:00pm exactly. I desperately needed a good night's rest. I was due to return to work the following day and Rochelle was already after my blood, in consequence of the days I had already spent at home. However, the night air had other plans: it was unforgivably moist and oppressively heated. As a result, I tossed and turned, curled and stretched and shuffled my pillows, over and over. *I'm going to be shattered in the morning,* I deliberated, all the while feeling more and more wide awake with each passing minute on the clock.

The red lights flashed, signifying that it was now 12:30am. That instant I was again struck by a brisk thrill of elation. I could feel myself rising, rising slowly from my earthly body.

'No, no,' I called softly. However, my soul was eager to journey back to its roots, back to face the past. Swiftly down the River Aire I floated, only slowing slightly as I reached the density of Hurst Woods.

All was still, save for the owls warning of their presence. Now and then there was a rustle, as some creature scuttled underneath the bushes. I glanced above me. I could see the night sky, seeping through the almost skeletal branches. The entire scene was murky, with the brushstrokes of tinted mists.

In no time at all I exited the woodland. I could distinguish the words *'Valerie Street'...* then number, *'13'*. Gravely, I hovered outside the chipped door. Tentatively, I went inside.

In the darkness, I could barely see the mottled brown wallpaper. It was the same paper my great aunt had hung years before. I took a few moments to regain the courage which, till now, had speeded my journey. I levitated higher and higher. I mounted the stairs. There was the room, shrouded in shadows. The door was slightly ajar. I peered through the space and into the gloom beyond. Inside, I could perceive the outlines of an old-fashioned hearth, with unused coals upon the fire. There was also a solid oak table, placed in the furthest corner. My soul leapt as the door moved slightly and rays from a nearby streetlight illuminated an object on the table, a bottle. *No.* I wrenched my spirit from the doorway. I was torn in two.

'My God Catherine, what are you doing?'

Shaken, I sat upright in bed. Marko was unfolding the blankets that had become twisted.

'You were having one hell of a dream by the looks of things, Cathy,' he laughed. 'Do you want a coffee?'

Without waiting for an answer, he headed off to the kitchen and returned with two steaming mugs of milky coffee. The time was 5:15am, too early to rise, yet, too late to return to sleep. So, we sat, drinking in the darkness. Patiently, we waited for time to pass. Eventually we got ready for work.

Soon, I was standing in the rain, waiting for the 7:32am, 621 to Bierley. Certainly, it was at times like this I really wished I had learnt to drive; just one more aim on my 'things to do' list that had never been accomplished. Some 10 minutes late, the bus arrived, steaming its way through the puddles, and splashing my legs with gushes of water. Even so, albeit saturated, I was on time for work; work that began with sorting the unusually high number of invoices that had piled up during my absence.

For the rest of the day I kept myself busy and my head down. I did not want Rochelle to notice my sudden appearance. 'Lister's, Little Comforts...' I muttered, as I sorted.

'Hi Catherine,' Helen whispered in my ear, as she rounded the table and sat down on a chair beside me, 'are you alright?'

'Yes, I'm fine. I just had a really bad cold, that's all.'

Being an extremely astute person, Helen was not convinced by my explanation. 'Well, if there's anything you need to talk about, you know I'm always here.'

In fairness, she always was; the ever faithful Helen, who was also accredited with the titles of fortune teller and mystic, someone in tune with the spirit world. That was why I chose to share my problems with her that afternoon.

'Helen, do you know anything about out-of-body experiences?' I enquired, as she tilted her head, slightly shocked by my swift introduction of the topic.

'Sure, I've read a great deal about them. Though, I've never experienced one personally.'

'So, do you think there real; not dreams?'

'Oh, I'm sure they are. There are too many reports, all of which outline the same symptoms, the same feelings that accompany the experience.'

I was hooked. Helen was indeed a mine of information. 'What feelings?'

'From what I've read, Catherine, people claim to have experienced feelings of intense ecstasy and being out of control. They also claim they were able to see and recall details of their surroundings and so on, facts that weren't available to them in their waking lives.'

'Why do they start, if you've never had them before?'

'Err…I'm not sure. Maybe the spirit becomes restless?' Helen guessed, as she began to laugh at the severity of our little chat. 'I really don't know.'

As we conversed it turned 5:00pm, time to go home. However, Helen and I remained in the office. I shared everything with her: all I could remember about my discussions with the counsellor and my own experiences during the night. Helen was sympathetically saddened when she heard of my lonely days at school. She also became edgy when the talk turned to the room at the head of the stairs.

'So, you spent days crying in the room? But that doesn't explain why you would be so frightened by it now.' She paused, and reflected on the facts. 'Something happened in that room, something that you're blocking out. If you really want my opinion, for what its worth, I think you should go back, go back to the room and find out what has been holding you back all these years. Whatever it is, you're being drawn there anyway. It's just a matter of time before you find out and, when you do, you must tell me everything, I'll help you through this Catherine.'

As she spoke these words, she took hold of my hand. I merely nodded, thanked her for listening, and set off home.

During the bumpy ride on the 621 I felt relieved, somehow freer. I had shared a problem with a true friend. I decided that, regardless of my apprehension, I would return to 13 Valerie Street and confront the demons of my youth. I also determined to have a special, hearty meal that evening – one that would ensure at least physical fitness for the trial ahead.

Chapter 5

Journey of Discovery – A Fractured Soul

In the event, fish was the dish of the day. This was the ultimate brain food, albeit, cooked in homemade batter and accompanied with chips and peas. I finished the meal with a piece of fresh fruit, a banana, decadently covered in custard. The hunger satisfied, I sat down to write for the first time in weeks.

As it happened, I wrote a diary entry; something I had never done before. Once I had outlined my nocturnal plans and the causes thereof, I flicked clumsily through the blotched, filled pages, which numbered six. *Six!* I had been so consumed by the need to put pen to paper, I had not noticed that the hours had passed quickly. Not until the old carriage clock chimed 12:00.

Marko had already gone to bed. I determined to spend the night downstairs. That way, he would not be disturbed by any occurrences during the twilight hours. My passage would be a sure one, there being nobody to call and no turning back. To further guarantee the success of my venture, I extinguished all the lights and turned down the volume on the television. Only a faint murmur could be heard. I then gathered a fleece blanket and feather pillow, from the cupboard of spares, and drank a full mug of hot chocolate, with just a hint of fudge. The time was now 12:30am. *It won't be long. If these things won't happen during the witching-hour, when will they?*

As it turned out, *'these things'* occurred much later. It was 2:25am when I sensed the first signs of release. I didn't try to struggle against them, not this time. I just lay there, as the wash of delight flowed unhindered through the depths of my body. Within seconds, I was drifting down the empty streets, down under the bridge and along the canal. There was no dawdling, no time to take in the scenery, not that night. You must understand the quest was everything. Even Salt's Village, a World Heritage site, was all but a blur, as I sped, cheetah-like, towards number 13. With haste, I was there. *Let's get this over with.*

As I entered the house, I wondered why it was so silent, unnaturally still, for an inhabitancy. With more restraint, I ascended the stairs, towards the room. Again the door was ajar.

'Well, here goes', I whispered to the darkness. I conquered my nerves. I entered the room. It was just a room. A room lit gently by a street lamp beyond.

I turned around and around. Here and there the beige patterned paper was torn, exposing rotten plaster below. The window was opaque with condensation, which was dripping steadily from the sill and onto the floor. The whole atmosphere was moist; moist from the damp, which was crawling like gangrene through the flesh and bones of the house. It was a sad, forgotten and neglected place.

'So, where is all the furniture then?' I questioned, seeing that there was only one piece of craftsmanship, an oak table, in the far corner of the room. As there was nothing else to view, I glided over for a closer inspection. However, as I did so, I came upon an object. It was an empty bottle of bourbon, left carelessly on the floor. 'It must be squatters,' I presumed. I attempted to lift the offending object out of harm's way. Yet, my hands went straight through it, from one side of the jar to the other. I lifted my hands up to my face. I could barely taste the liqueur upon my lips.

I continued towards the table. There was another item placed there: a small medicine bottle with a white label on the side. Fortunately the container was tilted, and I was able to read the information in full:

'P…Anti-depressant tablets
Take as directed
Miss Catherine Stanley
6 Thorneby Crescent,
Bradford.'

The medication was mine, why? *Think, come on think.* As I hung weightlessly in the air I did think, long and hard, about the significance of the pieces I had found. Sure enough, the awful truth, the profound importance of the room at the head of the stairs was revealed. Long repressed memories began to flow unhindered and I recalled the tragic event that had occurred at 13 Valerie Street.

It had been the holidays, a time for relaxation and play. The sun was glowing, somewhat brighter than can be seen in the summer skies of today. As usual, I had been excluded from the rounder's match, which was capturing the attention of all the children under 15 on Thorneby Crescent. I was perched on the sill, staring out of the window, wanting to play, wishing I belonged. Somehow I caught Georgiana's steely eye.

Instinctively I turned away. I didn't want any trouble. The truth was: I was more than a little surprised that she had condescended to ingratiate herself with the others, who were not quite of her standing or intelligence. Regardless, she had chosen the position of third deep; a suitable one which would ensure rest for most of the game, and all the credit for catching the odd ball that came her way.

Tap, tap, tap, I turned back to the window. Georgiana was smiling the sweetest of her smiles. This left me feeling apprehensive about what she was going to do next. I stepped back a couple of paces.

'Why don't you come out and play, Catherine?'

I shook my head, and was about to make a lame excuse for staying indoors, when she further implored that my services were needed. 'Oh, come on. You can't let me play on my own with all these boys. Besides, there's a place spare.'

'I'm not very good,' I called, through the glass. All the same, I tied my trainers tighter and set off outside.

It was clear, from the looks on the faces of all the other players that no one really wanted the charity case from number six to join in the games. I awkwardly walked over to third base, to which Georgiana was pointing, and the match continued.

True to the words I had uttered, my performance was pathetic in the extreme. I failed to catch all of the many balls that flew in my direction and when it came to my turn to bat I succeeded in being beaten to first-base by speedy Tom Scholes. What was worse, my actions had caused Darren Bucks to charge at full pelt for second-base. Needless to say, he didn't make it in time and we were both cast out of the game. Whilst I felt a little relief, Darren took his exclusion badly, and directed many expletives my way. Next, he approached Georgiana and whispered something in her ear.

'Never mind,' Georgiana comforted me after the game. 'I say, we were thinking of going to Marsh Rough, do you want to come?'

I didn't know what to say. Maybe she had finally given up on tormenting me? Perhaps she genuinely wanted to be friends? I decided to give her the benefit of the doubt:

'Yes I'll come.'

Marsh Rough was a shoddy plot of land that lay about two miles beyond the grounds of the old Moor View High School. Generations of children had been drawn to its barren landscape and pond, which housed various species of toad and frog. So, there we were, excitedly marching over the lush green hills, off on our big adventure. Georgiana seemed to have forgotten all her previous animosity towards me, and was even gregarious enough to offer around a large bag of assorted sweets. On that walk to the marsh I was happy, in a way I had not been for years. At last they were starting to like me. I was a part of something.

Finally, we reached the pond, in all its muggy finery. We were all laughing and sweating profusely from the excursion. Wisely we set to rest for a few minutes. Gary Smith, a chubby, blonde 11-

year-old, took the time to tell dated knock-knock jokes, which I, for one, had heard countless times before.

'Very funny,' Darren eventually clipped, sarcastically.

He then glanced, knowingly, at Georgiana, before nodding his head in my direction. Although I had seen this display, I pretended I had not. If I didn't acknowledge their secret mocks at my expense, they would leave me alone and everything would be alright.

At this stage Darren and Georgiana rose quickly and walked over to the edge of the pond.

'Shine-a-light, have you seen that Georgiana?' Darren gasped, as he pointed to something within the depths of the waters.

'It's massive,' replied Georgiana. 'Come and have a look at this Catherine.'

Like a faithful dog, I rushed to Georgiana's side, feeling more duty bound than interested by their find.

'Look it's there...' she exclaimed eagerly, as I lent over to look closely into the dark pit. I could see nothing. '*There...*' she stated, growing impatient.

Then, in a flash, the two pushed me ruthlessly from behind. My footing slipped on the grass and I fell, open-mouthed, into the frog-spawn infested slime.

Rapturous applause and laughter broke out. I struggled to pull weeds from my hair and spit the glue from my mouth. I screamed as my feet squelched in the soft jelly bed of the pool. When I eventually reached the banks, all the others had left. I was alone again, saturated and smelling of rotten gunk. I began to cry. Those tears were only vaguely noticeable amongst the countless droplets falling from my hair and onto my cheeks; cheeks that burned with embarrassment and despair.

The sun was setting when I left the marsh. I was broken. I wanted to disappear. My aunt's was the one place in which I could do this. So, I made one call from a nearby telephone booth, to my foster mother, to explain where I was going. Then I ran, ran from the vicinity of my enemies.

It took a further 20 minutes before I was able to knock on the familiar red door. My aunt appeared, dazed from sleeping on the couch. She began to protest: 'You shouldn't be out at this time of night Catherine. Well, come on, come inside and have a cup of tea.'

After a reprimand, about walking the streets alone, she set about preparing a hot pot of tea and some buttered toast.

'I'm not hungry, thanks,' I asserted.

She ignored my objections and forced the food into my hands. 'Nothing but bloody trouble those kids,' she snapped, angrily.

She was too well used to picking up the pieces after I'd been browbeaten by the tyrants.

Much later, following her traditional nightcap of whiskey, my aunt retired to bed. I quickly followed her, into my room at the head of the stairs.

Providentially, I had remembered my medication: anti-depressants, which I had been taking for more than three months – owing to the constant bullying at school. I opened the bottle and placed it on the chipped oak table in the corner.

'Oh, I'll need some water now,' I sighed.

I had to return to the kitchen for this and a glass. Unfortunately, the glasses were kept safely in the top cupboard, just above the sink unit. This meant I had to stand on my tip-toes to reach one. This I did, and, as my fingers rooted around in the darkness, my knuckles rapped on a bottle at the back of the cabinet, a bottle of bourbon.

I had never tasted alcohol before. Therefore, my unexpected yearning for the intoxicating liquor was strange. I took the glass and bottle back to my room. I began sipping, then gulping, the burning liquid.

Why won't they leave me alone? What have I done to deserve this? The more I drank, the more I wept. *I can't go on like this.* I grieved.

After a whole year or more of the relentless victimization, it all proved too much. It was too much for anyone, let alone a child.

'Why can't she just die?' I whispered. I quickly dismissed this sadistic thought, and turned on myself. Quietly I prayed to the void: 'I want to die, please let me die...'

There was no answer. There was no one there to help me solve my problems. I could not bring myself to hurt others, so there was only one way to end my suffering – I had to die.

I emptied the contents of the jar in my hand. I switched off the lights. It then took over an hour to swallow all the capsules, one by one, each accompanied with a mouthful of alcohol. When the task was completed, I settled down on the floor and went to sleep. It was a silent sleep, the sleep of the dead.

The next morning I woke, sickly and confused. It seemed that the assortment of tablets had not been enough. I had survived the night.

I hovered over the empty bottle. Sure enough I finally realized *I had died* that night. Or, to be more accurate, I recognized the simple truth spoken, when a person claims that a part of his or her soul has died. You see, a part of me did die, the good part. That was why my soul was torn in two. That was why I was forced to return to the room at the head of the stairs. I had to reclaim all that I was.

On the 15th July, 1990, the successful, jovial, sensitive, happy child had died. You have to understand that, all that remained of my soul after that tragic day was the hard, sober, level-headed Catherine – the part of me that could survive the demons of my youth, and would be satisfied, for a time, with an uneventful and unfulfilling life. For some reason, the pressure to perform academically had triggered the relentless pursuit of one half of my being for its counterpart.

Here was the problem. On the 15th July, 2006 I became whole again. However, that wholeness came at a price. There was a born-again sensitivity, and within minutes of the union a deep depression set in.

Understandably the rest of the morning of the 15th July was hazy. Apparently, I was found unconscious, by Marko, with an empty bottle and telltale paracetamol tablet at my side. For once, he had shown great presence of mind and had called an ambulance. I was rushed to hospital. I was caught in time. My stomach was pumped and the lethal liquid flushed away forever. Then there was the customary talk with a qualified Psychiatrist. After this I was discharged from Bradley Royal Infirmary.

Nevertheless, as this was my second 'suicide' attempt, I was referred to Hollbury by the Crisis Resolution team. To start with, this was only to be a temporary admission, just to ensure my own safety. Yet here I am still. What will happen to me, when I am finally released, I cannot say. For now I spend the hours crying: crying over a painful past; crying over a tormented present; crying over a lost future.

Miss Catherine Stanley, August, 2006.

Miss Susan Dane

Dr Milner's diary: 16th July, 2006

Today – I went for lunch with Miss Susan Dane. My goodness, she can be a hot-head when she wants to be. At least she's not dull, like some of the other workers at Hollbury.

Still, she doesn't have to be quite so forthright with her opinions. She's always so snappy whenever I reject the existence of the supernatural. Well, finally, I've found out why she is so convinced of the validity of her beliefs.

Sharp-tongued Sue has experienced paranormal phenomena. I can't wait to tell Isabella!

Note on the text: The following narrative is somewhat different from the rest, simply because Miss Susan Dane is not a patient at Hollbury Psychiatric Unit. On the contrary, she is a valued member of staff.

Miss Susan Dane is 28 years of age and has worked in the capacity of Residential Social Worker, a highly trained carer, in the unit, since May, 2005. During that time she has maintained her long-term relationship with a patient on Ward nine, Dr Adam Felts.

It should be born in mind that Miss Susan Dane is not only a work colleague of mine, but also a close friend. Frequently, over the last couple of months, we have lunched together. We have also enjoyed several evenings out, at fine restaurants, and sometimes in the bars close to the unit, when we have needed to let off steam.

During those thankful releases from the pressures of work, I have come to know and understand Miss Susan Dane very well. She has shared many of her private thoughts with me, on various topics. Although I have to admit, sometimes our discussions have turned into animated debates on the validity of Psychology and the existence of the supernatural.

Miss Susan Dane has much more time for the stories that the inhabitants of Hollbury have to tell, much more than me. Nonetheless, even I was surprised to discover that Miss Susan Dane herself has witnessed certain fantastic events, some in particular that have entered into the very sphere to which this book belongs.

The level-headed Miss Susan Dane, it seems, was touched by the supernatural some years ago, before she started her employment with the Aire Rise Hospital Foundation. According to her, these paranormal occurrences began in the autumn of 2003, whilst she was employed in the capacity of Senior Carer, at a private residence called Rubalt Hall, a Nursing Home previously owned by Dr Adam Felts. As for Dr Adam Felts himself, he has not commented on any of the facts given by Miss Susan Dane.

Since I know Miss Susan Dane is not a person susceptible to fights of fancy, I thought it only right that her account, written at my request, should be placed amongst the stories of the tortured inhabitants of Hollbury.

Dr Milner, Psychiatric Registrar.

Chapter 1

Rubalt Hall

Rubalt Hall has stood all alone on Baildon Moor for nearly 500 years. A truly impressive Tudor mansion, it is cloaked in ivy branches and decorated with elaborate stone carvings. At some stage in the 1970s, this fossil of Old England was converted into a nursing home, where those in the twilight of their lives could peacefully see out the short time they had left on Earth. Subsequently, a wealthy Surgeon, Dr Felts, took charge of the residence. It was for Dr Felts that I went to work, in the capacity of Senior Carer, during the tumultuous autumn of 2003.

Initially the position at Rubalt Hall was one I almost turned down; in light of the reaction I displayed as I approached the manor on my very first day. In retrospect though, my response to the residence was probably very similar to that exhibited by numerous visitors both before and after.

It was the 9th September, 2003, to be precise. Not a time of the year when nature's fruitfulness is at its most beautiful. Yet, even by such reckoning, it was a particularly dark and foggy morning, as I ascended the moor's steep incline, which led to Rubalt Hall.

'What a gloomy place,' I murmured, as my corroded means of conveyance choked upon the mists, which blanketed the barren landscape. *Maybe I've taken a wrong turn somewhere,* I mused, given that, aside from myself, there was no sign of any living creature, certainly no sight of any habitation, along the road upon which I was travelling.

Then, quite unexpectedly, the highway began to dip, and, as I descended further into the haze, I could perceive an entryway. Momentarily, the opening grew clearer and I beheld a pair of crusted, black, wrought iron gates. These were grandly overlooked by a crimson inscription, which read: *'RUBALT HALL, NURSING HOME'*.

At this stage in my journey I paused. Even though I was relieved at having reached my destination, I was reluctant to step beyond the cosy confines of my car; this primarily owing to the inhospitable climate that lay beyond. All the same, I had to open the portentous iron bars that restricted my access to Rubalt. So, I released the rusty car door, wrapped my woollen scarf tightly around my neck and proceeded to push the ice-cold metal railings of Rubalt with all my might.

Yet, the barrier persisted in irksomely preventing my entrance. It was after much pushing and panting that the obstinate iron finally gave way. Soon, I was once again back in the safety of my trusty rust-bucket and crawling slowly along a cobbled street that twisted this way and that through a scattering of oaks. It was only then that I stretched my neck onwards and upwards, so that I could see the ominous grey tower, looming over the east end of Rubalt. As I did so, my cheeks pressed, for an instant, against the frosted front windscreen. I felt a sudden compunction to apply the breaks with force. The car screeched to a halt.

'My God, what a malevolent looking place,' I mumbled to myself, as I perceived the entity in all its horrible finery. I cannot recall exactly how I managed to re-start the engine. Though, I must have done so for, seconds later, I was parked alongside an ostentatious convertible, just outside the main doors.

Normally happy-go-lucky, I was tingling with nerves, since my venture now required rapping on the tarnished brass knocker, elevated on the larger-than-life arched door. Even when I found the courage to do so, I immediately wished I had not. The gentle tap I had applied turned into a thunderous boom, which echoed, ungraciously, throughout the entire edifice.

After several minutes of waiting, the door creaked open, causing my teeth to grate and a shudder that set my hair on end.

'Hiya,' called a young woman, as she popped out of the darkness beyond, 'come in!'

I immediately complied and followed her obediently through a series of dimly lit corridors, which threaded through the fabric of the residence.

'Have you worked here long?' I queried, noticing that she was draped in the usual tabard and trousers of a carer, and wanting to acquaint myself with the other assistants as quickly as possible.

However, there was no reply. Instead, her pace increased rapidly, just as we neared a tight, shadowy bend in the hallway.

'Do you do power-walking in your spare time?' I jested, as the strands of her mousey hair were released from the tight bun into which they had been contorted.

At last she smiled. So, she was human after all and, in light of that fact, I struggled to keep up with her all the more. You see, I did not want to be abandoned in the maze-like passageways of Rubalt. Not for one second.

In due course, we neared a bright light shining at the end of the walkway. A single door was open. The carer rushed on ahead, pushing the entry open further, to reveal a reassuringly modern office suite inside.

'Haven't you heard of knocking, Judy?'

'There's someone here for an interview. Where do you want her to wait?' my companion asked, completely ignoring the comments of a man, sat well within the confines of the room and outside my field of vision.

'Oh, so she's here already? Well, show her in then,' he requested, as Judy grabbed hold of my hand and pulled me brusquely through the doorway.

'Hello. Welcome to Rubalt Hall,' said a strikingly tall gentleman, as he rose from behind a well varnished desk. 'My name is Dr Adam Felts.'

The said Dr Felts proceeded to take hold of my hand firmly, for a thoroughly professional shake. He then indicated to Judy that she was free to leave, sat back down and spent, what seemed like an inordinate length of time, staring curiously into my eyes. Without waiting to be asked, I seated myself upon a swivel chair on the opposite side of the escritoire.

I then began to babble, in the fashion that the nervous so often do, as I outlined all the most flattering features of my curriculum vitae to Dr Felts. Only those particulars that would demonstrate my suitability for the vacant post were aired:

'...I've also completed a Lifting and Handling course and a Basic Food Hygiene certificate, in September, 2000. I have since concluded my studies at National Vocational Qualification Level Two in Care Practices which, in addition to the practical experience I have gained, during more than four years of work within the field, more than equips me for the post of Senior Carer...'

'Oh, enough, enough...' Dr Felts protested, 'I'm convinced. When can you start?'

'As soon as possible,' I exclaimed.

'Well, there's no time like the present,' he maintained. 'We'll get your uniform ordered, a size 12?'

I nodded in affirmation and the 'interview' was over.

The remainder of that day was spent most agreeably. I was given a tour of the premises by the handsome Dr Felts. Indeed, to my shame, whilst he took the time to point out where all the fire escapes and extinguishers were positioned, I whittled away the hours by watching his every move. Consequently, I was impressed by the way he strode confidently down the hall. I was also taken by the way he combed his fingers through his dark, wavy hair. Most of all, I was put at ease by his eloquent, though approachable, manner.

'I think I'm going to like working here,' I whispered to myself, as we approached a sharp bend – the same bend I had passed earlier that morning. However, just as we turned the corner, I halted in my tacks.

'That's odd!' I stated to Dr Felts, who had continued on ahead.

'What?' he questioned, as he walked back towards me.

'Why there's no number six,' I explained, rather puzzled.

'That's right. When I took over the home it was the same as it is now. Don't ask me why one of the previous owners left out the number six. Maybe he or she simply couldn't count,' he laughed.

'Why have you never changed the room numbers? After all, it could be confusing for visitors,' I suggested, not entirely convinced by his clarification for the strange state of affairs.

'Well, as a matter of fact, "Miss Marple", I've often thought of changing the numbers. However, the residents seem to want things left as they are, especially the two in rooms five and seven. Yes, as I recall, it all caused a great deal of upset for Mr Lloyd and Mrs Radcliffe, when I tried to have the numbers changed...'

Dr Felts went on to express his own views on the conservative character of the populace at Rubalt Hall. Eventually we arrived at the staffroom, where all the other carers were taking a short break. As we entered, the happy crew were indulging in an intellectual debate on the appropriate care for one Mr Lodge, who was, from what I could gather, a new resident and dementia sufferer.

'I just don't know how the bugger managed to part with it,' giggled Judy, as she threw her head backwards and forwards in hysterics.

'It was the funniest thing I've ever seen,' seconded a dark, acne-prone teenager, who proceeded to collapse into an armchair. 'The chuffing pan fell out of the commode – it was that bloody big!'

Now the whole room rumbled with laughter, before one damp squid decided to pour cold water on the jovialities. She was a wafer thin nurse, with lank, red hair, pinched cheeks and a long, pointed nose. As was often the case, with certain members of her profession, she had chosen to isolate herself from the others, and was sat in a distant corner, listening with disdain to the prattle of the carers. Then, she could contain her indignation no longer and stated, in a condescending manner,

'Alright ladies, I'm sure poor Mr Lodge's ears must have burnt to a crisp by now. I really don't see why the conversation has to degenerate to the topic of stools *every* single afternoon.'

For several minutes the room was silent. The carers cast one another knowing looks. Soon the irrepressible Judy released her tongue.

'Boohoo!' she exclaimed, 'Listen to Little Miss Whitehouse. Look here, you blue-coats don't have to clean up all the crap. If you ask me, one of these days he's going to explode with all the capsules you insist on shoving up his arse!'

Yet again the workers rocked with laughter whilst the apathetic Nightingale made her exit from the room. As for myself, I found the relaxed and open atmosphere of the staffroom refreshing. It certainly made a difference from the formal talk of Ward 12, where I had covered endless nightshifts for the last six months. In truth, the girls were just having a bit of harmless fun. It was a way for them to make light of their duties, which consisted of assisting their elders with intimately personal hygiene tasks. It was a way for them to blot out the cruel reality of greeting a new resident one week and laying them to rest the next. It was a way for them to cope with death on a daily basis.

In time, the merry trio settled and I was more formally introduced to them by Dr Felts.

'Ok ladies. This is Susan Dane, she'll be your new Senior Carer,' he explained.

As he did, the others turned to inspect their supervisor closely. I smiled at each of them warmly, so as not to give the wrong impression and, fortunately, they all grinned back. Clearly, Judy, Siama and Trisha did not see me as a threat. I knew, instinctively, that we were all going to be good friends.

Once the introductions were over, I was told by Dr Felts that I was free to go home.

'We'll see you in the morning at 8:00am,' he called, as he waved to me from the main entrance, which somehow didn't look quite so stark anymore.

The Yorkshire sun was shining and the crisp green leaves, which caressed the walls, sparkled with dew. Thus, I was in very high spirits as I set off from Rubalt Hall. Well, who wouldn't have been? I had managed to secure a stable position: one that offered over six pounds per hour, a chance to practice my team management skills and gave the opportunity of furthering my qualifications to NVQ level three. In addition to these benefits, the new post required approximately 40 hours of my time per week, time which would normally be spent in my dismal third storey flat with Tom.

Tom was my old, scraggy cat, and the one to whom I boasted of my success later that evening.

'I got it Tom!' I screeched, as the balding tabby wrapped himself around my legs. 'Doesn't that deserve a celebratory drink?'

Naturally, this toast consisted of a bowl of milk for Tom, whilst I made do with a large glass of red wine. I then sat down to plan exactly how each and every wage packet would be spent over the forthcoming weeks.

'I think the first thing we need to get done is the bathroom,' I eventually decided, 'All that green has got to go.'

Since Tom had nothing further to add, I put him to bed in his basket and, much earlier than usual, headed for the bathroom for a thorough cleansing. In common with most newly inaugurated workers, I wanted to look and feel my best the next morning.

Therefore, it was more than half an hour later when I emerged from the water, crinkly and lobster red. I hurriedly dried myself and jumped, childlike, into bed. Embarrassingly, due to wood rot, the frame could not take the sudden impact and collapsed with a bang. I have to confess, it was to be a most ungracious end to an otherwise victorious day. I settled down to sleep on a mattress that was tilted to an incline of more than 30 degrees.

Chapter 2

'Poison Alley'

The next morning I was woken by the constant bleeps of my electric alarm clock and I sprang, gazelle-like, from the sheets. Wisely, I had set aside ample time to dress, in loose fitting trousers and a white blouse, feed the cat and tank-up my rusty Beetle at a local garage. However, in my quest to create a good impression I had been somewhat over-eager. I arrived at Rubalt Hall more than three-quarters of an hour early. This fact was crystal clear, seeing that the whole building was shrouded in darkness and only one other vehicle frequented the car park.

'Hello...,' I called softly, as I pushed open the huge arched door, '...is anyone there?'

The silence spoke for itself.

'The carers must be somewhere,' I stated, whilst I deliberated whether or not to open the various oak doors, which ran down the two sides of the corridor. In the end, though, I decided against this course of action.

'Well, I can't just go bursting into someone's room can I? I'd probably frighten them to death!' I whispered and, instead, made my way towards a solitary lamp that was glowing on a small table just a few metres down the hallway.

'Hello...' I called a little louder, growing more uncomfortable in the noiseless surroundings. Still there was no answer. Hence, I decided to follow the passage down to the office and staffroom area.

To keep a tight rein on my overactive imagination, as I walked, I analysed the décor. It was extremely tasteless and strangely menacing. A collection of mismatched art works were hung on the wood panelled walls, the sombre shades of which hardly served to warm the murky ambience. Even the carpet, quite soft underfoot, depressed the mood of the hallway; since it was dark maroon and indiscriminately streaked with the tire tracks of countless wheelchairs, which had run roughshod over the pile.

'The old place could do with a touch of house doctoring,' I grumbled, as I reached the most sullen corner, the shadowy bend that had unsettled Judy the previous day.

Approximating Judy's response to the turn, I automatically increased my pace.

Suddenly, I froze, hesitated for a moment and retraced my steps.

'What was that?'

I had heard someone moaning, or, more accurately, groaning in agony. It must be coming from number five, I thought, as I placed my ear against the door. There it was again. It was a woman, crying one moment and grunting breathlessly the next. There followed a faint whimpering. Then silence.

'Bloody hell, she must be having a fit,' I gasped, and I flung open the door.

There was no one there. Only the ruffled sheets clearly indicated that the bed had been slept in.

I felt foolish and intrusive. All the same, I glanced around the room. *You know better than that Susan, always go inside in twos,* I reminded myself, remembering the trouble Mary Howarth had encountered at the Belle Cross, when she was accused of taking 10 pounds from a patient's locker.

'What a performance!' I laughed, aware that the state of my nerves was pitifully amusing; amusing, up to the point when I heard the cries of distress again – this time apparently coming from the adjacent wall. *It must be the lady in number seven,* I concluded, and I dashed from room five and into Mrs Radcliffe's.

However, by the time I had stumbled through the doorway and leapt to her side, it became apparent that Mrs Radcliffe was, in fact, sleeping soundly. What was more, aside from her muffled breathing and the steady rise and fall of the blankets, the rest of the room was deadly still. Nonetheless, for several minutes I kept a vigil at her side, only determining to leave once I was completely satisfied that all was well.

'Maybe she was having a bad dream,' I surmised, as I carefully closed the door with a click.

'Hello there,' a woman greeted, tapping me on the back as she did so, and causing me to start, 'you must be Susan.'

Once I had regained my composure, I replied that I was, and gave a few words of vindication for my exit from number seven.

'I thought I heard someone screaming. All I can say is – she must have been having one heck of a dream!'

Having thereby clarified my position, I removed my fingers from the door handle and started to laugh openly at my own stupidity. Peculiarly, the nurse failed to see the funny side of the incident entirely, and seemed to be most concerned as she looked down at the floor.

'You said you heard screaming?' she inquired.

'Yes,' I replied, perplexed at the rather serious expression created by the worry-lines imprinted on her wide forehead.

'…And when you went into number seven Mrs Radcliffe was asleep?'

'Yes, well actually, I went into room five first, but there was no one there…'

'Oh that's just Mr Lloyd, he gets up at the crack of dawn,' she interrupted, outlining the truth behind that gentleman's absence, before returning to the original topic. 'You know, you're not the first one to hear noises outside rooms five and seven. I've heard strange noises myself. Sounded like someone dying. A woman, I think. The same as you, I went in and there was nothing. I suppose it may have been Mrs Radcliffe, but I'm not so sure…'

At last, here was someone almost as edgy as myself. Hence, we continued to discuss the subject of the ominous turn, whilst she escorted me to the staffroom for a coffee and a smoke.

'This is Rebecca, this is Rachael and my name is Bronwyn,' the nurse listed, when we entered an area that closely resembled a sullen tap-room. Inside, two carers were sprawled over a worn-out settee. 'This is Susan, she's new on days,' Bronwyn explained.

I nodded obligingly.

She then reiterated, for the benefit of the others, the strange shrieks which had been heard on 'Poison Alley', as she kept on referring to the area just outside rooms five and seven.

Eventually, most intrigued by the area's illustrious title, I ventured a question,

'Why is it called 'Poison Alley'?'

'I have no idea, everyone calls it that,' Bronwyn replied, as she supped her coffee.

'I bet Mrs Radcliffe knows,' chipped in Rachael, 'she knows all there is to know about Rubalt Hall. She's lived here for over 13 or 14 years, apparently. All the same, I wouldn't believe everything she tells you, Susan. She's as mad as a March hare that one!'

Rachael, a stout young Yorkshire woman with auburn tinted hair and a larger than average round face, subsequently described in detail why she had come to view Mrs Radcliffe in this unflattering way.

'It was all that writing you know, last year it was.' She paused for a moment, to light yet another cheroot and blow her nose. 'For one whole month she scribbled all over the walls of her room in black ink. Eventually Dr Felts had all the pens removed. Who could blame him? It was costing a fortune, to call in the decorators, every time she decided to scrawl all over the bloody place.'

At this point in her account Rachael's cold got the better of her and she sneezed, sending repugnant lime green slime shooting across the air in all directions.

'Oh…flip…I'm really sorry. What must you think of me?!' she apologized, profusely, taking a yellow hankie from her breast pocket to mop up the mess. She then completed her narrative. 'The really weird thing was, she still managed to continue with her graffiti, even when, and I would swear this on my mother's grave, there was not a pen, pencil, or anything else left within 100 yards of her room.'

'Don't be daft, Rachael. There must have been,' Rebecca argued, rationally, torn away from the contents of a magazine by the exasperating gibber of her work colleagues.

Unfortunately, Rebecca's cynicism infuriated Rachael and the room descended into silence. For an age the three ladies remained quiet, each one pretending to be busy with some little preoccupation, so that conversation with the others could be avoided. Some 10 minutes later, Bronwyn was still yawning, over and over, greatly in excess of the extent and needs of her fatigue; Rebecca was still flicking through the pages of a well-thumbed and obviously out of date newspaper and Rachael was gazing at the floor, intermittently tapping her mug and rubbing her nose till it shone Rudolf red with soreness.

I meticulously examined my coffee pot, feeling somewhat awkward amidst the frosty atmosphere which had been created. *Oh for goodness sake, grow-up,* I thought, as I earnestly awaited an attempt by one of those involved to break the ice. Then, finally, Rachael cracked.

'Look, I'm telling you there was nothing. Ask Carol if you don't believe me', she exclaimed, sulkily. 'It was Mrs Radcliffe's bath morning, so we checked every drawer and cupboard. Yet, when Judy took her dinner tray down the whole bloody wall was covered with crap.'

Not wishing to start a row, Rebecca withheld any opinion she may have had on the subject and continued to read the paper. All were eager for the arrival of those on the day-shift, who would relieve them of the current torment.

Sure enough, before long the motley crew, which comprised the day-shift workers, arrived. I was certainly glad to see that Judy, Siama and Trisha were amongst the seven carers who had gathered. I was even happier to see that sulky Rachael, Rebecca and Bronwyn were now on their jolly little way home.

At 8:00am sharp, morning briefing commenced. As was

customarily the case, this occasion took place around the main nurses' station, which in Rubalt was oddly situated at the back of the building. There, in the morbid surroundings, the nurse outlined the gripping events of the previous late-shift, which comprised the passing of four stools and the creation of one wet mattress. I pretended to be listening intently, whilst my eyes took in all the depressing details of the murky beige hallway; especially, its crowning glory, one feeble and quite dangerous looking spiral staircase, which rose up menacingly – as though sprouting from the nurses' desk itself.

'I'd just like to welcome a new member to our little team,' Caroline, the proficient nurse, interjected, as her chubby finger pointed in my direction.

I merely nodded obligingly, mumbling some vein attempt at reciprocation. Still, I could not avert my eyes and thoughts from the dismal welcome that the décor itself conveyed. *They really don't seem to give much attention to marketing their services in this place,* I deliberated, bemused by this unseemly placement of what was the most focal point in the whole establishment.

Suddenly, Judy grabbed my arm, in addition to my attention, 'Come on Susan – wake up. You're working with me on the West-Wing. You're going to love it up there!'

I had to admit, I was more than a little amazed by such a show of enthusiasm, especially so early in the morning. Moreover, I was confused by the glint in her eye and the glowing smile that was lighting up her slender, olive face. *Either she's crackers or she's planning something – some sort of mischief,* I guessed. We ascended the shadowy staircase to the West-Wing.

Nevertheless, everything looked in order. Judy showed me to the tiny store room at the top of the stairs, where all the necessary equipment was kept. There, she hurriedly piled an assortment of pads, wipes, flannels and towels onto a waiting trolley, before rushing off again down the corridor, with me in tow. *Must have had her Weetabix,* I conjectured, as I found it increasingly hard to keep up with my dedicated co-worker.

Thankfully, when we came to the very last room, number 40,

Judy's steps slowed. Here she paused for a moment, held her ear against the door, and then opened it carefully.

'Thank God for that!' she bellowed, to all intents and purposes, most relieved to find room 40 empty. She then took a magazine from the bed-side table and jumped onto the fluffy divan. When she was comfortable, she commenced her study of the said magazine.

After several awkward minutes I interrupted her reading.

'Shouldn't we be starting to help the residents prepare for breakfast?'

'Bloody hell, Susan, don't be such a stick in the mud. You've got a lot to learn about *work* at Rubalt.'

I was a little annoyed at her crisp remark, so I justified my position:

'Look, I just don't want to get into any trouble, not on my first day...Besides, I'm sure Dr Felts said that this was the easiest section. So, we don't want to finish after all the other carers, do we?'

As it turned out, Judy did not need to answer this question for, just as I finished my sentence, the door swung open and the whole troop entered.

'Lazy sod, I knew we'd find you here,' laughed Siama, as she helped herself to some chocolate mints which had been left to rot in a dressing table drawer.

I just stood motionless, uncomfortable and self-conscious. Meanwhile, the other carers planned a wheelchair rally down 'Frog Lane': the flattering title they had given to the upper corridor, owing to the close resemblance of one of its residents to the aforesaid amphibian.

After approximately 20 minutes of friendly banter, the great event took place. It was 8:35am and, as yet, to my knowledge, not one of the 39 residents of Rubalt had been dressed for breakfast. Regardless, the two passengers, Trisha and Judy, eagerly awaited the signal for the tournament to start.

'Ready, steady, go!' called Margaret excitedly, and the quartet set off at full speed down the hallway.

I had to snigger. It was silly but uplifting, to see four adults behaving like school children competing on sports day. I smiled and then gritted my teeth. The wheels of the two chairs screeched to a halt as they nearly collided some way down the corridor.

'Bloody cheat!' Siama complained, when the perspiring contenders returned, 'You forced us out of the way.'

'Well, let's race again,' Judy stated, pointedly, 'you're just a sore looser.'

Siama, predictably, took the bait and accepted the challenge. Trisha, however, withdrew from the rally. Margaret had nearly broken her neck and she was not about to let her have the opportunity to do so again.

Here, then, was a chance, a chance for me to become a fully fledged member of the team. I hesitated for one moment, considering whether, as a senior, it was unwise to join in the games.

'Why the hell not,' I concluded, and I rushed to take Trisha's place in the waiting chair. This was much to the surprise of the others, who had seemingly consigned my character to the realms of wet-blanket and spoil-sport.

'One, two, threeee...' Trisha yelled. I dug my fingers into the chair and closed my eyes. *What are you doing?* I thought, whilst the chair rocked too and fro and bumped, uncomfortably, over the uneven surface below.

'Holy shit!' someone cried, from behind.

The next instant, the wheels of the chair froze, and I was propelled head first through the air. I kept my eyes tightly shut. In time, with a deafening thud, I landed in a sorry heap on the floor; a heap, which upon closer inspection, was floundering just a few inches away from the head of the stairs.

'What the bloody hell are you playing at? Are you trying to kill me?' I shouted back to my dodgy driver.

A sickeningly acute pain shot through my wrist.

'Why, hello again Miss Dane,' the dulcet tones of none other than Dr Felts echoed. 'Looks like you need a hand.'

He passed into my field of vision and offered his own. I just couldn't believe it. I was sure to receive a verbal warning or maybe something much worse. I squirmed, most frustrated by my predicament. I had so wanted to impress my new employer. I certainly did not want to be reprimanded, not by him. Hence, with a dizzy head and throbbing arm, I reluctantly took the hand that had been offered and staggered like a new foal to my feet.

You scatter-brained idiot, I chastised myself. I hung my head low in shame, not knowing quite where to look or, indeed, what to say. In the distance a grandfather clock chimed 9:00am. Dr Felts remained silent, though I knew he was watching me very closely. My cheeks and ears burned, and slow tickling tears began to seep sluggishly down the creases of my face.

'Are you alright?' He asked hoarsely, taking my wrist and turning it over softly.

'It's your fault! Cheese on bread, man! You frightened the life out of Margaret! We were just having a bit of fun,' rambled Judy, who had taken it upon herself to assist the accident victim. 'You're lucky she didn't fall down the chuffing stairs or you would have ended up in court.'

Ever the tactful one, Judy continued to chew the boss's ear for several minutes. Dr Felts merely listened patiently, not that he could have got a word in edgeways had he chosen to speak.

Eventually, even he tired of Judy's incessant chatter.

'Come on Susan, I'd best take a look at this…just to be on the safe side,' he instructed, interrupting Judy mid-sentence. 'Let's go to my office.'

Without any further ado, I was escorted to his study, where Dr Felts diagnosed a slight sprain and applied a flint and bandage. In time the tears halted. Concurrently I stared, lecherously, at the mild mannered doctor, who was working his magic on my pain. I don't really know if what I felt at that moment could be called lust or love, but whatever the correct term, I was falling for the charms of Dr Felts. This was, perhaps, a natural consequence, of having someone in a position of power show a refreshingly human side and a concern for my well-being.

When the nursing was done he raised his eyes. I averted mine.

'Do you think you'll be alright to finish your shift?' he enquired.

'Oh sure, yes, I mean, I'll be fine, yes, thanks…' I answered, and left the room, before I made myself appear even more of a fool than I already had.

To my credit, I managed to avoid becoming embroiled in any other shenanigans for the rest of the day. Instead, I went out of my way to prove that the minor injury I had sustained was of no hindrance to the completion of my duties. Therefore, when the clock finally signalled the end of the shift, I staggered to my car. I was thoroughly drained from the pace I had adopted throughout the day; a day which turned out to be typical of those to follow – one during which I struggled to become one of the 'girls' whilst at the same time remaining a serious, detached senior.

Chapter 3

Signs

Although my work at Rubalt was both physically and emotionally demanding, in time, I did begin to feel more relaxed in my new position. A line was drawn, between the acceptable and unacceptable. As long as the carers kept their games out of my ear and eye shot, then we all worked harmoniously together. For several weeks work at Rubalt was both enjoyable and fulfilling.

However, such an aura of tranquillity was not to last. Winter took shape in all its lifeless glory. The mornings took on the apparel of a depressing night. Then my new-found security was to be rocked and my confidence shaken to its roots.

It was during my fourth week of employment when I took over the day shift cover on Section C, 'Poison Alley'. For the first morning of my work on Section C, I was set to shadow Michelle, one sturdy Bradfordian, who spoke very little and worked extremely hard. Compliantly, I followed Michelle down the shadowy passageway, where a sullen chill and stale damp hung in the air. I was far from looking forward to spending the next few days on this particular corridor, and my thoughts must have been written all over my face, for Michelle felt compelled to state:

'Crap, isn't it? Well, Susan, if you think this looks bad, wait till you meet Radcliffe. Now that should be interesting.'

Though, judging from the expression on her visage, I

gathered that *'interesting'* was, perhaps, not the most appropriate choice of term.

Before very long we were knocking on number seven.

'For God's sake come in, come in will you,' a croaky and impatient lady called from inside.

Michelle turned towards me and smiled. 'Well, let's see what the old goat has been up to now. Ready?'

I nodded in the affirmative and we entered the room. The décor inside was typically gaudy and inexpensive, the furniture being limited to a bed, a dressing-table, one wardrobe, and a chest of drawers. At least the normality of the surroundings brought some comfort and relief, after all the bizarre comments I had heard about Mrs Radcliffe. The only striking characteristic of her boudoir was the overpowering scent of lavender that dangled in the air and cloaked the newly pressed clothes hanging from the wardrobe doors.

'Are you going to stand there gawping all day or are you going to help me get dressed?'

I was irritated by this sudden interruption of my thoughts and found myself banging the bowl in the sink, running the water at full pelt and practically throwing the flannel into the soapsuds. *Why can't old people be polite? It doesn't cost them anything.*

'Haven't you finished in there yet? They'll have tidied the breakfast away by the time I get there. Can you hear…?'

She stopped as I approached the bed. I certainly didn't feel very caring or sympathetic towards Mrs Radcliffe. Nonetheless, I assisted her as best I could, whilst she grumbled about my technique, it being either too rough or too soft to be effectual. *There's no pleasing some people,* I concluded, and finally applied the lady's powder and paint in a fashion that would have only been appreciated in a waxworks. Ironically, Mrs Radcliffe was very impressed by my artistic flair – which had left her lips blood-red and her lashes matted black.

Meanwhile, Michelle covered her mouth, to conceal her chuckles at the old lady. When she could contain herself no longer, she left the room. Once she had exited, the place appeared darker and more sinister, somehow. The lavender fragrance faded, and was replaced by the smell of rotten damp. There was a definite chill in the air. I was eager to be done with Mrs Radcliffe, who was now quiet.

Abruptly she started and sat bolt upright in bed. 'Look, girl. Come on, look *over there!*'

My eyes followed the point of Mrs Radcliffe's scrawny finger to the wall. All I could perceive were the curves of a dated pattern upon the wallpaper. Mrs Radcliffe still persisted in wriggling her finger, just in case I decided to avert my attention. I, therefore, squinted in order to focus more precisely on the partition. Now I could see. There were faint damp patches pushing their way through the fabric. Slowly the patches turned into patterns. Steadily, the patterns formed themselves into symbols.

'What on earth are those? Hieroglyphics...?' I queried.

Mrs Radcliffe failed to reply. Instead she shook her head, evidently from a mixture of annoyance and disbelief at my lack of worldly wisdom. She then demanded her handbag, clicking her fingers impatiently. I passed it to her, in the manner of a serf, which she so obviously thought I was. For several minutes Mrs Radcliffe rummaged around in the depths of her moth-eaten, leather shoulder bag, tossing bits of paper and cosmetics across her bed as she did so. From what I could tell, she was greatly perturbed.

Finally, she breathed a sigh of relief and pulled her hands out of the depths. Within them she clenched a small paperback book.

'What's that then?' I enquired, as I tried to catch a glimpse of the front cover.

'Nosey, aren't you!' she stated, turning the pages of the text. 'I think that's it. Yes, that must be it.'

Satisfied with her investigation, she carefully closed the book.

Mrs Radcliffe was now gracious enough to offer a most fascinating explanation for the curious phenomenon on the wall and her own bizarre behaviour. 'Your name's Susan, isn't it?'

I nodded.

'Perhaps it's for the best that you are new to Rubalt. God

willing, you will look on the events here with fresh eyes.' She paused to wipe her brow and froth from the corners of her mouth. 'Those signs are runic symbols, a most ancient form of communication. I have recently become most interested in such things.' She patted the text that held the secrets of her new found study. 'You see, Susan, I believe that someone is trying to give us a message from the other side.'

I was lost for words. I simply did not know how to respond to Mrs Radcliffe's wild theories on the damp patches in her room. For once, my rationality presided over my imagination and I could not suppress a grin of superiority. Unfortunately, Mrs Radcliffe observed my actions and sighed. She had presumed there was a certain accord in our supernatural sympathies. Not wishing to cause offence, I tried my best to offer a few words; words which would demonstrate that, to a certain extent, our thoughts were in harmony.

'Well, you never know Mrs Radcliffe. I guess people sometimes die with unfinished business, I mean, when they haven't said all that they have to say.'

Yes, I know it was a pathetic statement. From the expression on Mrs Radcliffe's face, she was about as unimpressed with my oratory as I was, but it was all I could manage at that particular moment. So, I was greatly relieved when I heard someone knock on the door.

'Come in,' Mrs Radcliffe stated, quite icily.

'Hello, Mrs Radcliffe,' greeted Dr Felts, as he entered the room carrying a large package, 'your new zimmer-frame has arrived from Belle Cross. Do you want to use it straight away?'

Mrs Radcliffe nodded and, without casting me a second glance, left her room for the breakfast-hall.

Left alone with Dr Felts, I felt slightly embarrassed. For this reason, I busied myself in the en-suite bathroom, cleaning away the washing bowl and laundry. In truth, there was nothing I wanted more than to talk to the good doctor. However, I realised I was falling for his charms, and was mature enough to understand that such a man would have his choice of numerous attractive women. As a result, I set to avoid him. In any case, I supposed that Dr Felts would have much more important things to do, much more important than engaging in idle chitchat with an employee. I was, though, surprised to see that he was still standing by the wardrobe when I re-entered the bedroom. I headed for the door.

'Please, wait a minute, Susan,' he requested, 'I was just wondering, if you would like to go out for a meal sometime?'

He paused to hear my answer.

I just nodded and murmured, 'Err, yes.'

What else could I say? I had never been the most popular girl in school, or anywhere else for that matter. Yet, here was an extremely handsome, educated, well-mannered, not to forget successful, man, asking me out on a date. I had never been asked on a proper date before – not one that didn't include being dragged to the local for a pint, with the expectation that such extravagance would result in the satisfaction of some male's pleasures.

Indeed, given the experiences I had endured with the opposite sex, and my own consequential insecurities, I did wonder if perhaps Dr Felts was only asking out of boredom or curiosity. Maybe he had just asked in the heat of the moment? Tomorrow he would have forgotten all about it and he would henceforth keep me at a distance, in order to avoid any awkwardness. These thoughts occupied my mind for the rest of the morning, as I assisted the other, more accommodating, residents on Section C.

At 1:00pm Michelle and I headed for the staffroom. Judy had collected our lunches from the kitchen and they were waiting for us, slightly cold, on the scratched dining table.

'Grub's over there,' she indicated and, having already finished her own, flopped onto a settee to enjoy a cigarette.

At first I looked at my plate. Then I toyed childishly with my food, forming the mashed potato, carrots, green beans and chicken pieces, into various shapes and structures. Thereby preoccupied, I failed to notice that Judy was watching my every move, as she puffed smoke circles into the air.

'Well, are you going to eat that bloody food or not?' she

questioned, very agitated by my lack of enthusiasm for the cuisine prepared by the resident cook, who just so happened to be her boyfriend, Karl.

'I'm just not that hungry,' I replied, taking my fork and tapping it on the coffee pot in an irritating manner.

Judy suppressed whatever comment she was about to make and, instead, leapt towards the table, where she wolfed down my dinner. Within seconds she was again slouched on the couch, gasping for yet another cigarette.

'What?' she stated, as I shook my head, 'It's better than wasting it.'

Later that afternoon, I was to regret not having any lunch. All throughout Mrs Elsie Wilkinson's bath my stomach rumbled. The pangs grew even worse when it came to the delivery of afternoon tea and biscuits. Undeniably, poor old Mr Reginald Clark almost managed to lift his own withered right arm in an attempt to feed himself, having given up on waiting for me to put the tempting custard cream into his mouth.

'Oh, sorry, Mr Clark,' I apologised, taking my glance from the food just long enough to notice that he was about to slip from his chair with exasperation.

By the end of the shift I was starving. I had also concluded that Dr Felts had no intention of associating with one of his staff. Glumly, I fetched my coat and bag from the staffroom and sulked all the way down the corridor towards the main exit.

'Wait a minute Susan,' panted Dr Felts, as he approached from behind, 'I'm glad I caught you, I've been up to my eyeballs in paperwork this afternoon. I was hoping you would accept an invitation to dinner tonight at Delaney's?'

'Yes, I err, thought you'd forgotten.'

'Not at all,' he said, calmly, 'I thought you didn't want to come.'

'Why?' I couldn't comprehend why he would actually believe that I was indifferent towards him.

'Well, you haven't been to my office once today. It appeared that you were trying to avoid me. You were trying to say "no" politely.'

He stated the last word more precisely than the rest. True, he did have a point. Nearly every day during which I had been employed at Rubalt there had been some reason to visit the office, to order new pads and so on. I confessed to him now, that I had been taken by surprise by his invitation to dinner. I also hinted that one had to be careful when entering into a relationship with an employer. Not that we were entering into a relationship. Just that one needed to be careful. That was all.

He didn't seem to mind my babbling. He smiled warmly.

'Look, Susan, I've been wanting to ask you out since you started working here, and before you ask, no, I haven't dated any of the other staff at Rubalt.'

So without further ado, it was arranged that Dr Felts would collect me from my apartment at 7:30pm that evening. Elated, I left for home.

Chapter 4

Runes

As you would probably surmise, I pulled out all the stops for my evening out with Dr Felts. Legs were keenly waxed, and my hair and body bathed in luxurious raspberry scented toiletries. I chose to wear typically sophisticated attire for the meal. This finery consisted of: natural looking tights, stylish black suede heels and a black figure-hugging dress, which wasn't too revealing to detract from its elegance. My make-up was minimal: being a whisper of brown eye-shadow; a flicker of mascara; tinted moisturiser; pink lip-gloss and a brush of rose-coloured blush. I scanned my reflection in the mirror and was pleased with the healthy glowing young lady who looked back. The time was 7:25pm exactly.

I opened a bottle of Chardonnay that was cooling in the fridge and poured a tall glass. There was still a little time left. Hence, I decided to enjoy a favourite musical piece and a cigarette, which I preserved for such occasions.

The clock chimed 7:30pm. My anxiety rose. I looked down from the lounge window onto the car park below. There were the usual comings and goings of the neighbours, but no Dr Felts. *I wonder if he's coming. Maybe he's changed his mind.* Soon it was 7:45pm and there was no call on the intercom. I sat down on the recliner and supped my wine. I flicked through the pages of a TV magazine. I paced the room in circles. I then went to the mirror again, to check if my reflection had changed. It hadn't. Yet, I was not smiling as widely as I had on my previous inspection.

'Beep, beep, beep, beep...'

'All right, I'm coming,' I muttered, nearly falling over Tom, as I raced to reach the line before my visitor turned and ran.

'Beep, beep...'

I composed myself and lifted the receiver steadily. 'Hello,' I gasped, outwardly quite calm and accustomed to male callers, inwardly breathless.

'Are you ready, Sue?'

'Yes, come on up,' I instructed.

Before the knock finally came at the door, I had managed to brush my hair a further four times, pull down the hem on my dress six and clean my teeth twice! This being done, I checked my appearance, just once more, and opened the door.

Dr Felts stood gallantly in the hall. He was a truly impressive sight; dressed handsomely in a traditional black suit, tie and shoes, with an ultra clean, white shirt.

'I won't be a minute,' I informed him, taking my eyes away from his imposing form for a moment.

I then rushed to the couch, flung my wrap over my shoulders and grabbed my glitzy evening bag.

Now, not wishing to turn my tale of the macabre into one of romance, it is enough to say that I had a memorable evening. The meal was delicious, the conversation never stilted and Dr Felts was movingly attentive. What was more; this special evening did not end with the usual sticky fumbling, with which Western women have become so accustomed on so-called first dates. Dr Felts not only looked the part of a gentleman, but actually behaved like one. After driving me home, we kissed, like teenagers, at the door and he said goodbye.

'I'll see you tomorrow, Susan.'

For my part, I watched as he walked towards his car. I leered as he passed his hand through his dark mane. I was touched by the way he had begun to utter my name in deep intense tones.

Over the next few weeks our relationship grew steadily into

one of mutual understanding, respect and aching desire. The girls at work, although surprised when they first discovered the affair, soon tired of idle gossip and accepted that the new girl had hooked 'Mr Cool'. Work thus carried on as normal. I did not abuse the fact that I was the boss' lover, nor did I expect to be treated any differently by the senior nursing staff. The only actual privilege I was guilty of being granted, perhaps owing to my relationship with Adam, was that when I asked one of the nurses if I could be put on any section other than C they complied. However, even this privilege was curtailed, when the usual winter cold staff shortages forced me to complete Sections B and then C alone, on one frost-bitten morning.

It was the 1st December and five members of staff had called in sick with the flu. Consequently, the whole nursing home was in uproar, there being only four staff on duty and over 30 residents to get ready for breakfast. I had, therefore, been given both Sections B and C to finish before 10:00am. I was rushed to say the very least, and so were the unfortunates: Harold Beeton; Harry Travis; Emma Taylor; Joyce Jones; Alice Dickens and Jim Morris. These were the residents of Section B, who were practically hurled from their beds and sped down the hall to the smell of burning bacon.

In time, I steadied my pace. It was the turn of those on 'Poison Alley'.

'I'm going to have to tell Dr Felts to get better lighting down here,' I muttered, dragging my heels across the murky carpets beneath.

Timidly, I opened one door after another, each revealing a half naked elderly lady or gentleman, purple in the face with anger at being late for her or his breakfast. Quite on purpose, I chose to postpone my visit to room seven, the flighty Mrs Radcliffe's. For I knew that I was in for a verbal dressing down from that good lady and, in view of the morning I had endured, I was hardly in the mood. Nevertheless, the moment of truth finally arrived. I gritted my teeth before entering her room.

'Oh, so you've finally decided to turn up,' she greeted, as I made my way to the en-suite to procure her toiletries.

'Sorry,' I returned.

Although she still decided to pour further scorn on all my hard work.

'A few of the carers are off sick, I've had to do B on my own as well,' I offered, by way of vindication.

To this she said nothing, though the frown on her face suggested that she felt little compassion for the nursing team.

All the same, I washed her carefully, combed what was left of her hair and picked out a warm outfit for the day – the air being distinctly frosty.

Come on, hurry up, I prayed, as Mrs Radcliffe applied her war-paint with painful precision. I wanted to be out of number seven. I wanted to be done with Mrs Radcliffe as quickly as possible. I could see my breath drift through the air. I could feel the ends of my fingers and toes growing numb with the cold. *They're just wet that's all.* I rubbed my hands as hard as I could on a fluffy white towel. Mrs Radcliffe then began muttering to herself.

She paused as the lip-balm brushed across her lips.

'Saints preserve us, there it is again!'

She clenched my arm in a skeletal grip.

'Come on Susan,' she clipped, 'you think you have all the answers. What does that mean?'

I honestly didn't know. The walls had been completely clear. Now they were completely covered – covered with dripping damp. Squiggles and swirls, strange flashes and box-shaped patterns could be seen from one end of the room to the other. I was not so quick to laugh at Mrs Radcliffe's conjectures now, not now when the lights started to flicker then fade and a scent similar to sweet honey floated throughout. I felt sick inside. With the velvet curtains closed, the room was shrouded in sinister shadows.

'What...what do you think they are trying to tell us, Mrs Radcliffe?'

'It's not *they* Susan, it's *she*,' Mrs Radcliffe whispered, '*she's* been dead for 13 years or so. Oh look at that one, that one *there*...'

She pointed to the most curious of the signs, one that looked a little like a cross between a capital H and N, only upside-down.

'That's death. *Hegall*, it's the symbol of disruption, in this case premature death.'

Mrs Radcliffe hesitated then collected her thoughts.

'It's always the same, every time they appear. The symbols are always reversed, they always speak of murder.'

My knowledge of runic symbols was limited to one black and white film, *The Night of the Demon*. Therefore, I began to ask Mrs Radcliffe a series of questions, so that I could understand the writing on the wall for myself.

'What are runic symbols Mrs Radcliffe?'

'Well my dear,' she warmed to my enthusiasm, 'this is a topic I have learnt a great deal about. Runes were first used by Germanic peoples for spiritual and material reasons. You see, people believed that runes were a series of miraculous pictographs which symbolised powers and substances in the natural world. They also held that by utilising certain runes you could make contact with a particular energy.'

'So, runes are pictures used to command nature?'

'Not quite,' she smiled, grateful that she was given an opportunity to show off her greater knowledge to a youngster, one who thought they knew it all. 'The runic system developed into an alphabet. I think the first examples of runes being exploited to represent language appeared around the second century B.C. Today there are various different alphabets, though the most common one in use is the Germanic or elder *Futhark*. This alphabet has 24 letters, divided up into clusters of eight called *Tir's Eight, Hagall's Eight* and *Freya's Eight*. That,' she pointed to the wall, 'is elder *Futhark*.'

Sure, I now knew what the strange pictures were, though this information really told me nothing – nothing about why runes were gracing the walls of number seven, or what exactly the various signs were trying to say.

'Mrs Radcliffe, before you mentioned a *"she"*, who is she and why is she trying to contact you now? Can't she rest in peace or something?'

'She, my dear, is Martha, Martha Paris.' Mrs Radcliffe paused to capture her breath and wipe a tear from her eye, 'It was nearly 13 years ago. Poor old Martha used to have the room adjacent to mine.'

'...Number five?' I queried.

'Oh no, my dear, number six,' she stated, lowering her voice to a faint whisper. 'We all knew at the time that something was wrong, some sort of evil was at work. Died quite suddenly, she did. It was all very strange – had breakfast with old Lloyd and me one morning, and that was the last that we saw of her. Confined to her room, she was. No one was allowed to visit her, none of the residents anyway. The next news we had from Mr Felts was that she had died. A heart attack we were told, though I didn't believe it, not for one minute. God she suffered, how poor Martha suffered...'

Mrs Radcliffe was close to crying. I didn't want to upset her anymore, though my curiosity was ignited.

'How do you know she suffered, Mrs Radcliffe, if you didn't have a chance to see her?'

'Oh Susan, you didn't have to see her. I could hear her. I can still hear her moaning, sometimes even while I sleep.'

'So, you think that Martha Paris is trying to tell you something, something about her death?'

'Yes I do. You see, my dear, Martha was, I mean is, the only one capable of communicating with runes. It was her life. She was like a shaman. Had her own set of runes, carefully carved, they were, from fine oak. She used to do readings for some of the other residents, though I think the others were in it just for fun. Not Martha, she never let her runes out of her sight. She took it all very seriously.'

Mrs Radcliffe then went on to outline how Martha Paris, like others who have been involved in the practice of such magic, believed that her own rune set was imbued with her own life force. As such, her runes would take on whatever role she required of them, be that remedial, defence or divination. Mrs Radcliffe firmly believed that, even following Martha's death, her runes were searching for the truth, or to be more precise, assisting others in their search for the truth – the truth about Martha Paris' demise.

Mrs Radcliffe continued with my first lesson in rune reading. I came to learn the meanings of the various symbols still scattered on the wall. First there was the reversed *Perdhro,* which told of nasty revelations and evil secrets. Someone close had skeletons in his or her closet that were about to be exposed.

'We need to be very cautious at this time dear, *Perdhro* can signal danger ahead,' Mrs Radcliffe explained.

She had then pointed to *Nied,* the rune of impediment. As this symbol was also reversed, we were being warned about making snap-decisions, which could lead to tragedy.

In addition, there was *Jera,* so someone – we didn't know who – was going to be called upon to make some sort of recompense for past transgressions. The two runes, *Nied* and *Jera* were within inches of each other, which also suggested connections with the law. Justice was about to catch up with someone – the question was, who was that someone?

It could not be denied, the reading was inherently negative. All the signs had been displayed in murky yellow, which had altered to black right before our eyes. Again the colouring of the symbols heralded connections with the law and negative destruction. Yet, ominous as it was, I determined to find out for myself, with Mrs Radcliffe's assistance, what lay behind Martha Paris' calls for help. To find out exactly what had happened to the old lady who died most mysteriously within the confines of her room.

Finally, at 11:30am Mrs Radcliffe was escorted to the dining room. It was now cleared and empty, save for the cleaner, Joan, who was busy hoovering away in the corner. She cast a scornful look our way and shook her head.

'Make sure there's no mess, I'm not hoovering again,' she informed us and left the room.

I fetched Mrs Radcliffe her breakfast, since the cook had gone on strike and simply refused to prepare anyone breakfast so late. This done, I continued with my other duties, completed the daily report sheets and assisted residents who needed the toilet.

I saw little of Mrs Radcliffe for the remainder of the day, although I did find time to do a little investigating of my own, in Section C. In order to do this, I had decided to take charge of the tea trolley, which had to be taken throughout the home for those residents who chose to remain in their rooms.

Initially, I went along Section A, where a dementia sufferer, Mr Harry Taylor, was giving a noble speech to a crowd of invisible guests at his dinner party. Like many who are touched by this mental illness, he had, quite rightly, returned to better days, when he was the director of a large steel construction company, and hosted many a meal for other important businessmen. Next, I went onto Section B, where Miss Nelly Thorn and Mrs Hilda Bark were having their usual afternoon tête-à-tête as they watched *Fifteen-to-One*. Finally, as no one had chosen to remain solitary on Section D, I passed onto Section C, where only the private Mr Lloyd was awaiting his refreshments.

I knocked firmly at number five and entered with a steaming pot of coffee and two bourbons. The room reeked of tobacco, as cigarette smoke swamped the air. Petite Mr Lloyd was sitting comfortably in a chair: a chair that dwarfed him, for it had apparently been made for some giant.

'By, that's a grand cup of coffee, lass,' he thanked me, as he took a cheroot from a packet and relaxed back on his throne.

It had occurred to me that maybe Mr Lloyd had witnessed the strange symbolic sightings, or had perhaps heard Martha Paris' death groans, which had been so audible from number seven. At any rate, since he was the only other resident, apart from Mrs Radcliffe, who had been at Rubalt at the time of Martha Paris' death, I concluded that, at the very least, he might be able to cast more light on the tragic events of her last days. So, I perched myself on the edge of his bed and started to question him on the subject.

'You've been here for over 13 years haven't you Mr Lloyd?'

This question was just a way of broaching the topic, for I knew very well from Mrs Radcliffe that Mr Lloyd had been. When he thus answered in the affirmative, I continued, 'Do you remember Martha, Martha Paris?'

Mr Lloyd's face dropped. He was touched with sadness and his wrinkles crinkled into crisper chisels. He looked down at the maroon patterns on the carpet.

'Yes I remember her.'

For some time, I left him to his memories. Soon enough, he composed himself.

'Look in the top drawer, that one over there, if you want to see Martha,' he informed me, as he pointed to a faded mahogany desk resting in the corner of the room.

I walked to the drawers and opened the top one carefully. In the corner were two photographs, one black and white and the other colour. Firstly, I examined the black and white picture. It showed an attractive young woman with dark hair. She was posing on a stage, wearing a top hat and tails.

'Is this Martha Paris?'

Mr Lloyd nodded.

'Was she a dancer?'

Again Mr Lloyd nodded.

I then turned my attention to the second picture. This displayed an elderly lady dressed in tweed. It was strange how, regardless of the passing of time between the two pictures, the beaming smile and mischievous eyes obviously belonged to the same person. I tapped the picture with my index-finger, 'Martha?'

Mr Lloyd just smiled.

Over the next half an hour Mr Lloyd told me all that he knew about Martha Paris. She had been a talented stage actress and dancer in her youth, and an accomplished dance teacher during most of her adult life. As far as Mr Lloyd was aware, she had never married and had no children, for she had chosen a career at a time when women were expected to have one or the other, not both.

Still, she had been contented with her choices in life and showed no signs of loneliness or regret. She had a great many friends and acquaintances and had been a popular resident at Rubalt during her long stay.

'She was a character you know, lass,' Mr Lloyd sighed. 'She was always telling someone's fortune, reading palms and so on.' He added that, towards the end, Martha Paris had indulged in the occult and runic divination. 'Yes, it was all a bit much towards the end. Some of us became uncomfortable with it all. You see, lass, to begin with it was all a bit of harmless fun. Not in the last few weeks of Martha's life though. Used to lock the door, she did. Used to wail and cry, cry that she had read about her own downfall. I wish she'd never made those damn runes. Made her paranoid, they did. She was convinced that someone was out to get her. Within weeks she was dead. I never touched the runes after that. Just can't get the sound of her cries out of my mind, terrible they were...'

Mr Lloyd stared out of the window. He had begun to pace the room and now he paused. It would have been cruel to question Mr Lloyd further, but I simply couldn't resist just one more question.

'I'm sorry to pester you Mr Lloyd, but there is just one more thing I would like to know...'

He nodded in ascent.

'Do you think Martha Paris was right? Do you think there was anything *unusual* about her death?'

Mr Lloyd pondered momentarily and stated,

'I suppose I would have to say, yes. She was as strong as an ox that one. She never had any vices, drinking, smoking or the like. I, for one, thought she would outlive me. It all happened so suddenly...Well, one of the nurse's husbands, who worked as a Pathologist at the hospital, carried out the post-mortem. Dr Crabtree it was. Cardiac arrest, he said. Well, who would have thought it?'

I shrugged my shoulders, not knowing how to reply and turned to leave. Having bothered Mr Lloyd for quite some time, I surmised that he would be glad to see the back of me, when without warning, Mr Lloyd grabbed my wrist.

'Seeing that you're really interested in what happened to old Martha, perhaps you should take a look at this,' he exclaimed, mysteriously.

Still holding onto my wrist, he turned me towards the wall.

'What?' I queried, looking blankly at the chipped blue paper.

'This...' he nodded, as he punched his fist full on into the division.

I jumped on the spot, not really anticipating this swift action on the part of an old man. To my astonishment, Mr Lloyd wasn't hurt, not in the slightest. On the contrary, more damage had been done to the partition itself, which was merely constructed of crumbling plaster board.

I moved closer, to inspect the fracture that had been created by the impact of Mr Lloyd's feeble hand. A tiny hole had been made, which forced its way right through to the other side of the panel and the room beyond. I peered into the crevasse, half expecting to see Mrs Radcliffe's boudoir. However, a strange scene was illuminated before my eyes.

In the room beyond, time had stood still. White sunlight was streaming down, speckled with dust. In the centre of the space stood a rusted four-poster bed, shrouded with a mustard mottled spread and a fine film of powder. To the far right of the room, I could perceive a dressing table, covered with grey dollies and an assortment of boxes. One box in particular, a small silver trinket box, which was twinkling in the morning light, caught my eye. Its clasp was open and the edges of a piece of brown paper could be seen protruding from inside – an unusual object, I thought, to be forced into the tight space of so small a confine.

Eventually, I managed to avert my attentions from the neglected room and back to Mr Lloyd.

'Is that Martha Paris' room?' I enquired.

He nodded, and informed me that shortly after her death, the doors of number six had been boarded up.

'When Martha died the noises began, terrible noises which kept the residents awake at night. Soon enough, the boards were put in place. It was as if Martha had never existed, room number six had never been. If you want to know what I think, I think that Mr Felts was scared. He was scared of what Martha would tell.'

Mr Lloyd continued, further pointing out how he felt sure *Mr* Felts was somehow involved in Martha's death. After that, I simply said goodbye to Mr Lloyd and left. I didn't like what he had said, not one little bit. I refused to believe that Adam was somehow connected to some sort of crime; that he shared some complicity in Miss Paris' murder. I refused to believe that he held some sordid secret deep within.

Nevertheless, that evening, and for the remainder of the week, I was subdued and detached in Adam's presence. I just wanted him to tell me all he knew about Martha Paris. I wanted to know why he had boarded up room number six. I also wanted an explanation as to why he had told me it was Mr Lloyd and Mrs Radcliffe who had objected to the room's use for residential purposes. They, like me, wanted the secrets of room number six to be opened up for all to see.

Chapter 5

Adam's Sinister Side

When the weekend arrived, I was relieved. I was certainly looking forward to a couple of days reprieve from Rubalt Hall. However, as usual, Adam had taken the liberty of booking a reservation at a local restaurant for Saturday evening. Now, although this was something that I normally eagerly anticipated, I really didn't relish the thought of making romantic small talk. I even telephoned Adam earlier in the day, in an attempt to persuade him that I was not feeling my best and should give dinner a miss. Yet, he was having none of it.

'After all,' he rationalized, 'if you're run down, the best thing for you is a good meal, in good company, of course.'

He arrived at 8:30pm sharp and we set off for *The Tapas*.

Well into the feast an uncomfortable silence rested at our table. We ate, though failed to fully taste the cuisine. We returned home, without calling at the customary night-spots on the way for refreshments.

Finally, we arrived at my flat at 10:15pm. It was not that late, and Adam began to talk incessantly, about this and that. It was transparently clear that he was trying to coax me into a conversation, any kind of conversation. Though, it was a futile task. Eventually, enough was enough.

'Look, Susan, is something wrong?' he asked.

'No, why?' I replied, with as much certainly as I could muster.

'Well, if you're having second thoughts about us, you have to say so.'

'No, not at all!' I exclaimed, worried that he was about to call an end to our relationship before it had really begun.

'I've been thinking,' he paused at this moment, causing my heart to race nervously, 'it seems silly to me, you living here and me living in my bachelor pad in Bingley. I think we should take our romance to the next level. Would you consider moving in with me? Or, if you prefer, we could look for a new place together?'

He waited for my answer anxiously. I was stunned, yet excited. My worries became a nothing. We were forging a more secure, long-term commitment.

'Of course I would,' I blurted, and jumped on his knee, sending a shower of red wine droplets down onto the recliner and the carpet beneath.

Sure enough, by the following weekend I had moved all my belongings into Adam's immaculate new build, Ivy Bank. Finally, on Friday the 13th December, I said goodbye to my apartment for the last time. I felt no regret at not being able to carry out all my carefully laid plans for the old place. On the contrary, when I arrived at Adam's and began to arrange my clothes thoughtfully, in just one of Ivy Bank's walk-in closets, I was more than impressed. The décor was beautiful and the whole character of my new accommodation was spaciously grand. At last, I was in a residence that needed no correction, no time and money spent on making it habitable.

In truth, whereas Adam had always referred to Ivy Bank as his 'bachelor pad', it was in fact a spectacular piece of modern architecture. No expense had been spared on making its interior the finest, that I had ever seen at any rate.

Within no time at all, I came to view Ivy Bank as my home. However, I was a little at a loss as to what to do with myself there from the 23rd December, when Adam departed for France on urgent family business. 'Business' which had come to light during a 2:00am phone call: one that had woken me during the night; one that Adam had clearly not wanted anyone, even me, to hear; one he had chosen to take in the kitchen, even though there were more than three connection points closer to the bedroom.

Sure, I had suggested that, perhaps, his trip to France could wait until after Christmas. This idea met with a negative response. I had also volunteered to accompany Adam on his journey, since it would provide an opportunity for me to meet his family, a family he had not mentioned before. However, Adam's declinations became even more adamant – under no circumstances would he consider taking me to his brother's Maison de la Fôret.

So, I was left alone, except for Tom, in frost-bitten England, reeling from my apparent rejection. I was also rather bored in my splendid isolation, for the holiday season proved to be uneventful. Indeed, I spent most of my time cleaning the house; wandering up and down the corridors, aimlessly; and calling old friends who had not been contacted in years. However, I eventually gave up on the latter activity, when it became glaringly apparent that just about everyone in my universe was having a more marvellous time than myself. To relieve the monotony I, therefore, took to supping lager in the Jacuzzi, whilst watching the customary snow descend outside.

It was thus with a certain amount of relief that I returned to work on the 2nd January. When I entered the staffroom all the others were busy discussing the various visits they had made and parties they had enjoyed over the holidays. Naturally, Judy outshone them all, with her tales of drunken exhibitions on the dance floor and numerous propositions around the backs of seedy nightclubs.

'Oh, and what have you and lover boy been up to Sue?' she pried, as if knowing very well that we had been *'up to'* nothing.

'This and that,' I clipped, turning away to look out of the window, hoping that she wouldn't bother me anymore.

Unfortunately, Judy was not put off in the slightest.

'What do you mean, "…*this and that?*" Anyway, what did the great romantic buy you for Christmas?'

'Nothing,' I said quietly, 'he had to go away on business.'

There were no more questions. Judy glanced at Tracy, who in turn looked at Siama. All three remained hushed. It was obvious that the trio thought there had been some sort of lovers' tiff and I simply couldn't be bothered to put them straight.

Instead, I absorbed myself in my work. Never before had the residents in Rubalt been subjected to such a thorough cleansing; never before had I stirred the teas and coffees with such vigour; never before had so many people been rushed to the toilet in such a short space of time, whether they really needed it or not.

Such was my enthusiasm for my vocation that I hadn't noticed someone had been watching, while I had shipped more than 20 people up and down the corridor. The first I was aware that anyone was in the vicinity was when one wheelchair nearly collided with the gent as he emerged from behind a mahogany dresser.

'My God! Oh. Adam!' I stuttered, as the wheels ground to a halt.

'Slow down, Sue,' he laughed, flicking his hair from his brow, 'are you going in for the land speed record?'

'I am sure she bloody well is,' Mr Graham Johnson spat, singularly disconcerted with his carer, after having to haul himself back into position, to avoid slipping onto the floor.

I apologised to Graham and carefully escorted him back to the lounge. I said nothing to Adam. What I had to say could wait until the end of my shift.

That came soon enough and I made my way to the office. Adam was busy ordering a new commode for room 16. As he talked politely on the phone I clicked my fingers. When he finally put down the receiver I sat up straighter, placed my hands on my knees, for reassurance, and began the tirade. 'I had a *lovely* Christmas. Absolutely *great!* Still can't quite get over all the *excitement* I had. The only difficult thing was fitting all the *fun* into my bustling timetable. Oh and *thanks* for the present, I was truly *blown away* by all the thought that went into buying it.'

For once Adam was speechless. To be fair, it was the first time

I had chosen to unleash my caustic tongue on him. In my own defence, I was angry and hurt over how I had been left to rot. What really niggled was that Adam had not taken the time to telephone once while he was away. He had not even thought it necessary to send a greeting on Christmas Eve, or best wishes for a Happy New Year. I really couldn't see *what* would have been so mind-blowing that one could forget a so-called loved one back home.

Over the next three-quarters of an hour I explained my disappointment to Adam. He merely listened quietly and patiently.

'We are supposed to be in a serious relationship aren't we, Adam?' I continued, as he shook his head, to all intents and purposes frustrated that the whole discussion was turning into a blazing row, one he was in no mood for. 'You haven't even had the decency to tell me what you went over there for in the first place.'

It was at this point in the one-way conversation that Adam's usually flippant and easy-going character changed, completely. He leapt towards me suddenly, took hold of both my forearms and glared with a look of pure unadulterated anger into my eyes.

'Listen very carefully,' he grated, through clenched teeth, 'what happened abroad is none of your business, yes? Never ask me anything about my family again. Do you understand?'

His fingers were now practically digging into my arms. I was stunned and nodded in ascent. Without another word I feebly collected my handbag and went to wait in the car.

I didn't question Adam any further. That night, we hardly spoke at all. Adam was obviously preoccupied with what had happened in France. As for myself, I was starting to view Adam in a more sinister light. I felt uncomfortable about the secrecy that surrounded his trip and his family in general. I began to wonder if perhaps Mr Lloyd was right. Was Adam somehow involved in the death of Martha Paris? Before, I had rejected such an idea as nonsense. Now, all I knew was that there were things about Adam's past that he didn't want others to know. Added to this, I had witnessed a brutal and crueller side to Adam's personality, a side I, for one, did not want to see again. More than ever I determined to gain entry to Rubalt's room number six: to solve the enigma and reveal the mysteries, which were currently kept hidden well within its walls. I would help Martha Paris' spirit find peace.

Chapter 6

Death Leads to the Trinket Box

The following day, without waiting for Adam, I set off for work in my tarnished Beetle. It was a prophetically bleak morning and the heating in 'Beety' was failing. Intermittently, I shuddered, as yet another wisp of cold air shot through the vehicle. *Please, please don't break down,* I prayed inwardly. At least my prayers were heard and I pulled up outside Rubalt at 6:30am. For a second time, I was struck by the morbid character of the exterior. Once again, I was hesitant as I passed along Section C.

My first port of call that morning was number seven. I wanted Mrs Radcliffe's advice. I was also eager to know if she had seen any more symbols on the wall. I quickly approached her bed and tapped her gently on the shoulder. I presumed that she must have been sleeping, deeply, as there was no response. For a few moments I paced the room and fetched a cup of cold water from the en-suite.

'Come on Mrs Radcliffe,' I whispered, wiping the droplets from my mouth as I did so.

I pressed more firmly upon her cold, delicate arm. 'Wake up Mrs Radcliffe, it's Susan,' I called more piercingly.

Still, there was no response. I pulled the covers back slightly. What I then saw made my heart hammer and my lungs freeze.

Eyes wide-open, Mrs Radcliffe was staring at the blank wall.

One of her arms remained wrapped in my hand, whilst the other was crumpled under her left side. With a soft touch I turned her onto her back, so that she would *look* more comfortable. I ironed out the creases in her white cotton nightdress with my fingers and replaced the cover. Briefly I closed my eyes and took a deep breath. Mrs Radcliffe was dead.

A certain cloak of numbness matted my mind and body. In the style of an automaton I told the nurse on duty of Mrs Radcliffe's passing and she in turn notified the proper authorities, including Mrs Radcliffe's doctor and the undertakers Colton and Riditch. Having discovered the deceased, I was given the morning off work. Yet, I didn't choose to go home. Instead, I remained hidden in the confines of the staffroom, supping pot after pot of coffee, until the taste of caffeine became repugnant.

It wasn't till lunch time that I rose from my depressive stupor and went for a short walk around Rubalt's twisted maze. With shoulders hung and back aching, from being slumped over for the best part of the day, I sauntered along Section C. It was completely deserted. Earlier, carers had removed all the residents who usually chose to stay in their rooms. This was the done thing in the case of a death in a nursing home, in order to prevent the elderly from viewing yet another friend, or acquaintance, being dumped ungraciously onto an awaiting hearse.

If it were possible, the whole ambiance had taken on an even more spectral tone. The mouldy fabrics were somehow mustier, the shadows strangely sharper. An eerie silence crammed my ears. A sudden chill forced me to fasten the buttons on my cardigan. I headed straight for Mrs Radcliffe's room. As yet, she was still laid out on the bed. Her body had been dressed and cleansed, ready for the gents of Colton and Riditch.

Quickly and quietly, I rummaged through the dressing table drawers. You see, my visit to number seven was not only triggered by a desire to see Mrs Radcliffe at peace one last time, I also wanted to find something, anything, that would help with my search for the truth about Martha Paris' death. In addition, I wanted to make certain that Mrs Radcliffe had not met with a similar end. I wanted to make sure she had died of natural causes.

However, each search proved unrewarding. Aside from scores of knickers and bras, the compartments were empty. Moreover, as I was far from being a qualified Pathologist, I really had no way of ascertaining the trajectory of Mrs Radcliffe's last moments. How was I to say whether she had died of natural causes or not?

All the same, I stood examining Mrs Radcliffe's face for a time. As far as I could tell, there was no evidence of foul play. There was no apparent bruising, and the corners of her mouth hinted that Mrs Radcliffe had actually been smiling at the time of her death. *She was an old lady, 82, maybe she just passed away in her sleep,* I concluded. I patted her hand and said my goodbyes. I then set to leave.

Just before I did so, however, I glanced upon Mrs Radcliffe's old handbag, hanging over a chair.

'Of course, there's the book,' I called, excitedly.

Sure enough, there it was, wrapped inside a handful of rotten tissues. These were swiftly discarded and I took my find. At the very least, I would now be able to decipher any messages I received from the other side for myself.

I strode to the door and flung it open. Unfortunately, this sent a tall young man sprawling onto the floor.

'Oh, I'm really sorry,' I stated, as I helped Mr Riditch to his feet.

Obviously, my apology did not go quite far enough, for the serious looking gentleman grimaced as he nodded his head rather quickly and brushed down his clothes. He then began to ask Bronwyn, who had entered behind him, what was the best route to take with the body, so as to avoid upsetting the other residents in the main lounge. To her credit, Bronwyn was now a fountain of information.

She explained that, due to the charged religious history of the building, it having been constructed during the reign of Edward VI, it was graced with a system of secret passageways, which knitted through the underbelly of Section C.

'Many a time, I can tell you, we've had to stop the carers from messing around down there. It was that bad Mr Felts decided to shut off the whole cellar area. If you're thinking of taking the body out that way, you will need to be very careful. Some of the walls are a little unsteady. If you want my opinion, it would be far better to move the others into the dining room. That way it really wouldn't matter if you went through the lounge...'

As Bronwyn continued to protest, the undertaker retaliated, arguing that it would cause far too much fuss to move close to 40 people for just a few minutes.

'Besides,' he added, 'they're not stupid. They know someone has died and are bound to realise why they are being shipped out of the lounge.'

That said, Mr Riditch readied the body for transportation and called to his assistant who was waiting in the corridor. Meanwhile, Bronwyn went to the office to fetch a master key, which would be needed to open a huge timber door at the end of Section C.

When she returned, I offered my services to the two men, who, I suggested, would need doors opening, lights turning on and so on. In all honesty, I was simply eager to find out what lay beneath Rubalt Hall.

Once the men were set to leave, I led them down to the end of the hallway. It then took some time to release the rusted lock on a door marked *'Private – Strictly No Admittance'*. All the while, Masters Colton and Riditch sighed, as they struggled to keep hold of Mrs Radcliffe's body, which was now encased in toughened black plastic.

'Got it,' I chirped breezily, to lighten the mood.

However, it did no good. The two men continued to maintain their frosty exteriors, one even being so rude as to tut impatiently,

'Come on will you.'

I hesitated for an instant. Then, slowly the door creaked open.

Directly inside was a decrepit, darkened tunnel. Its cobwebbed roof was so low that the two undertakers were forced to bend their necks slightly as they entered. The walls were so damaged that, as I felt along them to find my way, pieces of rotten plaster broke away into my hand and sheers of the material could be heard crushing underfoot. At intervals, we took it in turns to sneeze and cough, due to the debris and dust invading our lungs.

'What a great idea this ...' Mr Colton sneered at his partner, though his sentence was cut short as he stumbled down a barely visible step.

'Sorry,' I apologised, having failed to inform my followers of coming hazards, 'be careful there're quite a few more.'

Thankfully, I eventually found myself on level ground, albeit, in a void.

'There's got to be a light around here somewhere,' I suggested, utterly unnerved by my surroundings. *It's bloody horrible down here.*

My arms reached this way and that in the hope that they would find a light switch or pull.

'Thank God for that,' I exclaimed, startling my two companions, when I tugged on a piece of string and brought the cellar into a certain amount of brightness.

At this stage in our journey, the two men set Mrs Radcliffe down on the floor, stretched their arms and arched their backs. I scanned the space, which was one great storage dump. Cardboard boxes of various shapes and sizes were scattered across the floor. Discarded items of dated furniture including: a moth eaten settee, a broken rocking chair, the remains of numerous sets of floral curtains and even a stainless-steel cooking hob, were crammed into all corners of the room.

'Let's get a move on then,' Mr Riditch indicated after viewing his watch, 'we're running late.'

No more time was wasted and we made our way to the exit door, which was positioned at the top of another set of stairs near the farthest wall. Obediently, I pushed open the fire escape, though I decided against escorting the two men to the waiting car. Instead, I remained in the cellar, to investigate a little longer.

It had occurred to me, if such an area had been constructed in order to allow Catholics to practise their faith without fear of persecution, there could be other tunnels. Tunnels that would, perhaps, lead to other rooms in the building, or even to room number six.

So my search of the cellar began. Initially, it was futile. Aside from piles upon piles of dated household appliances, and reams upon reams of poorly framed pictures, which I presumed had belonged to residents long dead, there was nothing out of the ordinary. Still, I was ill at ease, as the single ceiling light swayed, causing suspicious shadows to dance around the crumbling walls.

Suddenly, I heard the sound of wings flapping frantically. The noise appeared to be emanating from behind a pair of large curtains still attached to a pole, lent perilously against the chimney-breast wall. Without a flicker of fear, I pulled back the screens to release the wild bird cornered there. However, as the fabric shifted, no such creature was exposed. Rather, an open fireplace was revealed, to the right of which was a darkened passageway. Perhaps this would burrow its way under Section C?

Naturally, I was nervous about following the tunnel. Yet, I chose to ignore my racing heart and entered.

'If I'm correct, and this follows Section C, there should be some steps along here.'

There were and I rose up them.

'Number six should be a good few metres, on the right-hand side…Though I could be wrong…'

I waffled on and on, not wanting to hear any more untoward noises. I placed my hands on the wall one minute and removed them the next, fearful of what I might feel. I took each step slowly and with precision.

'What? … Yes, this must be it.'

I tapped upon a layer of plasterboard. I was right at the end of the passage. For my own peace of mind, I glanced back to make sure I could still see the light flickering in the cellar. Thankfully it was. So, I picked up a piece of stone, one amongst many other fragments littering the floor. Then, holding the clump firmly in my hands, I battered its point against the feeble partition.

For quite some time, I continued to pull the wall apart. Eventually, it submitted to my curiosity, and there was a hole just large enough for me to fit through. I hastily squeezed through the gap, and collapsed into room six.

Martha Paris' musty room was opened to view once again. It was the same as I had seen it before: everything cluttered – everything filthy – and everything frozen in time.

Carefully, I examined each and every object in the room. The pillows were lifted and removed from their cases, but there were no clues hidden inside. The quilt was thrown back across the bed, but there were no telltale traces of blood. The bedside cabinet was emptied, but there was no rope, knife or any other kind of murderous instrument.

Finally, I approached the dressing table. The chimes of *Pavane* echoed from a jewellery box as I lifted its lid. Inside were two gold bracelets, a pair of pearl earrings and a gaudy ruby costume ring. Frustrated at the futility of my investigation thus far, I quickly scanned the other items on the dresser. Only one, the tiny trinket box, captured my interest. Similar to when I had peered through from Mr Lloyd's room, the case was illuminated by gold and pink rays, which were streaking across from an elevated, arched window.

For one brief moment in time I turned to admire the floral patterns on the leaded glass. The effect upon my soul was calming, pacifying. Yet, this serenity of spirit was brief. When I returned my attentions to the table, on the wall above it, were coarse black symbols.

'Wait a minute. Just hold on.' I rummaged around in my pockets and procured the *Mystical Runes,* booklet. 'Now all I have to do is find them,' I explained to myself.

I then flicked over page after page for the significance of the given signs.

The first was *Tir,* the rune of triumph – that is, when it is placed in the upright position. However, *Tir* was given in the reversed position, and was shown as a huge arrow pointing downwards. *'This rune can indicate that you are about to struggle for what you see as right and just – some hitherto 'lost cause' or another, involving the forces of justice…'* I carried on reading the text aloud:

'...*Reversed Tir can indicate that you are experiencing a glitch in the solving of some mystery.*'

This was certainly true enough of my present situation. Though, I couldn't help thinking that the sign was also trying to tell me something else. *Tir* was pointing directly at the silver trinket box.

I continued to decipher the runes. The next symbol to the right of *Tir* was *Eihwaz*. Unlike *Tir*, this sign was given in the positive position. This foretold that things were going to improve. In addition, it indicated that a matter, which had been obscured for quite many years, was about to be resolved. Finally, the last rune sign was *Jera*. On this occasion it was placed in the result position, which hinted at a constructive outcome to a certain predicament. What was more, in the current reading, *Jera* also suggested that legal assistance would be sought in order to reveal the truth. Perhaps, this was the truth about Martha Paris' death?

The reading over, I picked up the silver case. I concluded that, somehow, this alone held the secrets that would assist me in my amateur investigation. Gently I released its clasp.

'Now I didn't expect that,' I muttered, since I found that the box was not intended for precious gems at all.

On the contrary, it was a solid silver, miniature cheroot holder and ashtray. A truly fine antique of the 1920s, it was elaborately decorated on the inside, with the outline of an elegant lady puffing on a cocktail cigarette.

'I wonder what this does...'

I pressed a minute button on the front of the piece. Immediately, the first level of the case opened to expose a second compartment underneath.

This layer measured no more than three by two centimetres. Its height was approximately four to five millimetres. In its corners, wrapped in a small fragment of brown paper, there remained particles of a greyish white powder, ash I presumed. I cannot explain why I now chose to test the composition of this substance, but I did. I licked the tip of my finger, so that the particles would cling to it, and rubbed it around in the case. Next, in the manner of an adept snuff specialist, I sniffed and tasted the rotten matter. It left a revolting chalky film in my mouth. It tasted of talc mingled with bitter lemon and almond. It was definitely not cigarette ash. I crudely spat the rest out onto the floor.

The time was now 3:30pm. The others were bound to be missing my services, especially since afternoon teas and toileting were due. I, therefore, placed the case into my pocket, watched the runic symbols fade and clambered out into the sultry passage. I swiftly retraced my steps: shot through the tunnel; crashed through the cellar and scuttled up the stairway to Section C.

'About flipping time,' Trisha scoffed, as the contents of the pan she was carrying swished dangerously close to the rim. 'Where the hell have you been?' she continued, 'Bronwyn's going ballistic in there.'

I mumbled some expletive, making it abundantly obvious that I was not interested in Bronwyn's opinion in the slightest. With that, I summoned all the speed I could muster, and rushed to the nearest bathroom. Once safe inside I was profoundly sick. Soon after, a knock came at the door.

'Are you alright in there?'

The answer was clear enough when I emerged. I was ashen in appearance and the corners of my mouth were covered with fragments of vomit, which were still clinging to the invisible bristles nestled there.

'I think you'd better go home, Sue,' Bronwyn suggested, and being in no fit state to carry on working, I complied.

A few minutes later I was heading for Ivy Bank. It has to be admitted, my journey took much longer than anticipated; in consequence of the stops I was forced to make on the way, to relive an excruciatingly painful churning deep within. Indeed, at one point, a poor pedestrian on Bingley Road was left in a state of shock and fuming anger, when my Beetle nearly mounted his foot and, to add insult to injury, I released my breakfast all over his leather boots.

The whole of that evening and during the long night, I was draped over the toilet. As you would expect, I got little sleep. Not that I would have felt like laying next to Adam, even if I had been well enough to do so.

Chapter 7

To the Station

Early the next morning Adam found me bleary eyed on the normally immaculate couch that was now covered with pillows and sheets.

'What happened to you yesterday?' he began. 'I tried calling you all evening but there was no answer.'

'I was ill Adam.'

'I gathered that,' he replied, 'why didn't you come to bed?'

'I didn't want to wake you,' I explained, tersely.

He didn't look at all convinced. 'Maybe you should see a doctor.'

I turned over on the settee, so that my back was to him. 'Maybe I will,' I stated, bluntly, and closed my eyes.

I really didn't want to converse with him and, luckily, he got the message; I heard the front door slam shut with a bang.

In truth, I had no intention of going to the doctor's. The only place I planned to visit that day was the local police station. I was convinced that my sudden sickness was triggered by the strange powdery substance contained in the silver box. 'It must be some sort of toxin. That's what it must be,' I aired my views to no one but myself.

'Maybe Martha Paris was killed with a dose of poison? Yes, that had to be the cause of death. Why else would Section C be known as 'Poison Alley'?'

After consuming two slices of dry toast and a pot of black coffee, I dressed in the smartest suit that I could find. I did not want the police to reject my information out of hand, as being the ramblings of a neurotic woman. I also determined not to mention any of the strange sightings of the runic symbols. I would tell the officers of my suspicions, hand over the trinket, and that was all. That settled in my mind, I brushed my teeth until the gums almost bled, applied an expensive eau de toilette, popped the case into a freezer bag and set off for the town centre.

There, every street hummed with the sound of shoppers, happily spending hundreds they did not have. I did my best to follow a quiet route from the car park to the station, but even the quainter alleys were teeming with other, more discerning, bargain hunters. On the way I stopped to buy a tuna salad teacake. I was famished. Technically, I hadn't properly digested a thing, aside from the toast, for two days. Thus, I devoured the rather soggy sandwich so hastily that half its contents spilled onto the floor. Regardless, I scurried on, guilty that some poor person was going to end up with fishy bits stuck to his or her shoes.

Sunbridge Hill Station was just around the corner. Its basement and first floor windows had been bricked up. Its exterior was like a fortress. I paused on the steps before entering. Maybe I was doing the wrong thing? What was I going to say exactly? Yet, there I was, standing still, whilst urgent faces huffed and puffed, as they scurried past into the building. Nearby, a clock struck 12:00pm. On the last chime I mounted the stairs.

Just inside the doorway was a small reception window. A very smart, uniformed officer peered out from behind the safety glass.

'Morning, do you have a crime to report?' he spoke, as he readied his pen to note the particulars.

'Well, I'm not really sure,' I stated, each word given cautiously.

The constable laid down his pen and studied my features.

'Would you like to speak to an officer on duty?' He queried.

'Yes.'

It was more than 30 minutes before I was escorted to a poky room by one Sergeant Philips.

He was a stout Yorkshire man, with a bushy moustache and a multitude of worry lines. He also had an extraordinarily profound, booming voice, which made me start each time he asked a question. However, I was on a mission, and was not going to be browbeaten. So, I raced to air my concerns. Initially, I told him where I was employed and how long I had worked there. I then explained how certain residents at Rubalt had suggested that there was something sinister about Martha Paris' death some years earlier. Finally, I revealed where I had found the cigarette case and how ill I had been on tasting its contents.

Sergeant Philips took the box, freezer bag and all. He smiled as he did so.

'I won't be a moment,' he informed me, as he left the interview room.

At this stage I was not optimistic. *I bet he thinks I'm crackers.* I began to tap my fingers and toes to a tune I detested.

It was 1:00pm when the officer returned. This time he was not alone.

'Hello Miss Dane,' another man greeted, 'my name is Cornforth.'

As he spoke he bent down to shake my hand. He was a large man, with powerful hands and arms. His hair was oily jet black and its matted waves flopped down and flipped back again, as he sat in the chair opposite mine. Despite his politeness, his countenance was serious and stern. He was no mere constable.

Without wasting any time, Inspector Cornforth insisted that I recount the facts, as I had already presented them to his colleague. As I spoke, he scribbled in an overly cramped notepad, and sifted through a folder of papers he had brought with him.

'So, Miss Dane,' he enquired, 'you're saying that this little trinket box…'

'It's an ashtray,' I stated.

'Yes quite. So, you're saying that this ashtray was found in Miss Paris' room?'

'Yes that's right,' I replied, becoming ever more than a little tired of the endless questions.

'Well, how was it that no one else has come across this find of yours in more than 13 years?'

'I've already explained to the other officer, the whole room has been boarded-up. I found an entrance to room number six by chance.'

'Just by chance?'

'Look, Mr Cornforth, Mrs Radcliffe had just passed away,' I clipped, impatiently, as he sent a frosty glance my way, none too impressed by my lack of deference to his authoritative position. 'The undertakers needed a way out which didn't involve walking right through a lounge crowded with elderly people. I found the room after following a tunnel that led out from the bloody cellar.'

Sure, I knew I was being rude to the Inspector. I didn't care. Cornforth had been talking to me in a condescending manner.

'Why don't you just test the powder?' I suggested, taking control of the conversation.

'Oh we intend to, Miss Dane,' he replied, all the while mulling over the contents of the file, which were, apparently, of much more interest than my information.

The clock heralded that it was now 2:00pm. Suddenly Cornforth put down the file. At last he had the decency to enlighten me as to its fascinating contents. What he had to say made a shadow cross my heart and the hairs on my skin begin to tingle.

It came to light that I was not the only person to have reported strange goings on at Rubalt Hall. Many years before, Martha Paris herself had called on the police to record her fears for her life. However, at the time her cries for help had been rejected as the ramblings of a *"senile old woman"*, to use the Inspector's words and not my own. In justification, Cornforth stressed that it was common knowledge Martha had dabbled in the occult and was an eccentric character. He also quoted statistics, on the scores of paranoid fantasies he had been forced to investigate over the years. Then, his tone became more serious.

'But, I'm convinced there's more to this case than that. Something else bothered me at the time.' He stared directly into my eyes.

'Are you aware that Miss Paris was an extremely wealthy woman?'

I shook my head.

'Do you also know that she left all her estate to the owner of Rubalt Hall, Mr Felts?'

Mr Felts, I shook my head more vigorously.

'And I ask you, Miss Dane, what kind of businessman would *choose* to lose hundreds of pounds in rent to board up a room for no good reason?'

It was a very pertinent question, though I chose not to answer. Instead I shocked the Inspector, by revealing how I was currently living with the said *Mr* Felts.

'Does he know you are here?' he asked, urgently.

'No,' I whispered numbly. Weak and deflated, I left the station for home.

Chapter 8

Frustrated Search

The journey to Ivy Bank was frustratingly monotonous. When I arrived, the house was quiet. Adam was still at work. I was relieved. At least I would have a little time to work out exactly what I was going to say to him. I had to tell him that the police were reopening the Martha Paris investigation; a case I was certain he would want to be forgotten. I wanted to see his reaction. I wanted some kind of explanation. I wanted him to confess to the crime now, before it was too late.

Yet, that evening, and during those that followed, every time I was set to raise the topic my nerves failed. It was, thus, over two weeks later when I finally realised the courage to question Adam.

That day I was off duty and had spent most of my time watching garbage on the television. Adam eventually arrived home at 5:30pm. It was already dark outside. I heard the door close softly with a barely audible click. I swiftly picked up a magazine and shuffled back on the cold leather chair. I could hear him slowly approaching. I gripped the pages tightly. I scarcely dared to move, let alone turn around to greet him.

'Hello Susan, had a good day?' His tone was calm and gentle.

'Yes,' I replied, though I couldn't bring myself to look into his eyes. I continued to read the magazine, desperately trying to make the love affairs of the rich and famous hold my attention. They did not, not that they would have done so under normal circumstances. Adam now relaxed on the opposite chair and, as was customary after a day's work, glared at the television. Prophetically, *Gaslight* was screening: the tale of a rich lady killed for financial gain.

As I watched, I pondered over the character of the heroine. She was a pathetically weak persona, who was convinced of her own insanity by a dominant male lover. I had to laugh. Though, it was more of a nervous chuckle. Surely, I did not vaguely resemble such a nauseating female?

'Adam, there's something I have to tell you,' I began, taking the control and switching off the dated piece of subservient hogwash, 'Do you remember Miss Paris, Martha Paris, who lived in room six?'

Adam stopped fiddling with his tie and perched on the edge of his seat. He remained mute.

'Well, you should be able to recall someone who was a resident at Rubalt Hall for a number of years,' I persevered, watching his features carefully in order to observe any indications of guilt.

'Look Sue, I've lost count of the number of people who've been in and out of Rubalt. Is there any reason why I should remember her?' he uttered, in a flippant manner. Though, he had started to fidget with the tie again.

'She died about 13 years ago Adam, under mysterious circumstances.'

'What do you mean? What are you going on about now?' His tone was harsher and he had started to pace up and down in front of the fireplace.

'I've been to see the police...You see, Adam, I found the cigarette case, you know, the one that the murderer put the poison in.'

I leapt to my feet as Adam charged over. His eyes flashed with raw hatred.

'What have you done?' he spat, menacingly, 'Do you have any idea what you've done?'

'That's enough Sir,' a man shouted, across from the hallway, 'stop right there.'

It was Inspector Cornforth. He was accompanied by two uniformed officers, who introduced themselves as Constables Edwards and Greenwood. All three strode confidently into the lounge and insisted that Adam should take a seat. He complied against his will, which I presumed wanted to fly far away. He then sat quietly, whilst his countenance fell to the depths of a broken man. Strangely, for the first time, I was fraught with feelings of regret. What if I were wrong about him?

How wrong I was only came to light during the ensuing conversation between the tired old Inspector and Adam.

'As I understand it Dr Felts, you took over the management of Rubalt in 1991?'

'Yes, that's correct. I was in partnership at Raymond Street Surgery before that,' Adam informed the officer.

'So, let's cut to the chase shall we? It would save us a great deal of time and lead to a better feeling all round, if you could inform us of your brother's whereabouts in France,' Cornforth explained, as he tweaked the corners of his slick moustache.

'He lives in the Maison de la Fôret. His old place is close to Versailles, just outside of Paris.'

Adam rubbed his forehead vigorously.

'Did you not think it was odd that your brother left Rubalt in such a hurry? Also, that he chose to emigrate, even though the distribution of Miss Paris' estate had not been settled?'

'I suppose so, yes.'

'You see, Dr Felts, new evidence has come into our possession. Your partner found a case, and what do you think it contained?'

'Poison,' Adam stated, and added, to neutralise the knowing look on the Inspector's face, 'Susan has already told me.'

'To be sure, Dr Felts, the case contained talc, mostly, which was just as well for your partner, here. Though, very miniscule traces of cyanide were also found in the cigarette case: particles of a chemical used by your brother, Mr James Felts, to murder Miss

Paris and thereby inherit her fortune to the tune of approximately two million pounds.'

The Inspector elaborated further, on how certain tissue samples had been retained at the time of Martha's death, and that, although there had been no toxicological screening of the samples at the time, a battery of such tests had recently been performed. A spectrometer had shown, beyond any doubt, that Martha's spleen contained five milligrams per litre of Potassium Cyanide – more than twice the amount required for a lethal dose of that substance.

As shocking as the information was, what was more so was Adam's sedateness. He took the information very well, too well. I could see that the Inspector's thoughts were following my own. He therefore questioned Adam more precisely.

'Is there anything else you can tell us, Dr Felts? Any information you have that could assist our enquiries?'

Adam shook his head firmly.

'It really wouldn't do you the slightest bit of good to continue to protect your brother. Not now. If you do, it could make you an accessory after the fact.'

The possibility of being stamped with duplicity in his brother's crime was enough to trigger Adam's swift recitation of all he knew.

Chapter 9

Exposed

It all began, as far as Adam was concerned, in January 1991. He had been working successfully, developing his practice and carrying out minor surgical operations at Raymond Street. This was when he had been approached by his brother, with an offer to take over Rubalt Hall. Certainly, he had been surprised at his, usually thrifty, brother's more than generous offer: to sell the business to him for a fraction of its value. Nonetheless, given that Rubalt was producing a profit in excess of 70 thousand pounds per annum, Adam had seized the chance to run his own business.

Shortly afterwards, James had relocated. Adam had presumed he did this using the payment he had given him for Rubalt.

'The name of Martha Paris meant nothing to me, you see, she died before I took over Rubalt,' he explained.

He also made it clear that he knew nothing about the particulars of her death. That was, he knew nothing about the murder until December, 2003, when his brother had telephoned one cold winter's night.

'He asked me to leave for France immediately, but to tell no one where I was going. He sounded desperate. I left for France the very next day. It was Christmas Eve…'

Adam's narrative stopped for a few minutes, while he fetched a glass of water from the kitchen. When he returned to the lounge, he could see that Cornforth and I were becoming impatient, so he resumed.

'When I arrived in France, James was waiting at the airport. He was scruffy, shattered. He drove me back to his house and on the way he told me all about Martha Paris. He admitted to the murder and how he had procured the cyanide from a friend at a metal plating factory... But, he only told me because of the signs on the wall. You see, Inspector, he thought that he was being haunted by Martha. It was probably a symptom of his twisted guilt.'

Next, Adam described how, for years, James had been safe in France; safe from the law and his own memories. However, this tranquillity had ended in the autumn of 2003. It was then that strange symbols began to appear on the walls of the Maison de la forêt. In addition, sickening noises, similar to those which had resounded through Rubalt as Miss Paris had died, echoed along his once silent corridors.

James had also confessed that this was why he had boarded up number six in the first place. This was why he had barred all entry to the cellar and the tunnels beyond; tunnels which had once enabled him to pass in and out of Martha's room undetected. This was why he had flown to France.

Adam admitted that he had been wrong not to report all that he had heard to the authorities. Yet, James was still his brother. The only family he had. This, of course, helped to explain Adam's gruff manner, whenever I had broached the topic of his family. It also seemed to settle matters for the Inspector, who now said his farewells and set off to pursue his target, with the two obedient officers in tow.

Adam and I were thus left alone, to pick up the pieces of our fragmented relationship. The truth was finally out. Regardless of a certain amount of relief, I felt deeply sorry for Adam. After all, he had only done what probably anyone else would have done in the same situation.

In due course James Felts was arrested, tried and sentenced for the murder of Martha Paris. Further charges were also made against one Dr Crabtree, an accessory to the crime. This particular piece of foul work was a fraudulent physician, one who accepted a bribe of 160 thousand pounds, to falsify the death certificate of a woman he hardly knew.

Police are still in the process of trying to track Dr Crabtree. He thus, as yet, remains at large, probably sunning himself in some foreign country.

Well, as anticipated, such events hit the national and local headlines. A media circus ensued, to feed the need for mystery and gratuitous violence amongst certain parts of the populous. The reputation of Rubalt Hall Nursing Home was tarnished forever. Adam and I could only watch hopelessly, as relatives arrived to move on resident after resident. Even the loyal Mr Lloyd was wheeled away to Rose Bank a few miles away. Soon enough, the hitherto soaring profits began to plummet and a gracious Tudor mansion became a shadow of its former self.

As a result, Adam succumbed to a nervous breakdown. True, at first he fought back. He changed the name of Rubalt to Sunny Bank, and put the entire estate on the market. However, when the old place failed to sell and finances became tight, to say the least, he was hurled head-first into an abyss of depression.

I have not forsaken him. On the contrary, far from destroying our relationship, the events I have recounted have made it all the stronger. I have, therefore, found different employment, working near Adam. I am currently employed as a Residential Social Worker, at Hollbury Psychiatric Unit. So far, I have found this post to be both rewarding and fascinating.

Just to sit and talk, to discuss the world with those who feel they have nothing to hide, nothing to hold back, is immensely enlightening. I have, thereby, encountered scores of people, like myself, who have been touched in some way by the supernatural or the macabre. I am never so flippant as to dismiss tales of the 'other side', as many who do not understand are inclined to do.

Miss Susan Dane, August 2006.

Mrs Hodgeson, on Kelly

Dr Milner's diary entry: 1st August, 2006

My soul was shaded with sadness this afternoon, when Miss Kelly Hodgeson was brought into my interview room. She was just a scrap of a girl. As for her mother, well, all I can say is that some parents have a lot to answer for.

Note on the text: For reasons that will become evident later, I have decided to include an exact copy of the Psychiatric Report completed on Miss Kelly Hodgeson. This is given below:

AIRE RISE HOSPITAL FOUNDATION

HOLLBURY PSYCHIATRIC UNIT

WARD 5 — CHILD & ADOLESCENT MENTAL HEALTH

PSYCHIATRIC REPORT

NAME:	Miss Kelly Hodgeson
INTERVIEWED BY:	Dr Milner, Psychiatric Registrar
DOB:	1st October, 1998
ADMISSION DATE:	1st August, 2006
HOSPITAL NUMBER:	99099…
DIAGNOSIS:	To follow

Kelly is the only child of Mr & Mrs Hodgeson, from the Keighley area. Mr Hodgeson is an electrician and Mrs Hodgeson works as a certified accountant for a building company in Bradford. According to those who know the family, Mr and Mrs

Hodgeson are devoted parents, who sincerely want the best for their daughter.

Kelly, who is nearly eight years old, has an above average I.Q. and has been described as a highly articulate, though 'troubled', child by her teachers. She was referred to the Unit by Rickensdale Social Services, after Consultant Paediatrician, Dr Westward, became concerned, as Kelly had reported various physical and mental symptoms. Numerous medical tests have been performed, all of which have proved inconclusive. These physical investigations have included: Full Blood Count (FBC); Urea and Electrolytes (U&E); Liver Function Test (LFT); EEG; MRI; Urine Test: to detect illicit drugs, infections and toxins...

As the exhaustive number of physical tests above (in addition to the psychiatric examinations, too numerous to list) have proved unproductive, it is Dr Westward's opinion that Munchausen's by Proxy is likely. He has stated that Mrs Hodgeson has displayed the classic attention seeking behaviour seen in sufferers of this condition. Mrs Hodgeson rejects the claim and insists that her daughter is ill.

It needs to be documented that, whilst in the care of Social Services, and here within the unit, Kelly's symptoms have persisted, which is not typical of Munchausen's by Proxy. According to staff on her ward, she has displayed highly disturbed behaviour with psychotic features: ranging from visual and auditory hallucinations, to delusions of being possessed. Such delusions have been reinforced by Kelly's mother, who too believes in possession.

Moreover, Kelly has also engaged in self injurious behaviour and, before being admitted, displayed a variety of physical injuries. Despite her symptoms, I am very reluctant to give a diagnosis of psychosis in one so young — especially in light of the fact that the ward staff, who have been monitoring Kelly, are convinced that there is a strong behavioural component to her condition.

I am certainly of the opinion that a thorough investigation of both Mr and Mrs Hodgeson should be undertaken; in order to establish if any emotional, physical or sexual abuse has taken place. However, as I am not a specialist in paediatric psychiatry, I have enrolled the help of eminent Paediatric Psychiatrist, Dr Wilson in this case.

The Interview:
Initially, when Kelly was interviewed, there were no obvious signs of psychosis. Indeed, she performed well in the Mini Mental State examination, answering all the questions put to her during play therapy. In addition, there was no mention of abuse during this first session. Her behaviour was appropriate to the setting and there was no evidence of a disregard for other peoples' personal space.

When the subject of injuring herself, through headbanging, was raised, Kelly insisted that she was not physically able to stop herself. Consequently, the likelihood of stereotypic movement disorder will also have to be discounted as a credible cause of these motor abnormalities.

Throughout the interview Kelly demonstrated a remarkable degree of insight. There were no typical symptoms of schizophrenia, depression or the rapid cycling bipolar disorder, which would have gone some way to explain the rapid fluctuations in Kelly's symptoms.

Kelly presents a perplexing psychopathology. Definitely, if her symptoms decrease in severity, then a conclusion for the case of Munchausen's by Proxy is highly likely. However, until then, I have instructed staff to specifically look for any evidence of behaviour disorders or pseudo-hallucinations. Current Medications: L10 mg.

The next review will take place on the 15th August, 2006.

Regretfully, Miss Kelly Hodgeson was not able to take part in this narrative study. The following text was written by her mother, Mrs Hodgeson, at my request.

Dr Milner, Psychiatric Registrar.

Chapter 1

A Personal Note

Loneliness, true unrelenting and stomach quenching loneliness, is a place commonly called the 'soul'. Just try, for a moment, to imagine a human being whose only source of recourse with the outside world is an accepted jargon, a jargon which it perceives as complete and utter pointless bollocks. Yet, this being clings to this 'bollocks', in the belief that, at the very least, it will be left without the pain of ridicule, rebuff and downright rejection – by the society to which it desperately tries to belong.

If this request seems peculiar, obnoxious even, just pause to consider the following: a 'woman' – I know, a derogatory term in the 21st century for over half the world's population – who finds that her only option in life is to find solace in the contemporary religion of her peers, or the 'truth' of science.

Unfortunately, contemporary religion only offers a means of relief for the selected few, to gain some kind of belonging to 'something'; a 'something' that is widely believed to be good and pure. However, what on earth was I supposed to do, when I saw certain fractures, contradictions, exposed within the very doctrines of faith that I was supposed to hold so dear, so sacred?

You see, the faith of Catholicism claims that: the only acceptable place for a 'woman' and her ideas is below that of the 'man' and his. Does it not appear odd to any educated and intelligent woman of the world that all 'gods' or should I say 'men' call for this belief? Most crucially, what they have proclaimed, and continue to claim, is that a woman's only true role in life is that of a mother. What was I meant to do when I failed in this one true 'calling'?

So, I decided that no one religion has penetrated the psyche of an all-knowing presence. No one can stake a claim to an unknowable God's omnipresent thoughts. Thus, for a while, I accepted the parts of my 'faith' which offered contentment, and rejected those points that did not.

At that time I also turned to the realm of science. Perhaps the good doctors of this planet could assist where my faith had not. How naïve I was to hold out such hopes. Science is simply the dogma of our time. One can see that, if one asks: exactly who was it who decided that these professionals held all the answers to the workings of the universe? What still makes these individuals so special that they, unlike the rest of us mere mortals, can reveal life's mysteries, which for most remain wrapped inside an enigma?

By now you have probably gathered that I have discarded all religions and scientific *truths*. More precisely, I have been shunned by my Catholic peers and vilified by members of the medical profession. It was important that you knew all this before I told Kelly's tragic story. This, I am ready to do now...

Chapter 2

Twisted Humour

'I am sick of being a parent.' These were the first words I uttered to Dr Milner.

I am sure they were as scandalous to her as they were to my conscience when I stated them. Yet, why is the rejection of one's offspring verbally such a sin? Have there not been moments in the lives of all parents when they have wrestled with such thoughts internally? When one has dared to imagine a parallel existence, free from the stomach wrenching guilt that only a child is able to ladle onto you without fear of reprisal? Maybe it was my soul that was sick. I am certain Kelly's was.

All the same, I did not disrespect the sanctity of life. On the contrary, like most put upon parents, it was the archaic system into which my child was born that I held in contempt, and continue to do so. It was this system of accepted rules that finally created an intolerable prison – one from which my only daughter was forced to escape.

Her troubles, and mine, began in October, 2002, on her fourth Birthday. We had decided to celebrate the event at a local laser and tenpin bowling centre, so had hired a children's suite to accommodate Kelly and her pint-sized friends. The evening itself went well, in so far as there were no major traumas; aside from the occasional spillage of lemonade onto the alley and a couple of tantrums, when egocentric Jack's bowling ball failed to hit one of the pins. The real 'event' of the 1st October was to come later that night, when we arrived home.

A gale was blowing hard outside, therefore we raced to the front door to avoid being drenched by the downpour. However, despite out best efforts, the three of us were sodden when we stepped inside. Kelly's blonde curls, which had taken more than an hour to prepare earlier, were unkempt and matted.

'Bath time for you, Miss.' I smiled down at my daughter, who was yawning and rubbing her tired eyes. 'We'll just make it a quick one,' I reassured her, as she attempted to slow our assent upstairs by pulling back on my arm.

Unfortunately, it took over 20 minutes to run the bath. For, we had been having some trouble with the boiler, owing to a leaking radiator. As a result, occasionally the water from tap ran cold, requiring it to be turned off, briefly, before being turned back on. I tapped my finger on the sink, frustrated at the multitude of sins our new house had revealed, since we had moved into it some five months before.

'Michael, you're going to have to do something about this. Call a plumber out or something,' I yelled downstairs.

I don't know if he heard me, he didn't answer at any rate.

'Come on lazy bones,' I chided, whilst struggling to pull Kelly's frilly attire over her head.

'I want bed Mum,' she moaned.

I was having none of that. 'Not whilst you're wet you're not, you'll catch your death,' I explained, lifting her carefully into the bath. 'You're a big girl now, make sure you wash everywhere,' I instructed, watching on from my place on the toilet seat.

Soon enough, Kelly had got into the spirit of things. She even took it upon herself to form her hair into a pixy's peak, three inches or more above her scalp and clogged with soap.

'Come on Kelly, it's time for bed. Get all that washed out,' I stated, somewhat gruffly, as my feet were aching.

Kelly stuck out her sulky lip. Still, she complied and was squeaky clean in minutes.

Bath time over, I turned to get the towel from the rail. It wasn't there.

'I won't be a minute. Don't try to get out on your own.' I pointed my finger at her as I said these words. She had to understand I was serious.

So, I left her. I left Kelly. But, it was only for the briefest of instants.

When I returned to the bathroom, I was horrified. Kelly was laying face down in the water. She was still. The room was silent.

'Michael...' I screamed, as loud as I could.

He shot up the stairs and burst through the door. He pushed me roughly out of the way and grabbed Kelly around the stomach. He whisked her onto the landing. 'Kelly...Kelly...Kelly...' he shouted, over and over.

She didn't move. In desperation he began to shake her. All the time he kept on calling out her name.

Then, just as Michael was set to attempt amateur first-aid on our daughter, she came to. She must have heard him. I am not even sure she had been unconscious in the first place, because she began to laugh. It was a nasty, cruel, grating laugh. Her eyes were alight with excitement. A false smile contorted her face. It was as though she had staged the whole scene. Kelly had pretended to be dead. Now, she found the looks on her parents' faces highly amusing.

I was unsettled, disgusted. I am sure I would have hit her, if Michael had not held me back. I suppose my anger was in part created by my own guilt. How could I have left her? What if it had been no joke? Nevertheless, I could not understand why my lovely four year old daughter had chosen to frighten me, us, in that way.

'Get into bed,' I said, numbly. There was no kiss for Kelly that night.

Subsequently, the following morning I eyed Kelly guardedly over the breakfast table. As she munched, I told her how foolish her little prank had been. I explained how she had scared me. Kelly just looked at me blankly.

'What's wrong, Mummy? Mummy had bad dream?'

She could not remember anything – certainly, nothing pertaining to her behaviour the previous evening. She only recalled the fun she had had at the bowling alley. 'Go again, please?'

For the remainder of the day Kelly was her usual, exuberant self. However, from the 3rd October, 2002 she was not the same. The little girl that I knew began to change into an unknowable stranger.

Chapter 3

The Voice of a Man

On the 3rd October, 2002, there was a training day at the Cherubs
Nursery Kelly attended, and I was forced to take a day's leave, so
that I could look after her at home. Uncharacteristically, I had also
offered to look after Lucy Gibbons' little girl, Holly, as a favour to
her mother, who did not have understanding employers.

Kelly had woken at first light, 6:30am to be exact. She was
eager to see her playmate Holly, as Michael and I rarely allowed
her friends from the nursery over to the house. In all honesty, I
was not the childminder type. I loved my daughter, but anyone
else's children sorely tried my patience. Still, when Holly arrived
with a bag of toys at 7:15am, I was relieved. Kelly had been
growing impatient and had been asking over and over, if and when
her friend was going to appear.

Within minutes of Holly's entrance the front room floor was
covered with a selection of dolls and games. I decided to leave the
two of them playing happily, whilst I prepared a light breakfast of
toast and tea. All seemed to be going well, so when Kelly asked if
they could go to her room with the dolls, I agreed.

'I'll help you upstairs. Call if you want to come down, I don't
want you messing around on the steps,' I insisted.

Once the two tots were deposited in the bedroom, I secured
the baby-gate and returned to the kitchen.

Throughout the rest of the day I periodically popped upstairs, to banish their hunger with my culinary delights and to check that all was ok.

'I'll have to ask Holly around more often,' I deliberated, given that her visit had provided Kelly with a diversion, and myself with much needed time to sort out the housework. The day seemed to thereby pass relatively quickly and it was soon time for Mrs Gibbons to return.

'You've been a Godsend,' Lucy thanked me, as she began collecting some of Holly's toys into a plastic bag. 'I hope Holly's been no trouble. The kids upstairs…?'

I nodded and described how I had hardly noticed the two children, since they had been playing in a world of their own. Why, for the last hour or so you would not have known that there were any kids in the house, in light of how quiet they had been.

'I bet we'll find them dozing, must have been playing sleeping-logs,' I maintained.

How wrong I was. How humiliating for myself. How upsetting for Mrs Gibbons. Sure, the two of them had been playing, but not any game a loving parent would have wanted.

When I opened the bedroom door carefully, so as not to wake them, if indeed they were sleeping, I realised why the house had been *so* quiet.

Holly was laid face down on the bed. Kelly was straddled over her, holding her still with her tiny hands wrapped around her neck.

'Shut-up you stupid tart,' she spat the words at her 'friend', lowering her head so that it was inches from the back of Holly's.

'What are you doing?' I screeched, and raced to pull Kelly from her embarrassing position.

Holly was now able to lift herself up. She ran to hug her mother, crying: 'I want to go home…I want to go home.'

My cheeks were burning. What could I say? Aside from reprimanding Kelly, relentlessly, for what she had done, there was nothing that I could do. As if things were not bad enough, whilst I was apologising to Mrs Gibbons and gathering Holly's dolls, I observed how each one of them had been vandalised. Especially a little china doll with large brown eyes and tight ringlets. Its clothes were torn and there were thick red lines painted around its fragile, glossy neck.

Needless to say, Mrs Gibbons did not ask me to look after Holly again. Not that I would have wanted to anyway. For, the events I have described so far merely marked the beginning of Kelly's problems. Her behaviour was to become increasingly unnerving over the next two years; so much so, that I was forced to go part-time at work.

It also signified the downward spiral of my relationship with Michael, who, typical of most fathers towards their daughters, was far too accepting of his Kelly's increasing tantrums. It did not overly worry him that Kelly was getting all the more erratic and aggressive during her fights with her mother; a mother who was desperately trying to save her. My feelings of distraction over Kelly, and frustration over Michael's inability to act, finally came to a head on the 9th September, 2004.

Two days prior to the event, Kelly had started a new class at St. Mary's Primary School, near Rickensdale. I was hoping that a new school would be a fresh start for Kelly. She would mix with her Catholic peers and become a 'normal' child again. For the first two days it appeared that she would. All was calm. There were no battles, no tears. Instead, Kelly had come home in high spirits and chatted happily about her new teacher, Mrs Bottomley. She also gushed with enthusiasm as she spoke of a friend she had met there. A girl called Becky, who was some years older and much bigger than herself.

The morning of the 9th September, Kelly was different. That day I had risen early, at 6:00am, to get myself ready for work, and Kelly ready for the childminder, who was to drop her at school.

'I'll let her sleep in a little longer. It's too early for a kid to be up and about at this time,' I told Michael, as he sat devouring his own breakfast.

I was quite taken aback, therefore, when Kelly entered the kitchen. I glanced at the digital clock on the cooker. It was only 6:05am.

Kelly's face was pale, her eyes sallow and bloodshot. She was clearly exhausted. That was not all. She stood silently, staring into my eyes. Eventually, she spoke.

'Mummy, I'm scared,' she mumbled.

I presumed she was nervous about school, so went to give her a big motherly hug.

However, just as I was about to enclose her in my arms, she spat in my face. I steadied myself, shaken, angry. She stared, smiling to herself. I hated that smile. It certainly was not the smile of my little girl. It was the one she gave me each time she was changing, changing into someone else.

I could never have foreseen what she was about to do next. Somehow I had managed to cope with the cruelty she showed to others, including her own mother. Now she directed this abhorrence at herself.

Like someone possessed, she started to call, yell. She grabbed at her hair, her beautiful hair. She pulled out a chunk and discarded it on the floor. Still, she screamed. I ran to her; to stop her, to hold her. She fled to the corner of the kitchen. Next, flinging back her head with venom, she ran out and into the dining room. There I found her: scratching her neck till it bled, banging her head remorselessly against the corner of the dining table.

'What are you looking at, whore?' she said.

Finally, she passed out.

I wanted to call an ambulance. Michael, who had done nothing but watch the spectacle dumbfounded, would not hear of it. He took my hand from the receiver. Kelly had come to.

She was crying now and calling for her mother. Cautiously, I observed her trying to put her thumb in her mouth for comfort. I knew that the episode was over. I had seen this happen many times before. One second she was like a wild beast. The next, her passion would subside; when whatever had taken hold of her tired of the sport. This was when she became my little girl again; the little girl who wanted a mother's love. This time, I simply could not give it. I stood studying her. I didn't understand what was wrong with her. I surmised that my child was sick. She needed help. Enough was enough.

'We've got to take her to the doctor, Michael.' I implored him, to acknowledge that for all our sakes, Kelly's 'condition' could not be allowed to deteriorate any further.

He, meanwhile, mopped up the mess with tissues and foul smelling TCP.

Once Kelly's injuries had been cleansed, Michael laid her gently on the sofa in the front room. He then returned to the table, where I sat sobbing.

'Look, Abigail, I'll ring in sick today and we'll go to the surgery, if that's what you want,' he started.

'Of course it's not what I bloody want. We have to...' I returned.

I resented the way he always tried to negate the severity of Kelly's problems, and suggest that, somehow, I was the one with 'issues' for noticing them.

'Don't all kids of her age have tantrums?' he suggested.

'No, Michael, they don't,' I clipped, exasperated by his lack of real concern. 'You're thinking of two year olds. Besides, even they don't try to ram their heads through sheets of glass.'

The conversation was stilted for a while. In his eyes, I was overreacting. If this had been the only incident, then his opinion may have been valid. However, it was not the first time I had witnessed Kelly's aggression, albeit towards others in the past. Moreover, there were certain facts I had kept from Michael. I was determined to share these with him now.

'There's something else you need to know Michael,' I began. 'It's not just that she does strange things, hurtful things, it's the voices as well.'

At last I had his attention.

'What are you talking about?'

'Do you remember her fourth birthday, the night when she slid in the bath?'

He did.

'Kelly's just not been Kelly since that night...'

'Now come on Abigail, I know you two have had tiffs, my god I have seen some of them...' he interrupted.

'Listen, will you,' I pleaded, 'You certainly haven't seen what has happened in this bloody house every bastard afternoon for the last two years.'

His eyes opened wider. He wasn't used to my using foul language. Hell, I wasn't used to it myself. I carried on regardless, 'She goes into some kind of trace, always at either 6:00am or 4:00pm. She's obnoxious, possessed. God, I don't know. All I do know is that I hear her, from upstairs in her room. Sometimes she screams; screams so loud it tears me to pieces. But, most of the time she talks. She speaks with the voices of others.'

'What? Whose voices...?'

'Children's I think. Though, not today, today it was different. I just don't believe she's physically capable of it.'

'What?'

'Do I have to spell it out for you? My God Michael, she sounds like a man.'

Chapter 4

Nosey Parkers

The journey to the doctor's was without incident. Kelly was shattered. Michael was quiet. Although he did, occasionally, cast a condescending glance my way. I pretended that I could not see. I chose to watch the town flash though the windows, illuminated by the crisp, white winter sun. It's strange, how in the midst of awkward situations, one can divert one's attention by analysing everyday particular details that one would normally ignore and cast aside in a careless fashion.

For the first time I saw how negatively the town had been affected by the closing of three local textile mills within the last 20 years. I passed by the house where I had grown from a child into a young woman. The garden was strewn with litter and overgrown with dandelions. To add to the insult, there was a rusted banger in the driveway that had black oil oozing from inside. The house whizzed by. It was much the same as the others on the shabby old street. *My parent's would turn in their graves if they could see this now.*

At last we arrived at the surgery. It was refreshingly angular, modern. I was the one who now felt out of time, dated and archaic; since my anxieties replicated those of a primitive specimen of the pre-Renaissance era. I just needed someone to help my Kelly. That was all.

Fortunately, children had always taken precedence at the Holy

Cross Surgery, so, once we were inside, we weren't kept waiting very long.

'Kelly Hodgeson, for Dr Baker,' the intercom called.

We were soon sat before Dr Baker, waiting for her attention, whilst she scanned through Kelly's medical notes in a flippant manner.

'Well, what can we do for you today, Kelly?' she drawled.

I paused. I didn't really want Kelly to hear what I had to say. Thus, I pointed to some toys in the corner.

'Look at that Kelly, why don't you go and cook us something to eat.'

She was happy to do so, and I was left with the difficult task of having to describe her past misdemeanours to the learned doctor.

I was relieved that Dr Baker did not smile. I was glad she did not reject my worries out of hand. On the contrary, she gave the impression of being as troubled by Kelly's challenging conduct as I was.

'I'm going to contact Dr Westward,' she informed me, 'he's a specialist in child development.'

This I was happy about. Yet I was far from happy, when she also instructed me that she was going to notify Rickensdale Social Services. I looked grave at that fateful moment.

'There's no need for alarm, Mrs Hodgeson. We're not making any judgements on you. They will simply be able to provide support for you at home.'

God knows, when I left Holy Cross I wished I had never been. Michael was of the same opinion. He had no respect for Social Services.

'What the hell do we want those damn nosey parkers prying into our personal lives for?'

I indicated that someone was listening on the back seat. I didn't want Kelly to know what was happening. I still wanted to protect her from the inevitable.

As it turned out, the 'nosey parkers' were out in force within the next week. An action plan was drawn, to solve my family's problems, which simply involved a carer spending a few hours a day with Kelly. Those hours were between 6:00am and 8:00am and 3:00pm and 5:00pm, to coincide with Kelly's departure for, and arrival home, from school and, more decisively, the times I had expressed as when she was at her most *'difficult'*.

It is appalling to confess, but I was relieved when Kelly turned her rancour upon Mrs Cindy Black, our *helper*. The way I saw it, it was better that Kelly released her torment on a stranger, rather than on herself or me. Though, I am not so sure that Mrs Black would care to agree.

She made her chubby self quite a part of the household furniture, during her first week in attendance. She even started taking liberties, like helping herself to biscuits without being asked and disappearing for a smoke in the back garden every 20 minutes or so.

'Any chance of a cuppa...?' she quizzed, from the backdoor.

I wanted to throw it at her. It was the fourth she had asked for within 70 minutes.

'As if I don't have better things to do... social *services*...? That's a laugh. I'm the one providing all the bloody services!' I cursed, under my breath.

All the same, I took the sickly sweet coffee out to her.

The instant the door was opened, a shrill winter gust swept inside. At the same time, the tones of Kelly's frosty friend crept from the living room. This offensive oratory lured Mrs Black to my daughter's side.

She clearly had never seen anything like it. Kelly was on her back, her hands straight down her sides. Repeatedly she cracked the back of her head on the laminate floor. Then, with the abruptness of the insane, she jumped up, grabbed at Mrs Black and pushed her onto a chair. She crawled spider swift up her legs and shoved her fingers into the hollow of her neck.

'Get her off...come on, help me!' Mrs Black croaked.

I pulled Kelly back. Purple lines and red squiggles were visible where she had been. I turned her tiny hands over in mine. Kelly's nails were cut back, blunt.

I am in no doubt that Mrs Black reported back eagerly, to her silly supervisors, on what had occurred. From that day on, there were two *helpers*; helping themselves to the contents of my fridge, when I needed to go into town to pay bills or call at the bank.

This situation was to last for several weeks. I struggled to fit in work, albeit part-time, household chores and caring for Kelly. Her 'fits' of aggression continued in a sporadic pattern. I was grateful for the days of peace, but then the powder-keg would explode. At least I didn't have to deal with it. I negated responsibility when the 4:00pm outburst struck. I tended to stay out of the way. I could not bear to see Miss Nicola Taylor, the second scrawny carer, use her cherished techniques of restraint.

'It's alright, Abigail, it doesn't hurt Kelly you know,' she maintained.

I certainly did not know.

I was getting desperate, even more so when further boulders were placed on my heart, in the form of a steady stream of calls from Kelly's primary school. The teachers had been made aware of Kelly's 'home visits'. However, they were unprepared for the torrent of abuse Kelly was to unleash on her tiny peers. At last, I was summoned to attend a meeting with Mrs Walker, the Headmistress.

'Good morning Mrs Hodgeson,' she stated.

It was far from it. It took her over 15 minutes to catalogue the incidents at St. Mary's Primary which had involved my little girl.

'…The last one was particularly alarming for the pupils and staff,' she read from her documents, '…she savagely bit a pupil and also her teacher's neck.'

I suppressed a smile. Mrs Walker failed to see the funny side. I had to.

'We're dealing with it…' I said, more seriously.

'*Well, quite,*' Mrs Walker scorned, 'you have to understand, Mrs Hodgeson, at St. Mary's we are ill-equipped for cases such as this. We have to consider the welfare of all of the children in our care…'

'What are you trying to say?'

I was tiring of Mrs Walker. Why couldn't she just get to the point? It was quite obvious where the conversation was going. She still hesitated.

'For God's sake, are you saying that she is excluded?'

'Not yet, Mrs Hodgeson, it's better for Kelly if you take a transfer form. That way she won't have a stain on her records.'

Mrs Walker sat back in her chair. She was relieved that the unpleasantness was over. For her it was. She handed me the form, recommending that I opt for Lillybank Primary. This was a Special School, one of only a few left that had the facilities to cope with 'little horrors' like mine. Having suffered enough of Mrs Walker's Christian charity, I left.

Chapter 5

Dr Westwood

In the event, Kelly saw little of her new school. Our waiting was finally over. The initial appointment arranged with Dr Westward arrived.

'Why am I going to see a doctor Mum?' Kelly had asked, as we set off for Millingham Children's Hospital.

I didn't answer. What was the point? She could never remember what she had done. Maybe she could, and would, with Dr Westward.

I admired this man the moment I met him. In his late thirties, sporting dark wavy hair, and a fine physique, he spoke with softness and sincerity. After leaving Kelly in the capable hands of a nurse, he listened to my tale from the very beginning. I am sure that at this stage in our acquaintance he believed that I was a genuinely caring mother, who was at her wits' end.

In turn, he called Kelly into the room. He proceeded with her interview.

'Hello Kelly,' he smiled, 'it seems you've been getting into some trouble of late.'

Kelly sat licking a purple lolly she had been given, quite oblivious to him.

'Do you get angry sometimes Kelly? I know I do.'

Still, she ignored him. I could see he was a little put out that his attempts to coax her into conversation were failing, and he tried a new tack.

'Your Mother's worried about you. Do you know why?'

'She says I get cross. I don't.' Kelly further denied that she had tried to hurt anyone, herself included.

'What about Mrs Bottomley. She was most hurt. Can you remember why she was hurt, Kelly?'

'I don't know. I like her. We do fun things in class.'

'I am sure you do…but, Mrs Bottomley has said that you bit her. Can you remember doing that?'

Kelly became agitated and fidgeted with the buttons on her blouse.

'No!' she said, almost defiantly.

It was useless, I explained to Dr Westward, given that, after her 'fits' she appeared to have no memory of what she had done.

Next, Dr Westward performed a physical examination of Kelly. This consisted of assessing the blue/black bruises that were visible around her neck. He also lifted her hair carefully, to see the discoloration of her skin and cuts that the numerous bangs had created. He then insisted that Kelly undress, though I didn't understand why he needed to further embarrass her by investigating her naked frame. Kelly just turned around upon instruction, as he checked that there were no other injuries evident on her body.

'Only the head and neck areas have been affected during the said episodes.'

He seemed to be talking to himself as he scribbled in his pad, so I was quiet.

At long last Dr Westward outlined what he was going to do about Kelly. He ran through a long list of tests which would be carried out, in order to establish the nature and cause of her outbursts. They all sounded very complex and important, and I could not even attempt to spell them for you now.

What each actually involved I do not know. Every time I arrived at one wing of the hospital or another, Kelly was whisked away. On the rare occasion I was allowed to go with her, to comfort her, she was shoved into some machine. Most times I was told to wait in the reception area. Whilst there, I have do idea how many of the cheap, frothy liquids, that they chose to call coffee, I consumed. Nor, for that matter, can I recall how many times I thumbed through the crumpled magazines which were more than a year out of date. I became so bored, so frustrated, that on one occasion, I followed another parent outside and practically begged for a cigarette. Suffice it to say, as a non-smoker, I choked for some time after inhaling its poison.

Eventually, Dr Westward made a final appointment to discuss his findings. I eagerly anticipated an end to the whole episode and some answers for Kelly's tribulations. This was not to be.

'The tests have proved inconclusive,' Dr Westward explained. There were no biological or physiological reasons for the fluctuations in Kelly's temperament. The eminent doctor was at a loss as to what could be done next.

'There must be something in Kelly's history that triggered these events. Some trauma of some kind...?'

I told him for the hundredth time that there was nothing. Kelly had been a happy, contented child.

At long last, the meeting concluded – Kelly was referred to Hollbury Psychiatric Unit for analysis, therapy, and possible medication, given the disturbing mental and physical symptoms she had displayed.

I can't help thinking now, that this consignment of Kelly to an asylum, was brought on by Westward's desire to separate the youngster from her mother. Had he not reiterated, repeatedly, during our last meeting, the fact that Kelly's instances of *'self-harm'* had increased in severity during her visits to the hospital? Why had he suggested that there must have been some *'trauma'* in her childhood that had instigated the anger he had witnessed first-hand during two therapy sessions he had held with my daughter? What was he really saying? That I or Michael had abused our child? I am confident that this was what he had been hinting at, though he never actually said it straight out.

Understandably, I no longer held Dr Westward in high esteem.

Chapter 6

Hollbury

You may have been wondering where Michael was throughout these months of torture. As usual, he was at work. He avoided the arena entirely. He only stepped into it once, to give me a lift to the psychiatric unit, because there was no direct bus route to Hollbury.

'Daddy will see you soon, Kelly.' He patted her as she clambered out of the car.

I was not acknowledged. The car drove off, before I even had the chance to wave goodbye.

Isolated and afraid, I pressed the button for access to the Child and Adolescent Mental Health Unit, Ward five. It was the 1st August, 2006: the date on which I met Dr Milner.

Initially, I was invited into her consulting room alone. This was when I shocked her with my defamation of family life. She probably thought the wrong person was being admitted for psychiatric treatment. I didn't really think a young woman of her age could appreciate why I was so tired of being a wife and mother. All the same, she listened, for a while, before I was asked to leave, so that Kelly's Psychiatric Report could be written.

I was not allowed to see the report at that time; that privilege came later when I demanded to see what the doctors had done for my daughter. It was a privilege I exacted before I would be willing to put pen to paper, for the benefit of Dr Milner's study. You have to look at this report for yourselves to understand why I still hold the medical profession in contempt.

I will never forget my daughter's face, when I told her that I would be going home. 'I'll be back first thing in the morning, Kelly,' I stated, and turned away. I was crying bitterly.

'No Mummy, no!'

'I have to go, Kelly, but I will be back,' I reiterated, as calmly as I could.

'Would you like to stay longer, Mrs Hodgeson?' the nurse enquired.

I was determined not to stay.

'Well, our normal visiting hours are, 1:00pm–3:00pm and 5:00pm–8:00pm daily,' she instructed, as I strode from the establishment.

I was set to go home and not to turn back. On I walked, for more than two miles. Until I came to the small town of Baildon. On the main road was a local taxi-rank, whose services I utilised owing to the blisters that my new ankle boots were creating. I needed to be home, so that I could give vent to my feelings of desperation. The easiest way I found to do this was by getting completely and utterly drunk on the home-made elderberry wine that had been fermenting in the cupboard under the stairs.

'Bloody hell this is strong,' I muttered, over the glass. My words were slurred and my eyes cherry red when Michael rolled in from the pub at 10:00pm.

I was, therefore, somewhat groggy when I arrived at Hollbury the following afternoon. Kelly was ushered into the visitors' room. Dr Milner entered close behind. She looked less self-assured.

'Mrs Hodgeson,' she began.

I interrupted her, 'I would like to spend some time alone with my daughter, if you don't mind.'

She clearly did, and failed to leave.

'I am sure, Mrs Hodgeson, you are interested in Kelly's progress?'

I indicated that Kelly's well being was my main priority.

'I'm glad to hear it...' she remarked. Dr Milner then informed me of her primary concern: what she had witnessed the previous day. The same as any child, Kelly had been disturbed by her mother's exit. This was to be expected. However, Kelly had also shown alarming mental symptoms at 4:00pm, when the evening meal was about to be served in the communal dining room.

To begin with, Kelly had tasted her vegetable soup. It seemed to be to her liking, because she took to dipping a crusty French-loaf into the broth and was soon gobbling away with childish gusto. Another patient, Chloe Johnson, then pulled her chair close to Kelly's and the two started to chat easily. It was the nature of this conversation itself which was rather strange for two young girls.

Dr Milner, observing from a discreet distance, could faintly hear the two discussing life after death. Soon, the topic focused on ghosts. Chloe admitted to suspecting that she saw one, just the once. Conversely, Kelly stated, quite calmly that she had been contacted many times.

'Who were they? What did they look like?' the other girl probed, excitedly.

'Children, mainly young girls, like you and me, I guess,' Kelly responded, continuing to chomp.

'I wish something like that would happen to me, it would be great,' Chloe confessed.

Kelly was most annoyed by this juvenile banter and set her dinner guest straight: 'It's no joke, stupid. Those girls died horribly – they were murdered.'

At this point Dr Milner admitted to intervening. She approached Kelly and introduced herself again. She then asked politely, if she could join her at the table. Kelly accepted, already bored with the youthful company the unit had to offer. Next, the doctor took it upon herself to question Kelly's firmly held spiritual beliefs, whilst pretending to sup her own bowl of soup.

'I could not help overhearing your talk with Chloe,' Dr Milner declared, '…so you have seen ghosts have you?'

'You can't see them silly,' Kelly chuckled, 'they have no bodies to live in anymore.'

'I see,' Dr Milner replied, 'how do you know they are there then?'

Kelly hesitated for some time. She toyed with her meal and started to look out of the window and into the dark.

'I hear them,' she stated, 'they talk to me. They tell me things.'

'What *"things"*,' the fool harassed her.

I knew she should have stopped right there.

'How they died,' Kelly snapped, flicking her spoon across the table towards the doctor. 'Just leave me alone,' she protested.

Dr Milner froze. The carriage clock chimed. It was 4:00pm.

Next, Dr Milner described how Kelly's face had turned and twisted with rage. She picked up her bowl and threw it at the wall, leaving carrots and peas to roll down at their own will. Yet, the rage did not subside. It grew worse, much worse. Screaming and pawing at her stomach she hurled herself to the floor. Then thuds echoed through the pathetic dining hall, as she crashed her skull mercilessly onto the, thankfully, carpeted surface.

'No, no, no!' she had yelled, lifting her arms to her face, in a vein attempt to stop her self-harm. She could not. She gave in and shouted insults at others in the room. The nurses were summoned and quickly arrived. It took three to restrain the little girl. Her cries of anger turned to tears, tears of pain and anguish.

If the good doctor had expected me to be surprised by this account, she was disappointed.

'I told you all this before, you're not telling me anything I have not already seen for myself.'

Dr Milner was silent. She was still in a state of shock and denial; for I knew she had not replayed all of the facts of the dining room scene. Nevertheless, she did have further information which added to my knowledge on Kelly's condition.

She explained how, later, she had visited Kelly in her room – just to make sure that the new resident of Ward five was settling down well on her first night. For the first time there was a promising conversation between patient and doctor.

'You see, Mrs Hodgeson, Kelly opened up to me last night. She told me of her fears, her dreams.'

I listened more intently.

'Have you any idea why she hates the colour pink?'

Obviously, I had not.

'The only request your daughter made last night was that we never put her in a room that was painted pink. Has your daughter got a pink bedroom?'

I remembered now how Kelly had always been so fussy, when her father and I had attempted to decorate her room. I had wanted to use reds, pinks, '...It's what all the other girls have,' I had explained to Kelly. She had been hysterical. Under no circumstances would she even enter a pink bedroom, let alone sleep in one. At the time I had rejected her protestations as childish ramblings. I never imagined that there was a genuine fear, a terror, behind her choice of unflattering green for the walls and carpet.

'No, she has not, she never has had,' I replied, at length.

Dr Milner then stated how Kelly had confessed to having vivid dreams: especially one recurring nightmare that dwelt on how she was going to die. According to Kelly, the setting was always the same: a room with a pink carpet, walls and curtains. She had seen her own slender body hanging from a noose tied to the metal bars placed over the windows of this room. The time on a nearby clock had read 6:05am.

'It must be here somewhere,' Kelly had suggested, 'I've seen bars on some of the windows. Am I in prison?'

Dr Milner had reassured her that she was not, and promised that she would never be asked to sleep in a pink bedroom.

In fact, the doctor had breathed a sigh of relief when she had left Kelly to sleep. The fact was: all the rooms on Ward five were pink, as only girls slept on this particular zone. The only exception was the room into which Kelly had been placed on her admittance. This one was still oppressive orange and brown. It had not been updated. Not yet.

'Call the decorators tomorrow, will you. I don't want room

seven done,' Dr Milner had instructed her subordinate, before heading for home.

'I see,' was all I could muster. Kelly had never shared her premonition with me. 'Strangulation,' I whispered. 'You have to make sure she is safe here. Don't let anyone leave ties, ropes in her room,' I informed Dr Milner.

She resented this commonsensical advice, which she pointed out was already part of the hospital's safety policy.

Chapter 7

Kelly Takes Dr Milner into her Confidence

Subsequently, over the next couple of weeks, Kelly took Dr Milner further into her confidence. In spite of the doctor's constant questions on Mum and Dad, she continued to maintain that her childhood had been a happy one. As a result, Dr Milner had to be satisfied that there was no history of abuse. I am grateful for that, at least. I was also appreciative when I was allowed to attend Kelly's second formal interview.

Kelly had grown more accustomed to her new surroundings and was more willing to discuss her experiences on this instance. Indeed, Dr Milner's questions were answered with an ease and eloquence of someone way beyond Kelly's years.

'So, Kelly, you were telling me yesterday about some of the things you had heard from 'spirits',' the doctor commenced. 'Don't you think that maybe you only thought that you heard them?'

'No, they were the voices of spirits,' Kelly replied.

'How often do these events occur?'

'All the time, everyday there is someone.' Kelly looked straight at Dr Milner.

'Well, what about here, can you hear anyone now?'

'No.'

'Why do you think that is, Kelly? If they can communicate with you, why can't they visit you now?'

'They're asleep, the dead people do rest at times. The living people are wide awake and they cannot visit me then,' Kelly stated, as a matter of fact.

Dr Milner needed some clarification on this last statement. She could perhaps understand that, in a child's mind, a spectral presence would need rest, the same as anyone else. What was puzzling was her comment on the '*living*'.

'I'm not quite sure what you mean, Kelly. You said that the voices you heard were those of the dead...' She checked her case notes.

'Yes, that's correct,' Kelly responded, firmly.

'Well, what did you mean when you stated "...*the living are awake*".'

Kelly was getting bored of the interrogation and jumped from her stool. She walked to the window and rapped on it gently, at first, though the raps grew louder.

'We've nearly finished, Kelly, just answer the question and I'll let you go to the playroom.'

That instant, Kelly stamped her foot, before giving the weirdest of answers; 'Some of the voices I hear are those of the dead, others are those of the living...When people sleep their souls are released, some anyway. When they are they come to visit me. They tell me things and I listen.'

According to my daughter, the spirits of the dead could walk the earth. They chose to communicate when their energies were at a peak. When they were lacking power they '*slept*', as she called it. Meanwhile, humans possessed the innate ability to fly from their bodies, but only in the twilight hours of unconscious rest. I suppose you would categorise her faith as spiritualist. Her convictions were certainly not learnt at home. Kelly had been raised as a Catholic, I assured Dr Milner. The second session was over and Kelly was allowed to play.

That night, I needed to distance myself from my troubles, so, for once, I relaxed with friends. Theresa, Kate and I went to the local bingo hall, to see if we could line our pockets with winnings. It gave me the opportunity to dress up, in a pale blue velvet waistcoat and royal blue trousers. It also gave me a few hours in the company of middle-aged females. We chatted about trivialities and gargled on lager, half forgetting to check the numbers on our cards as they were called. At the end of the evening I went home penniless, but all the happier for it.

Michael was waiting up. This was a refreshing change.

'Had a good night?' he enquired.

Of course I had. I sat down on the settee. He came next to me. He nuzzled his head on my lap and laughed up into my eyes, as he watched the latest comic blockbuster. Cautiously, he took my hand, rolled and kissed it. This was the most intimate that we had been for as far back as I cared to remember. I knew, in his own way, he was making an effort to say he was sorry. He had abandoned me for a while. Not any more. He was the one who had been in the wrong and he knew it. All he could do now was put things right, by protecting and supporting his wife.

In future my visits to Hollbury would be in Michael's company. This was fortunate, for those visits would become harder to bear.

The very next day, Dr Milner informed us that she had already held her third session with Kelly, the previous evening. Her reasoning behind this was based on information provided by the ward staff. They had indicated that, although the aggressive overtures of Kelly's symptoms were perceptible in the early hours of the morning and during the latter part of the afternoon, she had also displayed severe psychotic tendencies late at night. In short, Kelly, they claimed, had been suffering from visual and auditory hallucinations before falling asleep. What follows is an outline of the sequence of events that Dr Milner depicted to Michael and me.

She had entered Kelly's quarters at 9:00pm. Kelly was still wide awake and reading *The Princess and the Pea*.

'Hello,' Kelly had greeted her 'friend', who had sat down on a child-sized stool in the corner.

'You don't mind if I join you do you?'

Kelly shook her head. She was thankful for the company. It was a long time to be locked away, from 8:00pm until 8:00am.

Dr Milner sat studying her patient, quietly making notes, waiting for Kelly's eyes to tire of the text. Eventually they did and Kelly placed the book on the floor.

'They're here...' She looked beyond Dr Milner to the corner.

The doctor was disconcerted. She swivelled around to see what was grabbing her charge's attention.

'It's alright Kelly, it's just the shadows,' Dr Milner reassured her.

Kelly sighed and shook her head.

'I've told you before you can't see them...open your ears and listen.'

Dr Milner involuntarily found herself doing what she had been asked. The strain made her ears pop. All she heard were the faint clunks and clatters from down the hallways of Hollbury, nothing else.

Kelly began to giggle.

'What have they said to you?' Dr Milner asked.

'She thinks you look daft on that chair,' Kelly retorted.

'Who is "she" Kelly?' The doctor remained focused.

Kelly politely asked for the visitor's name and announced: 'Catherine...' She went on to elaborate that this was not the first time she had been visited by Catherine. Catherine had called on Kelly since the outset of her admittance to Hollbury.

'And...what does she want to talk with you about?' Dr Milner continued.

'She's very sad,' stated Kelly, frowning.

'Oh, and what is she sad about?'

The response was unexpected and unsettling for Dr Milner. This is exactly what Kelly had to say:

'She became whole again on the 15th July. She's too sensitive. You see? They put her in this place the next day. She doesn't like it here. Catherine Stanley wants to go to the other side.'

For the life of her, Dr Milner could not comprehend how

Kelly could have got this information. Miss Catherine Stanley had been admitted on the 15th July, and certain particulars given in Kelly's statement corresponded with the very words Catherine had said to the doctor on her referral to the unit by the Crisis Resolution Team. Yet, Catherine was on Ward nine, a section some distance from the child unit, owing to the severe mental symptoms of its inhabitants. There was just no way that Kelly could have seen or spoken to Catherine, who was still under constant supervision.

Intrigued, Dr Milner set to find out if Kelly had any further facts to share on the other residents of Hollbury. She did.

'David sees me the most. He's a bit scary, always shouting.'

'David who...?'

'David Lowe.'

Dr Milner put down her notebook and pen. What could Kelly know about Mr David Lowe? He had been on the secure Forensic Unit since October, 2005. It was impossible that this little girl had come into contact with an inmate of that wing, which was impenetrable and over half a mile down the road. *Maybe she's read about him in the papers,* the doctor conjectured, as it had been a high-profile case which had received much publicity.

She put her suppositions to Kelly, who was undeterred. Mr David Lowe had told her everything: all there was to know about his so-called crimes, his trial and his subsequent incarceration.

'He didn't do it,' Kelly maintained. 'There was someone else, a more powerful being than David. He controlled him during his last months of freedom.'

'...And who was that Kelly?' the doctor enquired.

'Hopline, it was William Hopline...' Kelly barked, as though she hated to say the name. She started to cry.

Dr Milner was staggered. Surely a child of only eight years would not have followed Mr David Lowe's trial so closely? Moreover, if she indeed had, she would have read the public apology that had been written to the maligned Mr William Hopline and his family, once Mr Lowe had been sentenced. She would not have been defending a child killer like Lowe. Dr Milner was *almost* convinced that the child was receiving messages. Eventually, she shook her head and the silly thoughts out of it. She concluded her recital.

I don't know what disturbed me most about this admission of the doctor's: that it showed how far my daughter's psychosis had plummeted; that Kelly may have been right, in which event she was the receptacle of messages of a distinctly adult nature; or that the doctor herself was perhaps turning out to be more twisted than some of her patients.

Michael was thinking the same and directed his disbelief at Dr Milner. 'Let me get this straight. You're telling us that you think our daughter is some kind of medium for crazy people?'

Dr Milner bit her lip. That was not what she had been trying to say, not at all. She simply wanted to put all the facts to the parents; all the facts, even the ones that she could not explain in her professional capacity.

In the event, it was a shame that Michael chose to belittle Dr Milner in this way. She was the only member of the medical profession who could have helped us. She never again expressed any feelings of self-doubt. She was once more the stereotypical objective psychiatrist. Whatever conjectures she had on Kelly that steered from the scientific path, she kept hidden deep within.

Chapter 8

The Final Session

Keep thoughts hidden deep within. This was precisely what Dr Milner chose to do on the 7th September, 2006. This was the date of our final session. This was the date on which I abandoned all my religious beliefs and my faith in science exploded. This was the date on which I witnessed the most terrifying scene involving my daughter. This was when I discovered the reality behind Kelly's condition.

To begin with, the doctor went over Kelly's crammed file, while she played in the far end of the consulting room. At this point, Dr Milner admitted to having held certain views which cast both Michael and I in a sinister light. Though, she added, as Kelly's symptoms had not decreased in rigour, during her stay, she had rejected this preliminary diagnosis.

Then, she requested that Kelly join us around her desk. She now focused her interview on the child, who had been asked to sit on an armchair next to her mother. The same mundane questions were put to Kelly for the umpteenth time. She rejoined with the same answers that she was increasingly weary of giving.

Eventually, Dr Milner prompted Kelly to demonstrate, to those assembled, her ability to talk with any one of the patients in Hollbury.

'They'll be awake, I can't do it,' Kelly grunted.

The doctor insisted; surely one of the scores of residents would be asleep, even if it was mid-afternoon. Kelly closed her eyes for a while. She saddened and a tear trickled down her cheek.

I felt like slapping Dr Milner. Her constant pushing was too much for Kelly, or so I thought. Yet, this was not so. Kelly soon shared with us the reason why she had been crying. It was because of Catherine. Kelly maintained that the medication this woman was on was dulling her mind. She was weak and needed sleep. Kelly added that Catherine had often come to share her grief, her loneliness, with her. Dr Milner also reminded me of previous 'auditory hallucinations' Kelly had endured involving this persona.

The doctor then appealed to Kelly to contact any of the spectral voices she had encountered.

Kelly sighed, 'I'll try.' Indeed she did. She crumpled her lips, rubbed her forehead and repeated, 'Is anyone there?'

Soon enough there was.

According to Kelly, the spirit of a young girl was with them.

'Where is she?' Dr Milner demanded.

For Kelly this was hard to ascertain, though she eventually concluded that the ghost was somewhere to the right of her.

'And what does she have to say today?'

It came as a shock when Kelly informed us that the little girl wanted to tell us for herself.

I rubbed inside my earlobe to determine that I was hearing right. Kelly's tones were lower. It was not her voice. I watched the doctor, to see what her response would be. She was singularly unimpressed with this display and continued with her objective analysis. Regardless, it was quickly established that Kelly was possessed by Rebecca Galloway.

'She was murdered wasn't she?' I needed to know.

Dr Milner insisted that I would have to remain quiet or would be asked to leave. I complied.

It was then that Rebecca utilized her hold over my daughter to reveal the ordeal she had endured in the last minutes of her life. How she had suffered; how she had scratched and fought; how she had called for her mother. No grisly details were spared. Not even when the perverted animal had shoved a cigarette packet into her mouth to silence her screams. As she spoke, you could sense the breath being choked right out of her lungs. As she spoke, red rope marks were visible on Kelly's neck. Slowly the struggle subsided. Kelly was still. Her eyes were wide open, blank. In fits she came back and called out in her own high-pitched voice,

'Hopline did it. He killed her at 4:00pm.'

Dr Milner explained that she was convinced this was why Kelly's behaviour at 4:00pm had always been so erratic. It was possible that she had read in the papers, or heard on the TV, how Rebecca had died. Young, developing minds being very vulnerable, Kelly had been haunted by the tale of a young girl's death so close to her home on the outskirts of Keighley. She had forthwith internalised Rebecca's torture.

I believed this was utter nonsense and told her so. I stated that Kelly had never been allowed to watch such things on the television. Besides, I had heard Rebecca's voice before, when Kelly was just four and playing in her room. She would not have understood the events of Rebecca's death at such a young age, never mind been able to fake the voice of a girl who was more than six years senior to her.

In view of the fact that Dr Milner did not trust in my daughter's story, I suggested that the interview should cease. It didn't. The doctor would not be deterred from her final line of investigation.

'Now Kelly, are there any others?' She chewed her pen and shuffled to the edge of her seat.

Yes, there was just one more. Kelly looked anxiously at Michael, then at me.

'He's here, but I don't want to talk to him Mummy.'

She took hold of my arm. She wanted the interview to stop. She was terrified, and sweat dribbled down her forehead.

'For God's sake, that's enough…' I stood up to leave and was set to take my daughter with me.

I could not. She was held back. He was there alright. I know it now. He held her, hurled her back onto the chair. She clawed at her stomach in agony. Suddenly she was calm.

'Who are you now, Kelly?' Dr Milner asked, cautiously.

'Kelly's not here you stupid woman.'

For once, the doctor was stunned. She lifted her glasses, put down her pen and swiftly picked it back up.

'Who are you?'

The visitor merely stated that we already knew the answer to that question.

'Mr William Hopline...?'

He nodded in accent.

'And *why* are you haunting Kelly, Mr William Hopline?'

The reply was shockingly direct:

'That's painfully obvious isn't it? I loved my vocation. Killing children was my life. Can't seem to manage it in person anymore...Now, I can get inside their heads. What better way is there to kill kids than to get them to do it for themselves?'

Poor Kelly was left to reject the fiend on her own. Michael was useless. Dr Milner strained to keep up her professional pretence. She waffled on about how she had discovered Mr William Hopline's death had occurred at 6:05am; the point in time when Kelly's behaviour was at its most sinister. She concluded that this information must also have been filtered through to Kelly by certain media:

'She must have heard it and projected the events onto her own consciousness. This formed the basis of her psychosis...'

Her speech trailed off. It was useless trying to convince us with her scientific jargon. I could see she didn't believe in it herself. We had all heard Hopline's voice; the voice of a man devoid of conscience; the voice of a man and certainly not an eight year old girl.

Dr Milner finished by informing us of how she was passing Kelly's case onto another: Dr Wilson, an eminent Child Psychologist from a fine institute in London. In reality, I could tell that she was washing her hands of Kelly once and for all.

Chapter 9

The Keyring

So, now I come to the last day on which I have to report: the 9th September, 2006. The tragedy which unfolded on the morning of the 9th was due to one stupid mistake. One phone call could have saved my daughter's life.

As I have recounted earlier, Dr Milner had insisted that room number seven should not be updated, even though this would put it on a par with the others on Hollbury's Ward five. She had stated such to Mrs Bury, the efficient Secretary, who was responsible for sorting such matters.

However, the non-descript piece of notepaper on which the message had been left, to be dealt with in the morning, had been misplaced. Mrs Bury had forgotten to call Burton & Sons Painters and Decorators, who turned up on the morning of the 8th September to complete their work. Dr Milner was not around that morning. She was busy on another ward, completing an initial Psychiatric Report on one Mr Edwards.

Therefore, when she arrived on Ward five, for her afternoon duties, she was furious to find that room number seven was glistening with white gloss work and fresh pink satin.

'You'll have to do it again. The patient cannot possibly sleep in here,' she informed Barton senior.

Yet, he was unrepentant. He had another job on at the other

side of Leeds and was not going to waste anymore of his time. In any event, the paint was still dripping wet. If she really wanted to have the place done in a different colour, she would have to wait until tomorrow, when the paint was dry.

This was Dr Milner's dilemma: where could she put Kelly? All the rooms on Ward five were the same. There was no question of her being sent to the boys' unit. This would have been a serious breach of regulations. So, Kelly was taken to her own room at the end of the evening.

As the staff endeavoured to get Kelly into number seven, she had kicked and scratched at them. They didn't listen to her appeals: that she should be allowed to stay on the couch in the playroom.

'I'll sleep on the floor,' she pleaded.

But they closed the door behind her.

I find it very difficult to talk about, let alone write about what happened next.

I was told, later, that she had cried for more then two hours before room number seven descended into silence. Carer, Mr Carnelley, reported that he had heard Kelly calling for Dr Milner at 11:50pm. This was the last time anyone heard my daughter's voice.

They found her body at 8:00am on the morning of the 9th September, 2006. Kelly was found in her teddy-bear pyjamas, hanging from a dusty brown rope that was tied to the bars which covered the windows – bars that were meant to keep her safe. The carers rushed to take down my little girl. Her legs were still warm, from being rubbed on the radiator as she had swung. They tried to resuscitate her. They failed.

Michael and I were immediately called to Hollbury. We had to identify the body. It was surreal. It was her face. It was sleeping. I hoped that she would wake and laugh, even if it were the laugh of another. For over two hours I stood over my child: stroking her arms and flicking her blonde curls from her face, so that they would not go into her eyes.

'She just wanted to be left alone…' I wept.

I took hold of her fragile hand one last time. It was colder now and clenched. I prized the fingers open, so that I could hold her tightly. At that moment a small keyring fell from her grasp; a small gold pen keyring with the inscription *'W.H.'*

No one has ever been able to explain to me, convincingly, where this object came from. No one has established why Kelly was holding it when she died. No one has taken responsibility for leaving the murderous rope in Kelly's room. Personally, I am of the opinion that no human inhabitant of Hollbury can.

Mrs Abigail Hodgeson, September, 2006.

Epilogue

Dr Milner's Conclusions

I finished the logging of these six narrative studies in late September, 2006. The primary aim of the project was twofold: to bring comfort to the residents and carers who had taken part, and to build upon my knowledge of the facets of mental illness. In the end, I cannot say whether the venture helped any of my patients. As for me, the outcome was not what I had expected. True, I developed, but in ways I could not have foreseen.

Most significantly, since I received an offer of publication on this text, I have resigned from my post as Psychiatric Registrar at the Hollbury Unit. My pursuit of a new position, in a field theoretically opposed to Psychology, was primarily due to two important factors. Firstly, I have concluded prolonged mental study is an inane practise. Psychology itself is just pseudo-science, a method by which doctors fumble in the dark, only to find more shadows. More importantly, I left behind the world of white coats and lexical logistics because my perceptions of life and death have transformed entirely.

Still, I am hesitant to reveal my inner thoughts on the supernatural. I remain, after all, a qualified psychiatrist, and understand that any expression of sensitivity to such fantasies would result in ridicule by my peers.

You should be made aware, however, that, of all the disturbing and baffling psychologies I have encountered, that of tiny Miss Kelly Hodgeson will haunt me forever.

'Hallucinations' were her particular vice. Hallucinations triggered by an unrelenting belief in spooks and possession.

Yet, as perplexing as these features were, they would not have caused me a problem, had it not been for the fact that I am half-inclined to believe that she was, indeed, possessed.

You see, I was there. I witnessed certain 'psychotic episodes'. Two in particular have plagued my mind. On both of these occasions, I could have sworn that I heard a masculine voice. An eight year old girl, one Miss Kelly Hodgeson, talked like a man!

Moreover, this girl's claims of conversations with the souls of others were strangely insightful. I know it sounds ludicrous, but Kelly clearly knew things about people. Things she could not possibly have known.

So, let's just say, for argument's sake, that she was right and the medical profession has got it wrong. The worrying part of this conclusion is that it means there is an innocent man incarcerated within Hollbury. Moreover, it could suggest that other patients' experiences were not as far-fetched as I had previously thought. It pains me to say it, but the acknowledgement of such beliefs would make me either a despotic gaoler or one twisted physician who fed upon the psychosis of her inferior inmates.

Obviously, I have not mentioned any of this to my senior, Dr Peel. Certainly, he would have had me committed. Though, I surmise even his ultra-logical mind would be at a loss to explain away the pen keyring that I continue to store in my bureau. I doubt that anyone living in Hollbury is capable of that.

So, for now, I have decided to take a short holiday. Devon is my destination. A place where I hope the fresh, sea air will provide a cleansing atmosphere, one in which I can find myself again and, hopefully, a new career...